Fast Balls

Fast Balls

Erotic Tales of America's Favorite Pastime

edited by
Jesse Grant

alyson books
NEW YORK

© 2007 BY ALYSON BOOKS. ALL RIGHTS RESERVED. AUTHORS RETAIN COPYRIGHT TO THEIR INDIVIDUAL PIECES OF WORK.

MANUFACTURED IN THE UNITED STATES OF AMERICA

THIS TRADE PAPERBACK ORIGINAL IS PUBLISHED BY ALYSON BOOKS, 245 WEST 17TH STREET, NEW YORK, NEW YORK 10011. DISTRIBUTION IN THE UNITED KINGDOM BY TURNAROUND PUBLISHER SERVICES LTD., UNIT 3, OLYMPIA TRADING ESTATE, COBURG ROAD WOOD GREEN, LONDON N22 6TZ ENGLAND

FIRST EDITION: JUNE 2007

07 08 09 10 11 **a** 10 9 8 7 6 5 4 3 2 1

ISBN 1-59350-029-7
ISBN-13: 978-1-59350-029-0

LIBRARY OF CONGRESS CATALOGING-IN-PUBLICATION DATA ARE ON FILE.

COVER DESIGN BY VICTOR MINGOVITS
INTERIOR DESIGN BY CHARLES ANNIS

CONTENTS

Introduction   vii

Capping the Season
by Ryan Field   1

Locker Room Home Run
by Morris Michaels, Jr.   17

Pitcher and Catcher
by Armand   30

Right Field
by Simon Sheppard   42

Glory Days
by Shannon L. Yarbrough   54

Juego de Pelota
by Charlie Vazquez   68

Island Ball
by Neil Plakcy   77

Robert Strozier's Toilet
by Shane Allison   93

Summertime
by Curtis C. Comer   100

Home Run at Madgecull Park
by Lew Bull   112

Locker Room Heat
by John Simpson   124

Bat-and-Ball Wager
by Jay Starre   134

Contents

Rain Delay
by T. Hitman   150

Bennington Boomers
by Joel A. Nichols   162

Jock Sniffer
by Bearmuffin   171

The Bird
by Erastes   180

Phenom
by Todd Gregory   189

Team Player
by Brian Centrone   198

Switching Positions
by Brad Nichols   213

About the Contributors   223

INTRODUCTION

My question is this: why do they call them the "boys" of summer, when it's so clearly obvious to me that those people playing on the baseball diamond are all man. Muscled bodies, scruffy faces, thick arms, it's a veritable feast of the flesh. And those uniforms! I love the way they mold to a player's skin, highlighting those bubble butts, those finely chiseled chests . . . Oh wait, I think I'm getting ahead of things here. Or at least getting ahead of the writers.

But you get my point. Baseball players are hot. And as I write this, it's the off season, so I haven't been getting my daily fill of those homoerotic images of pitchers and catchers, free swingers and contact players. What better way to wait for the next fantasy-fueled season of baseball than to read a bunch of stories where the sexiest players come into our minds, our hearts, and our . . . well, I don't think I need to go there, do I?

The great group of writers I've found have hit home run after home run here, with a wide variety of tales that take us from the days of innocence to the heat of summer, from the playing field to the locker room, to the heights of passion and the realization of dreams. So, sit back, relax, become an armchair commentator, and play the field the way you want to. Read a story between innings, and if that turns you on enough, well, there's always something more to do during the seventh-inning stretch . . . or a rain delay. Just be sure to pick up someone who plays on our team.

I'll say no more. Batter up!

—*Jesse Grant*

Capping the Season

Ryan Field

───

The day Hunter sold the "big house," he took a deep breath and patted himself on the back when he signed the final contract. And it wasn't because he'd sucked off the hot, married real estate agent in the back seat of a black Mercedes SUV an hour earlier, either. A deep breath because the atrocious Mc-Mansion on six acres had swallowed his hard earned money for five years, and a silent pat on the back because the sale actually helped him attain his original goal, which was to own a smaller home without a mortgage before turning thirty years old. With money he'd inherited from his grandfather, Hunter had purchased the "big house" with a small down payment and a huge mortgage a month after he'd landed his first job at a law firm. He'd known it would be a struggle, and that he'd have to make huge sacrifices, but he'd also suspected the investment would pay off in the end.

He walked away from settlement that morning in late September with the sweet taste of straight-guy dick in his mouth and a savory cashier's check for more than twice what he'd originally paid; a twenty-eight-year-old financial success, now the proud owner of a three thousand square foot luxury town house that didn't have a claim against it.

The only thing he'd miss about the "big house" was the location: six acres of green lawn, the farthest rear section backing up to a baseball field that was part of a large corporate insurance complex. Not like the typical baseball field—with sand, bare patches of unkempt grass, and faded white lines—the field behind Hunter's mansion resembled a country club, with lush, emerald sod, thickly mulched, manicured gardens, and perfect white lines connecting the bases. An expensive sprinkler system kept the field perpetually fresh; landscaping crews, with dirty young guys in baggy shorts and black sneakers, primped and prodded the faultless gardens daily. Because he couldn't afford a landscaping crew for his property, Hunter had mowed his lawn and maintained his own simple gardens year round, never too shy to linger at the back of the property during baseball season, wearing nothing but skimpy cotton shorts the landscaping boys could practically see through.

Hunter's sex appeal came in that innocent way dark, rough men always seem to notice. About five eleven, with blond hair and large blue eyes, he had a slim body frame enhanced by working out in the basement with free weights and push-ups. Though his arms weren't particularly large, his chest muscles responded to bench presses and push-ups to the point where they rounded and popped like unbreakable ostrich eggshells sliced directly in half. But most men noticed one thing first: his round ass, a protruding cushion begging to be pounded and slapped and plugged.

The landscaping guys, always on the down-low, would furtively watch while he pruned and trimmed hedges, parading his naked torso, sometimes pulling the sheer shorts so far below his waist that half the crack of his smooth ass could be seen. Though it didn't happen often (most of the time this was just a show), when Hunter noticed one of the guys seriously watching, he'd gradually arch his back, stretch his arms, and then nod toward the garden shed. The guy would follow him to a private place behind the shed, where Hunter would slip off his shorts and lie face down on a pile of mulch. He'd then spread his legs wide, arch his back so his engaging ass would be in the air, and the guy would pull down his zipper for a quick afternoon fuck. In a white enamel pail with chips around the rim, Hunter kept lube and a full supply of condoms. Once, on a rare, unforgettable afternoon, when four Spanish-speaking studs had been drinking too much beer on the job, Hunter spread his legs and arched his back while all four took turns nailing him into the mulch pile. It took a week for the reddish handprints, where they'd squeezed his supple ass so hard, to disappear.

Though he'd miss the summertime romps and capping off the baseball season with the landscaping boys, living a mortgage-free life was far more exciting. The new townhouse, in an exclusive community of only thirty large units, had year-round landscapers included in the monthly community fees. Hunter would never have to push a lawn mower, dig with a shovel, or rake a leaf again. He wouldn't have to work out at home in the basement anymore either; he could now afford to join a gym like all his friends, where he'd prance around naked in the locker room for men who were just as horny (and dirty) as the landscaping guys. He also portended he'd be able to distract at least a few of the guys who landscaped in the new townhouse community, too, by walking around on his rear deck in nothing but a short towel.

He drove directly to the new house after settlement and saw the moving crew had arrived on time: three overweight guys in Dodger baseball caps with yellow teeth and man breasts. In the back of his mind he'd been hoping for fierce and rugged moving men, with shaved heads and pierced nipples, who would only be too happy to pull down their zippers while he sucked them all off consecutively in the back of the truck: an unfulfilled moving van fantasy that caused his hole to twitch.

The moving guys had been waiting for him to arrive from

settlement, standing beside red brick front steps, with their hands in their pockets. They were talking with a fourth guy who stood out, wearing tight, white workout pants and a white cotton shirt that had the number sixteen written across the back in blue letters; a specific uniform for baseball from what Hunter could see. The guy in white was smiling, and writing on small pieces of paper, using the back of his black leather briefcase as a writing desk. Hunter didn't care. Someone had parked a huge black Cadillac Escalade behind the moving van, and he didn't have a place to park his own small Jaguar convertible to remove the few boxes of personal items he'd wanted to transport himself. Parking in front, on the circle, was only for temporary loading and unloading.

Without a choice, he parked in the back, near his new garage, and walked around to meet the moving men. It was one of those perfect, brisk California days. The winds had finally died down and the sunshine reflected against the brass hardware of his black front door. He knew he'd made a wise decision with the town house. He'd looked at dozens, but this group of homes were classic, with red brick, white trim, and black shutters, and red brick walkways in a herringbone pattern leading to front doors and garages, flanked with well-trimmed ivy and juniper hedges. If you didn't know you were in southern California you would have thought you were in Cambridge, Massachusetts.

He pulled two large boxes from the front seat of his car and walked around the side of the house, toward the front door where the moving men were waiting.

"Sorry I'm late, guys," Hunter said, noticing the guy in the white shorts was gone, "the settlement took longer than usual because the seller showed up late." It was a lie. Hunter had spent thirty minutes blowing the married real estate agent. Poor guy, so eager and needy; and Hunter loved hungry dick.

"No problem," said one of the fat guys.

Hunter looked at the sidewalk, toward the Cadillac. "Does that car belong to you guys?"

"I wish," said another moving guy. "I'd kill for a car like that. It belongs to the guy who lives next door, Roddy Kent. We just got his autograph."

The comment caught Hunter off guard. "Who's Roddy Kent?"

"Dude, Roddy Kent is only one of the best major league ballplayers who ever lived," said the third moving guy. His eyes sparkled with excitement.

"Oh," said Hunter, disappointed. He'd been hoping for a gay neighbor.

The moving guys worked fast and surprisingly well, and Hunter was all moved in by four o'clock that afternoon. When he walked them to the door, handing the leader a check, he noticed the black Escalade still parked out front.

The next morning, just before Hunter left for the office, he looked out the front window and noticed his neighbor, Mr. Baseball, carrying the black briefcase and walking toward the car. Clearly, it had been parked there all night. As Mr. Baseball walked around to the driver's side, he stopped and stared at the windshield for a moment. There was a piece of paper attached, a parking ticket, Hunter assumed. He yanked the ticket from the windshield, crumpled it up, and tossed it over his shoulder.

That night, on his way home from work, Hunter stopped at a home decorating shop on Melrose for some new linen. It was Friday, payday, and he felt like spending money. He'd always been so cautious, shopping online at smartpurchase. com, selecting simple, inexpensive bedding. Now that he had the extra cash he wanted to splurge on real dupioni silk; something sexy and sheer in dark gold and bronze that needed to be dry-cleaned, so when he slept naked the softness would rub against his shaved balls. But when he pulled up to his garage the good feeling suddenly disappeared. There sat the black Escalade, parked to the side on an angle, just far enough over to block Hunter from parking his own car.

One thing Hunter had learned in law school: handle a problem the minute it happens. Don't wait; be firm. So he walked around to his new neighbor's front door and knocked.

It took a moment, but Mr. Baseball finally came to the door, wearing white boxer shorts and skimpy white ankle socks. He was cute at a glance, for a straight guy in his late thirties, with a good, strong torso slightly covered with light brown fleece. Not an articulate weight lifter, but large and athletic and powerful in a natural, manly way. His hairy legs, slightly bowed, were well proportioned. He had a minor belly, but didn't seem concerned about showing it to anyone. His short brown hair suggested the military.

"I'm your new neighbor, Hunter." Hunter spoke with purpose and conviction, as though he were just another straight dude talking to a buddy. He was by no means feminine, but he didn't want Mr. Baseball to suspect he was a nelly queen.

"Waddaya want?" Mr. Baseball asked, his words slurred, one hand pressed against the doorknob, the other holding a martini glass; large hazel eyes cloudy and red.

Hunter smiled, always believing it best to be nice at first. "Hate to bother you, man, but your car is blocking my garage and I can't get inside."

"Hold on," said Mr. Baseball, leaving Hunter to stand at the open door while he walked back into his hallway. His head shook, as though he couldn't understand why he had so much trouble parking in the tight-assed community.

He returned a minute later. "Here's the keys. You can move it. As you can see I'm in no condition to drive." Mr.

Baseball laughed, tossing the keys and slamming the door in Hunter's face.

It occurred to Hunter he was missing his old house, where although he had a huge mortgage he didn't have to deal with neighbors like Roddy Kent. It also occurred to him he could call the police and make a big deal out of it; however, in spite of the fact Roddy had been drunk and extremely rude, he had trusted Hunter with the keys to a very expensive automobile. The innocence this exuded made Hunter pause. So he moved the car himself and decided to wait before he did anything that might cause hard feelings. When he tried to return the keys no one answered the door, so he left them under the front mat and slipped a short note beneath the front door so Roddy wouldn't be alarmed the next day. He doubted the guy would remember anything.

That night, after putting his new bronze and gold silk bed together, Hunter decided to google Roddy Kent to see if he really was as well-known and famous as the moving men had claimed. While Hunter enjoyed watching baseball (not to mention big, strong baseball players) every now and then, and knew the game, he'd never been a die-hard fan who knew teams and names.

The things he read online about Roddy were outrageous. He'd gotten into fistfights during games, cursed and spit at umpires without a second thought, tossed his bat several times during a game in a fit that could only be described as a little-boy tantrum, and he once got so mad at a comment a sports writer made he pulled down his pants and mooned the press box on live TV. Worst of all, he had attacked and berated his own teammates more than once. He'd been with six teams in his major league career, that year with the L.A. Dodgers. And it had been a bad year. He'd been forced to sit out the remainder of the season for a rib injury, and his wife of only one year (classic bimbo) had just filed for divorce. At first Hunter wondered if Roddy Kent was dangerous, and then, after reading between the lines, he surmised that all the gossip and comments about him were based on the fact that he had a hot temper when pushed to the limit. From what Hunter concluded, thinking as a logical lawyer, every time Roddy had lost his temper it was because he'd been right (like when he ripped a team member last year for "not hustling the base paths"). He just hadn't known how to be diplomatic, was all.

Hunter spent the following day, Saturday, unpacking boxes and getting the new place organized. He wanted the house set up and ready by the end of Sunday night. By four o'clock that afternoon, just when Hunter had decided on a nap, there was a knock at the front door. He'd been working in his underwear all day, so he pulled on a pair of jeans and peeked through the side window next to the door to find Mr. Baseball standing at his doorstep.

Hunter opened the door and frowned. "Didn't you get my note?"

"Ah, yeah, man," said Roddy, "I just, yanno, wanted to apologize for yesterday." He wore a blue Dodgers shirt and white cotton shorts. The apology didn't come easily; his head bowed, his hazel eyes staring at the brick steps. His voice was deep and throaty, but his words were surprisingly soft and humble.

Hunter smiled. "Well, thank you."

"I need a ride, man," Roddy said.

"But I put your keys under the mat," said Hunter.

"Oh, yeah, I got them, man," said Roddy. "I went to practice this morning but I sort of, I guess, forgot to get gas and now my car is down the road."

He reminded Hunter of a bad little boy who'd forgotten his school lunch. "I have a gallon of gas in the garage. I'll go get it." One thing Hunter had learned from the "big house":

a gallon of gas came in handy for a multitude of things, like weed whacking, lawn cutting, or even burning leaves.

Later that night, around seven, there was another knock on Hunter's door. When he opened it, he looked down and saw the red gas container filled to the top and an expensive bottle of vodka with a card that read THANKS, ROD. There was something both awkward and adorable about the gesture, the way the items had been placed so cautiously. The handwriting on the note was large, bold script—masculine, without frilly corkscrews or wisps. *Funny,* Hunter thought, as he walked the gas container to the garage, *the guy is a famous baseball hero, everyone who loves baseball is terrified of him, and he's nothing more than a lost little boy.*

On Sunday afternoon, Hunter decided to stop working and take advantage of his new rear deck. With all the work he'd done at the old house, there'd been very few days for lying in the sun and relaxing. He hadn't even purchased outdoor furniture yet, but all he needed was a bath towel and sunscreen. At first he'd opted to wear a Speedo, but then he looked around and realized no one could see him; a huge wooden fence separated his deck from Roddy's. The only way Roddy could see anything was from an upstairs window, and he doubted Roddy would care one way or the other if he decided to suntan in the nude. Roddy, he figured, was probably drunk and passed out on the sofa, poor bastard.

Two hours later, turning on his stomach and spreading his legs so he wouldn't get little white tan lines beneath his ass cheeks, a loud crash came from Roddy's deck. He heard a shout: "Fuck me bitch, damn it!"

Hunter rose to his feet and wrapped the leopard print bath towel around his waist. He walked to the other side and cautiously knocked on the fence. "Is everything okay?"

"I cut my fucking finger," Roddy answered through the

wooden slats. "I don't know, I might need fucking stitches; won't stop fucking bleeding. It's bad."

Hunter frowned, wishing he hadn't heard the crash, or the expletives. "Why don't I come over and take a look."

Each deck had a rear gate, so Hunter tightened the towel around his waist and walked next door. When he opened the gate, he saw Mr. Baseball sitting on a black iron chair holding his right arm in the air with his left hand. He'd anticipated a bloody mess, and Roddy delirious, but aside from a broken glass vase, things looked normal. Except for all the boxes of baseballs, twenty or more, stacked neatly and ready to be autographed for Roddy's adoring fans. There was an open box, and the aroma of new baseballs smelled of leather and chalk. It wasn't the type of deck you'd expect a major league ballplayer to have; no hot tub for trashy, fake-titty bimbos, not a plastic palm tree in sight.

"Let me take a look," Hunter said, kindly taking Roddy's right arm in the palm of his hand. He noticed Roddy was still wearing the same white boxer shorts, unwashed with dried yellow pee stains near the fly.

"I need stitches, man . . . fuck, I hate the sight of blood. This is all I need, first the broken rib and now my pitching arm."

Hunter's brow creased. "It's hardly a scrape. I thought you'd sliced off your finger. This is nothing more than a prick on your middle finger." He was amazed at how strong Mr. Baseball fretted over a small cut. "Do you have Band-Aids and alcohol?"

"No Band-Aids, but plenty of alcohol," Roddy replied, joking about his full supply of booze. He wasn't drunk. Hunter could tell by the way he spoke.

"Just sit tight," Hunter said. He went next door for a Band-Aid and rubbing alcohol.

When he returned, Roddy was still holding his arm in the

air as though it were ready for a tourniquet. "Can't you just put on the Band-Aid, man? The alcohol will hurt."

"Don't be a pussy," Hunter scolded. He gently took hold of Roddy's pitching arm as though he were handling fine porcelain and began to dab the small cut with alcohol. Roddy's large fingers were thick.

"That doesn't hurt at all," said Roddy. "Feels kind of nice." His voice was soft and deep, not a hint of panic. He seemed to enjoy the attention.

Hunter smiled. "I think you'll live." Then he vigilantly wrapped a small Band-Aid around the wound and gently pressed it to make sure it wouldn't fall off. While he was still leaning over, Roddy reached around with his left arm and slowly began to run the palm of his rough hand up Hunter's smooth leg, under the towel, resting it on Hunter's bare ass.

"How come you're being so nice to me?" Roddy asked, his hand now gently patting Hunter's ass. "I've been such a pain in the ass to you since you moved in."

Hunter stopped breathing. When he looked down to where Roddy was sitting, he noticed a huge erection had pitched a tent in Roddy's pee-stained boxers. His brawny, hairy legs were spread wide, moving back and forth as though he were ready to jump up and pounce on a fresh kill.

"I don't remember giving you permission to put your hand on my ass, Mr. Baseball," Hunter said.

"I'll remove it if you want," Roddy said, sliding the tip of his thick middle finger toward Hunter's pink hole, lightly circling the opening.

Hunter didn't respond, and Roddy knew from the size of the erection poking through the bath towel that Hunter wouldn't resist.

Roddy stood. A thick, eight-inch donkey dick popped from the opening in the unwashed boxer shorts. He smiled, proud of his big baseball bat. "C'mon, let's go upstairs." He placed his palm on the small of Hunter's back as they silently walked through the first floor and headed upstairs to the master bedroom.

The room was a smelly mess. Unwashed jockstraps and soiled underwear were tossed on the floor and furniture, dirty sweat socks and used athletic cups were piled near the end of the rumpled bed. Leaning against a large glass desk were three baseball bats covered with autographs. Hunter felt as though he were actually standing in a locker room inhaling the ripe onion and vinegar aroma of sweaty baseball players—a combination of unwashed dick and hairy armpits.

They didn't waste time with "what are you into, man?" or other banal questions so often asked before sex between men. For Hunter this was unusually simple. He let the leopard towel drop to the floor, and then slowly went down to his knees. Placing the palms of his hands gently on the hard, hairy thighs of the baseball player, he buried his face in the pee-stained boxer shorts, inhaling the acid aroma as though it were worth a thousand dollars an ounce. Then he cautiously placed the wide dick back inside and lowered the shorts. Roddy stepped out of them awkwardly, pouncing his large feet in a rough-and-tumble manner. Hunter began to lick the soft, hairy place on the inside of Mr. Baseball's right thigh, licking upward, until he reached a heavy ball sac. He carefully inhaled both bull-sized balls and rolled them around his warm mouth, tasting the salt and sweat.

The moist balls eventually slid from his mouth and he placed them in the palm of his left hand. Hunter then wrapped his warm lips around the tip of Roddy's cock, a large dick head with a wide slit that reminded him of a frozen mushroom. His lips slowly went down the shaft, sucking the hard bat all the way to the back of his throat, and then with his tongue he began rhythmic suction, as though his mouth were an electronic machine designed to suck big baseball player cock. Roddy's precome oozed and Hunter swallowed each small, sweet drip.

When he finally released the big sopping dick, he placed his hands just below Roddy's slight potbelly, pushing the strong baseball player onto the bed.

"We have to go easy, baby," said Roddy, "I have a broken rib and this thirty-eight-year-old body is more like forty-eight."

Hunter smiled. It occurred to him that Roddy needed to be treated like a king—in charge, but pampered and babied and adored. Normally Hunter liked his sex fast and coarse, with lots of dirty talk and ass slapping, but with Roddy he only wanted to be placid and articulate. There was something about Roddy—his jarring baseball player movements, the way he crushed the floor like an awkward teenage jock when he walked through a room—that turned Hunter on so much he didn't need rough slaps on the ass or orders to "suck my dick, bitch."

"Don't worry, Rod," he whispered, "the only thing you have to do is lie back and close your eyes. I promise I'll take very good care of you. And, I'm clean, man . . . no diseases."

"Me too," said Roddy.

When Roddy was on his back, Hunter climbed on top and straddled the rock-firm dick. He then spit into his hand and began to lather the erection that rested on the crack of his ass. His hole was already wet and begging for cock, but he wanted the meat to slide in easily so that when Roddy felt the inside of the warm, velvet hole, he'd gasp. Men always did that when they entered Hunter's ass; his tight box was always referred to as a velvet cock trap.

Hunter pressed the tip of the large cock head to the pink opening and slowly pushed it past taut anal lips. With the head inside, Hunter arched his back and lowered his ass gently so the entire dick would be sucked into his body. As predicted, though his eyes were closed and his brows knitted together, Mr. Baseball moaned and sighed when the cock reached bottom. Hunter cupped and squeezed his own chest, always sensitive and orgasmic when there was dick up his ass.

Roddy opened his eyes and stared. "God, I've never felt anything so soft and so tight at the same time. Hot tits, man, I wanna bite them."

"Close your eyes, buddy," Hunter said, as he slowly began to rock back and forth, squeezing and releasing the big hard baseball bat as though his hole were giving Roddy a blow job.

While Roddy sighed, now paralyzed, Hunter continued to rock, holding his own erection. He looked down and noticed a large black-and-blue bruise on Roddy's torso; the broken rib he assumed. He stopped rocking, spread his legs wider, and leaned forward to gently lick the sore spot.

"That was nice," Roddy said, raising his eyebrows. "I didn't expect that."

"Close your eyes, handsome," said Hunter, his ass slowly beginning to rock and suck and squeeze the baseball player's dick toward what he hoped would be a stunning climax. Hunter suspected it had been a long time, if ever, since anyone had treated the poor guy so affectionately.

The rocking and ass fucking intensified, to a point where Roddy began to wiggle his large feet as men do just before they are ready to blow a full load. Hunter did all the work; his legs spread wide, a smooth ass riding large cock toward climax. Roddy didn't need to move a muscle, or return any of the fucking motions; just lie still and bust a nut up Hunter's ass.

"I'm close, dude," Roddy whispered. His eyebrows knitted together, toes beginning to curl.

"Go, buddy," Hunter said, while he began to jerk his own cock in the same rhythm as the fucking.

Roddy leaned forward to squeeze Hunter's round chest muscles, closed his eyes evenly, and moaned, "Ah . . . Ah . . . Ah." The baseball player went into spasms, his hairy legs vibrated, while Hunter drained every last ounce of juice, a full load of cream that Hunter could feel splashing inside his body. Barely jerking his own dick, Hunter climaxed with Roddy's great hands squeezing his tits—a double orgasm as the large cock banged against his prostate.

Roddy threw his arms behind his head, exposing hairy underarms, and stared at the ceiling for a moment. "Man that really was good. Dude, I needed that." He seemed surprised, as though he'd never had an orgasm.

Hunter lifted his right leg and eased the cock from his ass, come mixed with ass juice now dripping down his ass crack toward his balls. "Don't move. I'll go into the bathroom and get a wet towel."

"Wait," Roddy said. "C'mere." He leaned up, placed his palm on the back of Hunter's blond head, and pulled him forward so they could kiss. Not a peck, he stuck a thick, sloppy tongue down Hunter's throat and shoved it around for a minute. Rough, five o'clock shadow felt like sandpaper against Hunter's smooth face while they swapped spit.

After the kiss Hunter went into the muddled bathroom, noticing dark yellow pee stains on the rim of the toilet, and he wet two small towels with very hot water: one for cleaning the come and ass juice and the other for massaging and relaxing Roddy's empty balls.

"I like that," Roddy said, while Hunter ran the hot wet towel inside his groin and all around his balls. "No one ever did that. Damn, it's almost as good as fucking."

"Take a nap now," Hunter said. "You need rest." For some reason he felt the need to take care of him, to protect Roddy from the world and himself.

"My body is tired," he said. "I won't argue; that's all I

ever do. Later we're going out to dinner for a couple of big juicy steaks."

"If you're not tired," Hunter said. He meant it, too. Though he wasn't sure whether or not he and Roddy would ever become an actual couple, he was sure they would become very good friends.

"Oh, no," Roddy said, drifting off to sleep, "we're going."

"But you have to get up early tomorrow for practice. You'll be capping off the season soon. We'll have plenty of time for steaks." He reached down and removed Roddy's sweat socks, lightly massaging his feet.

"I'm capping the season off with your hot ass and a couple of juicy steaks tonight."

Hunter licked the bottoms of Roddy's feet. "We'll see, man."

Locker Room Home Run

Morris Michaels, Jr.

Monty walked into the locker room, his bat over his aching shoulder. Here he was, a forty-something corporate vice president, and after the first practice of this season's company baseball team he wasn't sure he would survive the second. The company team had won the championship of the informal league they played in with other businesses in midtown, and it had been quite a long shot that he would be selected when he had first tried out for the team. But he had made the cut. He had always wanted to play ball, but after playing on the high school varsity team he had never seemed able to find the time. He hadn't been quite good enough for his college team and after graduation his life had gotten busy—as it did for his friends, as well. He had played the occasional one- or two-inning weekend game with some of the guys in the first few years after college, but one by one they all scattered to the four winds as graduate school and jobs and relationships came to dominate those years. He had himself gone back to graduate school and then ended up a mid-level executive who traveled a lot and never seemed able to really put down roots, even when he was able to stay in one city for a few years. His work defined his existence now and he couldn't really think of himself as anything other than who he was at the office. But he was feeling the lack of an outside life. Those baseball days had been some of the happiest in his life. He never felt more connected with other people or the universe than when he was standing in the outfield, reaching to catch the ball hurtling toward him from the sky, or when the bat met the ball with a firm *crack!* and he sent the ball soaring out and above the players on the bases spread before him. Since his travel schedule had made long-term relationships—or any kind of friendship outside the office—difficult, he had decided to join the company team as a first step to enlarging his world and maybe connecting with a new group of "the guys" for a beer or two afterward. He wanted to recapture that connection with the world he had always felt through baseball.

A lot was riding on this team he had gotten himself involved with. But could his body take this kind of punishment? Even though he had kept up his membership at the gym, he hadn't swung a bat in the almost twenty years since that first promotion either! Running? Hardly. Although he was not exactly overweight, he had put on a pound or two since college as well. Was it really the exercise on the field that had been so grueling or was it the tantalizing—no, exhausting!—possibility of connecting with one of his fellow ballplayers?

"Great hit, Monty!" A big hand firmly slapped his shoulder. "You smack the ball like that a few more times and we'll be in the championship again for sure!" Monty turned to see who among all the guys around him had praised his newly resurrected skill.

It was Dave, the big, strong guy from accounting. About Monty's same height and weight but slightly younger and in much better shape, Dave had been on the team for as long as Monty could remember and always had a good word for everybody. He was sandy blond and had all his hair, whereas Monty's had begun to thin a few years back. His solid arms rippled with thick muscles, and a thick pelt of that sandy blond hair that looked as though it could ripple in the breeze like a field of ripe wheat or a lion's mane on the African savannah. His pale blue eyes and deep golden voice only added to the impression of a great lion or other creature, friendly and outgoing but with a reservoir of strength and ability just waiting to spring into action. It was that strength and ability that he had demonstrated on the baseball diamond as he manned second base or served occasionally as pitcher. He had agility as well. No one could scoop up a ball or pluck it from the sky with such seemingly effortless grace, or send the ball sailing over home plate, racking up strike after strike. Dave seemed like one of those guys could have been destined for the major leagues in his younger days, if he had wanted it. But instead he had wound up in the accounting department and had won the respect and admiration of everyone there. He handled numbers with the same skill that he handled a bat and ball on the field.

"Uh . . . thanks." Monty's response stumbled out of his mouth. "It's been a while since I really swung a bat, but it must be like riding a bicycle. You never really forget, I guess." He chuckled.

"No, you don't," Dave agreed, taking off his cap and running his fingers through his sweaty hair. "No, you don't forget and it comes right back—if you let it." He flashed a wide grin at Monty and chuckled with him. The dark wet stain under Dave's arm seemed to grow darker and larger as he lifted his arm higher to scratch the back of his head. The rich, fragrant scent clutched at Monty's senses and his reaction caught him by surprise.

There was another reason, if truth be told, that Monty had been hesitant to reach out to other people during his career or to invest much emotional energy in building and maintaining relationships outside the office. It was the same as the deepest, darkest, most secret reasons he had finally succumbed to the drive to join the baseball team this year: his desire to be with men, to see other men up close, to touch and to be touched had finally been more than he could withstand. Sure, he had worked out in gyms and had seen guys in the locker rooms, but always at a distance. An emotional distance if not a physical distance. Some of them had been so close that he could have felt their warm breath on the back of his neck if he had allowed himself to enjoy (or even notice!) that physical proximity. But his fundamentally shy personality, which he was able to cover up with the bravado of his office persona, had never allowed him to relax in those situations that might—even slightly—bear the potential of becoming "social." So if he could begin to bridge the gap (which was really a chasm) between himself and other guys, between his actions and his desires . . . . Why, that would be an even greater success than the thrill of getting his first promotion almost twenty years ago!

"Yeah, well . . . it might come back and I want to let it but that doesn't make it hurt any less." Monty smiled at Dave and swung the bat down as he reached inside the front of his blue-and-white striped uniform to rub his aching shoulder. "Ouch."

Dave swung his powerful arm around Monty's shoulders. "I can't argue with you there, Monty," he agreed. "Those muscles can hurt like hell when they get asked to do things they haven't done in years or move in ways they haven't moved in ages. But it does 'em good to get put to use again." He flashed another broad grin at Monty.

Electricity ran up and down Monty's exhausted frame. Could this be the connection he had been hoping for? Not only was Dave talking with him, he had reached out to touch him and Monty hadn't flinched or gotten so nervous and tongue-tied that he came off feeling or looking like an awkward, stupid adolescent again. Monty took a deep breath and swallowed.

"You know, Monty, you can't let yourself get dehydrated out there on the field or ignore those aching muscles. The pain will only get worse the next time unless you give those aches and pains the attention they need after each workout."

"Yeah, I've been going to the gym but I guess I haven't been swinging those weights quite the same way you swing a baseball bat." Monty nodded in agreement with Dave. "I guess I should go home and soak in a hot bathtub and maybe wrap this shoulder with an Ace bandage before I try to move it again."

"Yeah, that would be good. But you know what works even better? A good ol' fashioned massage. Rubs those aches and pains right out. I always get myself a massage after the first couple a practices each season, just 'til I get back into the swing of things again before the real games start. Because there's no time to recover in between those games once they start really going in earnest. And then, if we reach the play-offs, well . . . That's when a poor start during practice can send you into the hospital, because you never got the right foundation to build on during the season. You sure as hell don't want to miss the championship you help us reach, now do you, Monty?"

Monty shook his head. Getting that far with the team and then ending up on the injured list was not a good way to wrap up his first season back in the bullpen.

Monty suddenly realized they had reached the back of the locker room, where the showers were located. Clouds of steam wafted aloft and the hiss of hot water filled the air as the drops of water and suds of soap splashed off the sweaty bodies gathered under the showerheads. Laughter and conversation swirled in the air around him. He hadn't even noticed the other guys as he and Dave had navigated their way through their teammates. It was as if he and Dave had been the only two men in the locker room.

"That doesn't sound like a half-bad idea, Dave. Thanks for mentioning it. I'll have to sign up for a massage when I go to the gym again tomorrow. It's been awhile since I treated myself to that kind of post-workout reward, but I think you're right—it might be just what the doctor ordered this time 'round!"

Dave looked around, his arm still draped casually over Monty's shoulders. "You know, you can't let the muscles get too stiff before you get the kinks worked out by a good rubdown. Why not let me give you a little working over right now, before we hit the showers? I've gotten enough rubdowns in my life to have some idea as to how they should go. This way your aching muscles will get the attention they're telling you they deserve and you can follow it up later with a longer, more regular massage at the gym the next time you go." Dave glanced around again, apparently orienting himself to the outside world as well after his stroll from the playing field with Monty. His eyes found what they were looking for. "There. Right over there. That's the massage room." Dave moved toward the door, and Monty had no real choice but to let Dave's body guide his to the rubdown room.

No real choice? No real objection, was more like it. No objection at all. A rubdown or massage or whatever from Dave after this first practice was a greater connection with the outside world than Monty had ever dared let himself dream of. Dave unhooked his arm from Monty's shoulders and opened the door.

They stepped into a small cubicle, not unlike the massage rooms Monty had seen in countless gyms over the years. A square space, painted white, with a black leather-covered table filling the middle of the room. There was a pair of chairs against one wall, a stack of white towels on one of them. A few hooks were fixed to the wall above the chairs.

"Here, you hang up your uniform over there," Dave motioned to the hooks, "and get on the table with one of those towels. There must be some oil or lotion or something here somewhere." He turned his back to Monty and reached for a shelf behind the door, rummaging around the bottles and tubes collected there.

Monty turned his attention to the hooks on the wall. He took a deep breath to settle the butterflies in his stomach. He stripped off his soaked uniform (*Funny, I didn't realize how sweaty I was,* he thought) and hung the shirt and pants over the hooks. He paused a moment before taking off his jockstrap and then draping it in what he hoped looked like a casual manner over the back of one of the chairs. He propped up his bat and reached for one of the fluffy towels to wrap around his waist.

"Here's a good one," Dave announced, turning back to Monty and holding a squeeze bottle of some lotion or oil. "So, what 'cha waitin' for? Climb up on the table and let's get to work!" Dave smiled even more broadly than he had before.

Monty climbed onto the table and lay down on his stomach, adjusting the towel under him. He laid his face down, closed his eyes, and waited. He heard the rustling of a uniform being unbuttoned behind him and the sound of something being draped over another hook, then the sound of a bottle top popping off, and the scent of baby oil filled the room. He heard the oil sputter out of the bottle and Dave's hands rubbing together.

Then electricity sparked up and down the length of his body as Dave's strong hands began gliding along his shoulders, rubbing the knots and kinks out of first his left and then right shoulder. The tug as Dave pulled Monty's left arm felt both good and bad as joints popped and muscles stretched. As Dave worked his hands down the length of Monty's arm, his manipulations caused nerves to contract reflexively in Monty's hand and Monty realized that he was cradling Dave's sac in his palm; Dave's large and furry sac, filled with two oversized major league quality . . .

"Got the bat to go with these?" Monty murmured, turning his face to the side but keeping his eyes closed and speaking half to himself and half to the massage table.

"As a matter of fact . . ." Dave muttered, and shifted himself slightly, placing his half-engorged—and growing stiffer by the minute—bat into Monty's outstretched catcher's mitt. It certainly did match the rest of Dave's proportions and rivaled the wooden bats they had just put down by both strength and size. A caught pop-up fly ball had never settled so naturally into Monty's grasp. A contented sigh escaped his lips as he relaxed into the massage, fondling the equipment of his masseur.

There was a sudden vacancy in Monty's hand and a deep, golden growling as he felt the weight on the massage table shift. Dave was hefting himself up onto the table, straddling Monty's ass cheeks and reaching over and across his outstretched back to continue massaging the right shoulder. Monty felt Dave's strong hairy legs flex on either side of his own. His left and right arms readjusted themselves, enfolding Dave's well-defined legs between his hands and his own outstretched legs. Dave was trapped there now, as surely as a base runner caught between bases as he had tried to steal second. The stiff bat between Dave's legs brushed and grazed the cleft between Monty's cheeks and Monty flexed his ass in response. Although Monty could not see it, a thin sparkling filament of come traced the emptiness between the tip of Dave's now fully engorged equipment and the pale white pitcher's mounds beneath him. Dave held his breath and hovered in midair a moment to avoid a premature bunt. No reason to clear the bench yet. "Charging the mound" would have a whole new set of associations for him in the future.

Dave's hands worked the muscles just below Monty's right shoulder. "Think of this as first base," Dave's rich voice purred quietly. "These muscles need to be worked and relaxed before anything else, just like a batter needs to reach first before even hoping to get further than that." Dave's fingertips prodded under the shoulder blades and Monty sighed contentedly. He felt himself slipping deeper and deeper into a relaxed connection with his friend, with the team that Dave personified, and with humanity as a whole, all thanks to their common love of baseball. Could life get better than this?

"Now the runner heads toward second," Dave continued his sports announcer monologue. His hands glided down Monty's right side, working the muscles between his rib cage with one hand and those along his spine with the other. Dave breathed deeply with the exertion and gently rode the ass beneath him, his cock continuing to occasionally brush Monty's ass and send another tingle up Dave's horizontal spine as he worked on the vertical one before him. The deep breathing of the two men came to border on moaning in tandem with each other as each gave himself to appreciating the touch of the other. Dave's broad hands engulfed the mid portion of Monty's back, kneading the muscles there. Monty had never appreciated another player's large hands as fully as he did now. Large hands might be a decided advantage in handling the bat as the pitcher sent a ball hurtling through the air, but that advantage seemed minor league compared to having such hands work the "second base" area of Monty's mid and now lower back.

A wordless gurgle of appreciation rose from Monty's throat. Dave shifted slightly back on Monty's ass. Now

Dave's cock seemed aimed right at Monty's increasingly re-laxed (and ready?) asshole, which twitched as Dave shifted his weight and position.

"The runner rounds third," Dave announced to his one-man audience. His hands slipped easily down Monty's lower back and love handles, molding themselves around the firm top of the cheeks he straddled. He pressed his legs tighter against Monty, who responded by pressing back with his own. Monty grasped Dave's thighs more tightly with his hands and began exploring the firm ridges and valleys of Dave's muscular, fur-clad legs. Even with his eyes still closed, he could see the gentle rolling dips and ridges of the lush grassy outfield he had played ball in as a boy at school. He flexed his ass cheeks again and felt Dave's long, thick bat trapped there a moment before it slipped free, the precome leaving a shiny, slippery trail behind.

Dave continued kneading the muscles under his hands, including both pale mounds beneath him in his ministra-tions. Rocking gently in rhythm, both Monty and Dave felt the excitement and tension building between them. A sta-dium full of fans, waiting with bated breath to see if the ball suspended above would be a home-run or fall just short into the outstretched glove of a waiting outfielder, could not have been so electrified.

Dave unexpectedly reached up and over the open field of Monty beneath him and took the back of Monty's neck in both hands. Dave's pecs and tits brushed the shoulder blades beneath him and his cock plowed up the lower portion of Monty's back. The masseur's hands swept around Monty's neck and along both his shoulders, and then in one graceful movement not unlike that ball gracefully arcing through the summer sky over the stadium, down Monty's spine and out along the top of the hips beneath Dave's own pelvis. Monty could sense, if not really feel, the fur that enclosed Dave's groin like a jockstrap but that allowed the equipment to swing free and bump into the ass rising to meet them. Dave pulled himself upright, arched his back, and twice repeated the electrifying flight over the fields of Monty's back. He then trace the runner's route around the bases of Monty's shoulders, lower back, and ass. With just as graceful a motion, Dave slid off Monty's back and stood at his side again. The thrill of Dave's touch left Monty gasping with ecstasy. Would he ever get his breath back? He wondered if he would ever want to.

Dave reached under his friend's pelvis and pulled Monty's stiff bat and not inconsiderable bag of hot, salty popcorn down so that the mushroom head poked out between his thighs, nestled on the big sac and between the testicles it contained. As the dick head scraped along the surface of the once-plush towel, the rough scratchiness was not unpleasant. Tickled, kind of. Nicely. Monty shivered. Dave kept hold of the dick with one hand while reaching for the oil with his other. Monty heard the gurgle of oil and felt it splash against his dick, balls, thighs, and the thick fingers that held them all.

Dave began massaging the tip of Monty's cut dick with both hands, gliding his thumbs along the short portion of the shaft available. Knuckles massaged Monty's prostate from the outside, pressing up and down along the infield between Monty's sac and asshole. Mmm, mmm, good. Just like the commercial. Then one thumb reached up and into Monty's ass, exploring the waiting asshole hiding within. Monty sighed and gave himself over completely to the final stage of his new friend's therapeutic touch. He pressed his ass back against Dave's thumb and it gently entered the dugout.

Undreamt of, indescribable bliss washed over Monty. How could he have denied himself this connection with his fellow players for so long? Dave's hand continued to manipulate the balls and dick head nestled so cozily in the bullpen between Monty's cheeks, while with his other hand, the thumb, and then two fingers slid up to massage the virgin prostate. Dave wrapped his fingers around the sac, as close to the base as he could reach, and pulled. His slick hands traveled down the thick folds of skin until they were unable to slide around the twin bags of salty honey-nuts trapped within. Snacks sold at the stadium concession could not be so diverting or so sweet. Monty pressed back with all the energy he could muster, pushing both his dick and prostate closer to the source of those angelic sensations.

Dave's massage became quicker and more intense in response to Monty's pushing back, the expert nonverbal communication like that between a pitcher and catcher deciding between themselves the route of the next ball over home plate. Signals were sent by each man and received by his teammate, as surely as the concealed sign language that flew between the pitcher's mound and home plate. Quicker. Harder. Gasping. Moaning. Pressing. Pushing. Exploding . . .

Monty shot wave after wave of steaming come into Dave's hand, like the rapid fire repeating shots in a batter's cage. It spilled over his knuckles and pooled on the towel tangled beneath them. Dave held his friend's spurting virility for a long moment, allowing it to finally slow and then lie still within his sticky palm. The fingers massaging the prostate gradually slowed their attentions and then pulled out, allowing the throbbing prostate and ecstatic cheeks around it to collapse and rest. Mutual sighs contentedly filled the air.

Dave finally released Monty's newfound team spirit and reached for another towel on the nearby chair. Monty heard him wiping the oil and come off his hands. And then—finally—he opened his eyes and propped himself up on his elbows to look at the man beside him. He saw the handsome player standing there, his broad and richly carpeted chest heaving as Monty's had been. Broad grins blossomed across both their faces.

Monty's eyes slid lazily down the muscular torso and came to rest on the still half-engorged cock that hung to one side of the masseur's hips. Dave flexed those hips and his cock swung tantalizingly.

"You hit one hell of a home run, buddy," Monty muttered, swinging his head from side to side, mesmerized by the cock swinging like the bat in the hands of a star hitter waiting for his turn at bat. "Care to play a double-header?"

Pitcher and Catcher

Armand

I was the only gay player—or at least the only out player—on our college baseball team. During my senior year, thanks to some new transfer students and improved training, the team had effectively evolved from an inconsistent, mediocre group of guys into a fierce, cohesive unit, and no one cared that I was a homo.

When I was recruited out of high school, I worried about how the other players would react to my sexuality (and I refused to be in the closet). Though they were all straight, the guys turned out to be extremely cool about the whole thing. I couldn't ask for better friends. They didn't seem uncomfortable being naked around me; they often asked me about my love life; and they never used the word "fag," except in play. Though I knew they didn't require it, I held to certain boundaries for my own peace of mind: I never showered with the guys, unless there were private stalls; I never made out with a boyfriend in front of them; at parties, I stayed sober, so I didn't make any unfortunate passes at my fellow teammates. And in four years, I'd never slapped another player on the ass or jumped into his arms.

My teammates, however, seemed to have no boundaries and loved to play with me. They'd mooned me, groped me, kissed me, stripped me, and humped me. One time the whole team even took a trip to a gay bar. A couple of times, a drunken teammate put the moves on me, but it was always a feeble attempt by a lonely, horny guy to relieve his pent up sexual frustrations. I never allowed anything to happen, because these guys were my friends, my family, and I didn't want anything awkward between us.

The other players were always asking me questions that were naïve yet cute, and I often fought to stifle a laugh. Mostly they wanted know if the popular axiom is true: gay guys give better head than women. Every one of them asked me if I'd ever slept with a woman, to which I always replied, "Have you ever slept with a man?" (Some of them coyly responded, "Maybe.") Probably a dozen or more had asked me, in a roundabout way, if I took it up the ass. Straight guys are so curious about butt sex, and it cracks me up. One of the guys actually asked me how he could loosen his hole because his girlfriend wanted to fuck him with a strap-on. He was anxious about it when we talked, but after it happened, he told me that he liked it so much that he'd shot a huge load while she was plowing him.

Everything with my teammates was done in good fun and without malice, so I never took offense because none was intended. Hey, they were curious straight guys trying to be supportive, and I was flattered that they felt comfortable enough to joke with me, pinch and tickle me, and ask such intimate questions. They treat me like just one of the team, and that was exactly how I wanted it.

I guess lots of gay baseball players would have gone for it—messed around with their bi-curious teammates—but I never had a thing for straight guys. I wanted another gay boy to sweep me off my feet and satisfy my lust. It would be icing on the cake if he loved baseball, too.

I never dreamed I'd find the guy of my dreams on the

opposing team. As the breakout team of the season, we were about to face our greatest rivals on their turf.

The game was in Chicago, a six-hour trip from Ohio. The night before I'd gone out clubbing, and had spent the whole night trying to avoid this sixty-year-old troll who kept trying to buy me drinks. I went to bed horny and woke up crabby, so I folded up my coat for a pillow and went to sleep on the bus. I expected my teammates to do the same, but when the bus hit a pothole, I awoke to find a crowd surrounding me and knew they were up to no good.

When I'd fallen asleep, I had the whole seat to myself, but when I awoke, the centerfielder, Tommy, was next to me. I looked over to ask what he was up to and realized that his fly was open and my hand was wrapped around his penis.

"Damn, Evan, that feels good." Tommy began to undulate his hips.

My teammates roared with laughter and called out "do me" or "yank it off, Evan" or "let me show you what a real dick looks like."

I jerked my hand away. "Geez, Tommy. What the fuck!"

"I guess I might have to go gay, too." He closed his fly and bound his penis inside his jeans.

"I don't think your girlfriend would like that." I gave him a shove, but he didn't budge.

"She don't know how to take care of me like you, lover boy," he cooed before leaning over and kissing me on the cheek.

The other guys patted my cheek, pinched my nipples, and kissed the top of my head, and one by one they drifted away.

"A guy can't even sleep around you jokers." I fluffed my jacket under my head and turned toward the window.

"Oh, Ev, I'm just playing. You know I didn't mean anything by it." Tommy patted my thigh. "You mad at me?"

I tried to feign anger, but a smile threatened to crease my face.

"Come on. I want to sleep, too." Tommy laid his head on my shoulder and fell asleep.

It was a great team, and I loved these guys, but sometimes their playing around fired up my libido and made me horny as hell. This was one of those times, and I knew that I'd have to go on the hunt when we got to Chicago to see if I could find a cute gay guy.

When we arrived, we checked into the hotel and the guys fought—literally arm wrestled—to see who would room with me. It was their game every time we had an overnighter. This time the shortstop, Denver, won.

I'm just shy of six feet and close to 180 pounds, but Denver scooped me onto his shoulder, carried me to the room, threw me on the bed, and pretended to hump me. Nearly the whole team followed, and before I knew it fifteen guys were piled on top of me, the bed groaning in protest.

"What is this?" I could barely get enough breath to speak. "A gay baseball team?"

A bunch of them whistled and called out, "Yeah give it to me."

"Get off me, you bunch of homos." I couldn't help but laugh at their crazy antics.

Each guy slid off the heap until I was blissfully alone on the bed, where I remained pressed like a gingerbread man.

"We love you, Ev," one of them called, "but we got to go find some pussy."

"Yeah, yeah. Go get some pussy before you all turn gay."

Jumping on one another, the guys ran from the room.

"Come on, man." Denver scooped his big arm through the air.

The guys always tried to drag me on their expeditions,

and sometimes I'd give in and go. Inevitably, they'd try to pair me up with a woman. Then they'd get jealous because I ended up with all the hot chicks around me.

"Hey, Evan." Denver stopped at the door and closed it so the other guys couldn't hear.

"Yeah." I sat up and threw my legs over the side.

Looking like an Abercrombie model, Denver chewed his lip in hesitation. There was no reason to rush him, so I casually kicked off my shoes and let him ruminate over what he wanted to say. Then he plopped down next to me.

"If I ever have a girl who wants to have a threesome with another guy . . ." With his soft brown eyes, he looked into my baby blues. "I want it be you."

For a moment I debated how to respond. Do I make a joke? Do I dismiss this as folly? Do I give him a serious response? Ultimately, I opted for a smile and a slap on the back. After all, it was the greatest compliment a straight guy could give me.

Then Denver darted to join the pussy-hunting brigade. Not to be outdone, I cleaned up and left the hotel on a hunk-hunting brigade.

In the student center, I found the GLBT student organization office and a group of students, including the president, Krissy. As luck would have it, their weekly meeting was about to start in the auditorium, and they dragged me along with the promise that it would be hot and fun. Turns out that the speaker was a cute, cheery woman who was a sex educator, and she'd brought along props for demonstration. This would be good.

On my campus, the average GLBT meeting had about twenty-five students, but on the Chicago campus the room was filled with one hundred or more students, and I felt exhilarated and overwhelmed. Needless to say, when I entered the room, I drew a little attention. Trying to remain inconspicuous, I selected a seat in the back of the auditorium. As Krissy introduced the speaker, a gorgeous Hispanic man entered the room. All male eyes, including mine, followed his movement, and I expected him to take one look at the crowd, realize he was in the wrong room, and do a one-eighty.

Instead, the Fates delivered him to me, probably to make up for all the ribbing I took from my straight teammates. The Hispanic man walked up the stairs and down the row, moving closer by the second. All attempts to look away were futile; I leaned back in my chair to appear cool and collected. The stud sat down next to me, leaned close, and whispered, "I'm Eduardo."

"Evan." I tried to whisper, but my voice cut out, so I repeated it louder and accidentally interrupted the speaker.

"Nice to meet you, buddy," he responded with a wink.

Eduardo extended his hand, took mine almost delicately, and pumped it firmly three times. The sensation of touching this man was undeniably erotic. When I looked at his thick brown fingers, the desire to suck them threatened to make me launch from my chair and pin him to the ground.

"How many of you know how to properly put on a condom?" the sex educator asked while I was still admiring Eduardo's hands and muscular forearms.

Without hesitation, Eduardo raised his hand, so I absently followed suit and shot mine proudly toward the heavens.

"Good," the perky sex educator responded. For someone who talked about cunnilingus, birth control, and STDs, she was certainly ebullient. "Can you two come up front and demonstrate on this banana?"

What! I had to have heard her wrong. In front of a hundred people with this hunk as my partner!

"Sure," Eduardo responded, already out of his seat. "Come on, Evan. I'll let you hold the banana." His smile was so glorious that he could have convinced me to cluck like a chicken in front of this entire crowd.

So there I was holding a banana while the hot Latin man pinched the tip of the condom and deftly rolled it down the shaft. I dared to glance out into the crowd and saw the lust on the faces of every gay man in the audience. We were eye candy for the masses. My condom buddy brushed his hand against mine and leaned so close I could smell his Nautica cologne. To my horror, I realized that my cock was straining against my 505s like a seventies porn star.

The sex educator lauded our efforts, rewarded us with a pack of flavored lubes and some free condoms, and the crowd exploded as if we were Britney Spears lip-synching "Hit Me Baby One More Time." As we proceeded back to our seats, Eduardo put a hand on my shoulder, and all gay eyes followed our walk of fame.

After the presentation, the president of the GLBT organization covered the bylaws on elections, which was as exciting as the accountants at the Emmys.

Eduardo leaned over and asked, "You want to go out for coffee?"

"Sure."

"That was easy." Eduardo again put his hand on my shoulder, and the nerve from my shoulder to my groin charged like a heart defibrillator.

"I love coffee." That was a lie, but I'd eat mud for this man.

As we exited the room, one of the gay boys said, "Hey, Eduardo. Good luck tomorrow." He was apparently the spokesman for a group of five pretty twinks, and the sycophants eyed us lustily.

"Hey thanks." Eduardo was gracious, which endeared him to me.

"We'll be there," another pretty boy added.

"Great. See you guys then."

I didn't understand the whole exchange, but I was foolish not to figure it out.

In the food court, Eduardo and I talked for over an hour. Coffee turned into burgers and sodas. My new Hispanic friend was funny, bright, wry, and fucking adorable. I felt like I'd been selected for Make-A-Wish, and I completely forgot about my hetero teammates, who were probably still hunting cheerleader pussy.

Eduardo and I were yin and yang. His hair was black and wavy, his eyes were the color of hot chocolate, and his arms were like a power lifter's. My hair was light blond, almost white, my eyes were blue, and my musculature was more like a swimmer's. His skin was a perfect brown while mine was creamy ivory. Eduardo stood about four inches shorter than me, but he weighed about the same. He was fucking hot. Just what I needed.

By the time he asked if I wanted to see his room, I had already picked out our honeymoon destination (Bali), our children's names (Bettina and Javier), and our favorite song ("Beautiful" by the semi-Latina Christina Aguilera).

To my surprise, his room was adorned with a unique mixture of Mesoamerican art and baseball trophies. Clearly, he had respect for his ancestors and his culture, and he loved my sport. Great start!

"You like baseball?" I asked.

"Yeah. And you?"

"Love it. Been playing since I was a kid."

"Me, too. Actually, I'm the catcher on our team."

That was it! I laughed at the irony. "I'm the pitcher on the visiting team. Guess we go to battle tomorrow."

Eduardo's eyes lit up and he moved close to me. "No shit. This is kinda awkward."

"I guess."

"So you're a pitcher, huh?" With his Hispanic accent, he sounded like Salma Hayek, who was so sexy she could tempt me to be straight. I wanted to hear what Eduardo sounded like in bed. Would he speak in Spanish?

"Uh-huh. You a good catcher?" I moved even closer to him.

"Whatta you think?"

It was my turn to smile wickedly.

"So what're we going to do?" he asked.

Rarely the aggressor, I nonetheless grabbed him and kissed him straight on his plump lips. It was the best first kiss I've ever experienced sober, and I knew there was something to be said for Latin lovin'.

Time to go to second base. I slipped my hands under his T-shirt and felt his glorious belly hair. As my hands traveled toward his nipples, he groaned and bit my bottom lip. When I pulled his shirt over his head, his black curls danced and fell back into place perfectly. His dark body hair was clipped and shaped, and the sight of it made me horny as hell. His brown nipples were erect and begged to be sucked, so I obliged.

With an animal ferocity, he yanked my shirt and tore it from my body. My hairless chest and pink nipples were a perfect contrast to his.

Eduardo didn't stop there. He pushed me back on the bed, where I fell onto the lubes and condoms we'd received for our banana demonstration. I pulled a packet of mango lube from beneath me and brandished it as an invitation. Goaded by the lube, he removed my pants with the passion and zeal of a Latin lover. My cock made a *thwap* as it slapped against my belly. Eduardo reached down and rubbed my heavy balls then moved my cock from side to side. After a moment of bewilderment, I realized he was fascinated by my blond pubes.

"I want to see yours." My voice was so husky, I sounded like a male Jessica Rabbit.

Eduardo stripped off his jeans and briefs and proudly displayed the clipped black bush crowning his thick brown penis. When he turned to kick his pants away, I saw an ass so round I couldn't believe it was real.

After another kiss, we flipped into a sixty-nine position and started showing our ample cock-sucking skills. While he tried to deep-throat my eight inches, I tried to accommodate his tree trunk organ. His foreskin gave me a particularly pleasing distraction.

He wiggled a finger against my tight hole and flashed me a smile. "Will you catch for me?"

"Uh, I usually do the pitching." I stroked his thick member in my hand and wondered if I could even take it up my ass. He wet a finger and worked it slowly into my hole.

The catcher wanted to pitch to me, so I'd have to let him do it, no matter how thick his cock. "If I let you fuck me, can I fuck you next?" I quickly added, "But I want to be on top."

"Just how I like it." Eduardo offered me that killer smile, and all hesitation faded.

So I put the yellow condom on his cock and coated it in strawberry lube while he fingered my tight hole. Then I straddled him and wiggled the head of his hard organ against my cherry hole. After a minute of serious effort, his cock breached my rectum and slipped inside. Though I made a better pitcher, I was bound and determined to relax my hole and catch for him. As I rocked up and down, his eyes rolled back in his head and he muttered something in Spanish. Gradually my ass loosened up and allowed me to bounce on his cock, making the bedsprings squeak. It actually felt good and I surprised myself as I slammed down on his big dick. When he took my cock in his hand and stroked, I realized that I was leaking precome.

After I'd ridden his cock for a few minutes, he sat up, kissed me hard, and asked, "So you going to pitch to me now, buddy?"

I nodded.

"Good. 'Cause I'm a great catcher. That's how I like to get off."

He didn't need to convince me. I had the condom and mango lube on my dick before he'd even removed his condom. Then he lay back, lifted his leg, and showed me his round ass. Eduardo pulled his muscular ass cheeks apart so I could see his pink pucker surrounded by a wreath of black hair. Though my cock was about to explode, first my tongue had some exploring to do, and my hot Hispanic friend responded with loud moans.

Unable to stand it any longer, I lifted his legs higher and placed the head of my cock against his wet hole. Clearly, Eduardo loved to be the catcher because he was wiggling his hot butt to try to work himself onto my eight inches. Happy to make his wish come true, I slid my dick inside and it felt like warm Jell-O.

"Fuck me, Evan."

I picked up pace and watched his eyes roll back in his head again. Then I leaned over him and sucked on his luscious lips. As I pounded him harder, he whimpered in pleasure.

"You like that, Eduardo?" I asked.

"Fuck yeah. Fuck my ass, buddy. Fuck it good."

Since he'd given me permission, I pushed his knees toward his chest so I could pile drive his ass, and I saw the precome leak from his cock. The whole bed rocked with the momentum.

"Yeah, buddy," he cried. "Show me your fastball!"

I laughed. "You like it fast?"

He chewed on the corner of the pillow as I fucked him fast and deep. "I like it any way you give it to me." His words were muffled by the pillow.

So I gave him a slider, a screwball, a curveball, a sinker, and every other pitch I knew.

"Yeah. Yeah. Yeah. Oh yeah, fuck me."

"God I'm getting close." I wanted to hold out longer, but there was no fucking way. His ass was just too pleasing.

While I held his legs aloft, he shot his load all over our bellies, and I'd never seen come fly like that. Then I pulled out and mixed my white goo with his as I shot the biggest load of my life.

"Was it good for you?" he asked.

"Hell yes! That was amazing."

After some clean up and a few more deep kisses, we fell asleep in postcoital bliss with Quetzalcoatl and Johnny Damon looking down on us.

The next day, during the game, my teammates kept goading me to tell them where I'd been the night before. Though I'd endured graphic accounts of their conquests with women, all I told them was, "I was practicing my pitching."

From the dugout, a beautiful Hispanic catcher watched me with a smile.

Right Field

Simon Sheppard

███████

When he was a kid, he hated May.

May was the start of softball season. It wasn't that he was bad at everything in gym class—although he was, more or less. It was that he was really, really rotten at softball. And, unlike, say, volleyball, or even football, softball was a sport where, whether at bat or fielding a ball, you were on your own. Which, for Jeff, meant mortification. Individualized, repeated, lasting, hurtful mortification.

He already—always—knew he was different. More intelligent than almost all the other kids. Even different in his religion, one of only a few Jews in his class. But mostly it was his desires that gave him trouble, made him feel isolated. Though he was in the running for a National Merit Scholarship, so were Deb Larsen and Ricky Sanchez. His family went to *shul,* and not just on the High Holy Days, so he knew there were other Jews out there. But when it came to what he wanted, or rather *whom,* he was out there in right field, all by himself.

That's where they always put him: right field, where he'd have almost nothing to do for most of the game . . . if he was lucky. They always chose him last for their teams, too, the other boys did. Well, there were a couple of others—Larry Farkas, who was mildly retarded, and the morbidly obese

Steve Schwinn—who were usually chosen after he was, the dregs of the dregs. But he was pretty sure that no one else experienced, under the somewhat malignant supervision of the gym teacher, Mr. McFarland, the same degree of shame.

Eventually, he knew, school would let out for the summer, and he could blissfully ignore the baseball season. He liked to swim, diving into the chlorinated silences of the pool at the "beach club" the family belonged to . . . though it was, of course, hundreds of miles away from anything that could reasonably be regarded as a beach. Actually, he'd never been in the ocean, and so had to settle for the experience of gliding through cool water, almost weightless, holding his breath, the outside, dry world just a wavering blur over his head. He could only hold his breath for so long, though, and eventually he had to surface, returning to reality.

He was finally able to breathe freely when he headed off to college. He enrolled in a small, weird liberal arts college in the Pacific Northwest, not the least because he could fulfill its meager phys ed requirement with classes in folk dancing and tai chi. The school didn't even have intercollegiate sports teams, something that suited Jeff Rosen just fine. Freed from the pressure to fit in, he pretty much blossomed. He even discovered that distance running—something Mr. McFarland had doled out as punishment—was something Jeff not only enjoyed, but was good at.

And he discovered he was good at cock sucking, too. He first found that out on a moonlit night when he and a couple of the guys got drunk and stoned and he and Ken Kim ended up sprawled on the floor after the others had staggered out of his dorm room. Somehow, one thing had led to another and he ended up with Ken's almost-hard dick in his mouth, his nose buried in the other boy's dark, silky pubic hair. The next day, Ken acted like nothing had happened, but the blow jobs soon became a semi-regular thing. Ken never sucked him off, though, the arrangement being strictly a one-way thing. Which was okay with Jeff.

It was a time of change for being gay, and the college was an outpost of liberal tolerance anyway. By the time he graduated, Jeff had had sex with maybe half a dozen other students and a townie or two, and even had a boyfriend for a while. Though he and Kristofer drifted apart before graduation, Jeff went out in the world pretty much accepting himself, and prepared to find the man of his dreams. It took several years in Chicago to find him. Chad was amazing—or at least it was amazing that he could fall for Jeff. Or at least that's what Jeff thought.

Chad might have been a big old bottom, someone even more eager to suck Jeff's cock than vice versa, but he was also a jock. He'd been a wrestler in high school and college, and still had a wrestler's thick, muscular body. He played touch football on Sundays with straight guys from his office. And he was a huge Cubs fan. Even Jeff, no reader of the sports pages, knew from the first that loving the Chicago Cubs was an exercise in frustration. But Jeff figured that the team was another of Chad's unreasoning enthusiasms, like Jeff himself, and he did his best to go along. It was okay to be a queer jock, of course. There were the Gay Games. And, he knew of *Take Me Out,* a Broadway play about a gay baseball superstar. Hell, someone somewhere was probably putting together a book of baseball-themed gay porn.

He would cuddle with Chad in front of the TV, watching baseball, doing his best to get into the game's tranquil, Zen-like pacing, the long stretches of nothing, punctuated by the thrill of a homer hit, a crucial base stolen. In contrast to the bulked-up, macho violence of pro football, the deliberative pace of America's favorite pastime had an almost nostalgic appeal. Chewing tobacco! He even managed to eroticize the players, who were, thankfully, neither the well-padded behemoths of football nor the giraffe-proportioned mutants of basketball. They were just guys, pretty handsome men, some of them, with nicely rounded butts beneath those white uniforms.

Chad even persuaded him to go out to Wrigley Field a few times, where he ate hot dogs he knew were bad for him, mused on the unnatural greenness of the field, and watched the Cubs self-destruct, as was their habit. Even if they put *him* in right field, Jeff figured, they could scarcely do worse.

Still, Chad loved the Cubbies with the devotion of the true fan. So for their anniversary, Jeff fucked Chad while wearing a secondhand baseball uniform he'd found at the Salvation Army. It had been almost unbearably hot to see the look on Chad's face when Jeff surprised him, walking into the room like a ballplayer in rut. Chad had dropped to his knees and buried his face in the pinstripes at Jeff's crotch. He maneuvered his lover's hardening dick from the cup, then licked and kissed it until it was fully erect. They had ended up on the floor, Chad totally naked, Jeff still fully in uniform, from cap to cleats. But Jeff"s cock (*hard as a Louisville Slugger,* he thought with a smile) protruded through the fly of the jersey pants, and it wasn't long before he was fucking his boyfriend, pounding his cock home.

Shortly after that, though, Chad began to get sick. His once-powerful body withered away and then, with a final kiss in the hospital room, he was gone.

Jeff managed to pick up the pieces of his life, though he never could bring himself to watch the Cubs again. Not that there was, most seasons, much to watch.

There were a few men after Chad, but nothing lasting. No home runs. Jeff went to work, came home and watched TV, went out to bars on the weekends and sometimes got laid. The Cubs almost made it to the Series in '03, but fucked up in game six of the play-offs. And Sammy Sosa left. Jeff still found himself unexpectedly in tears, sometimes, when the sports news came on. He began to go the bars less, watched HBO more. Though he'd run a few marathons, always feeling triumphant when he crossed the finish line, the training tore up his knees. He settled for Pilates classes, instead. Right field.

The envelope came as a surprise. He hadn't realized anyone at his old high school even had his address—maybe his mom had sent it on. There was a reservation form for the reunion, and a form to fill in for the "Memory Book." Questions like, "What were some of your best high school memories?" to which Jeff had an awful temptation to reply, "Being gay-baited, forging notes to get out of gym, and getting the hell out of there." But he figured that would be excessively mean-spirited, and besides, they'd never print that in the book.

He was curious about what happened to a few of his schoolmates, but he wasn't about to attend the reunion. Too far to go, too risky, too potentially boring, and maybe even upsetting. He meant to fill out the form as innocuously as possible and send it back, just in case someone wanted to get in touch after all those years, but it sat around in one of his piles of papers, and when he finally came across it, it was just past deadline. *Oh well,* he consoled himself, *if I'd really wanted to send it back, I would have.*

That was the last he thought of high school for months. And then his mother phoned. Her usually strong voice sounding suddenly terribly old, she told him, forthrightly, that she'd been diagnosed with early-stage Alzheimer's and would be moving into a managed care facility. Fortunately, Jeff's father had left her well provided for. It was more a matter of getting ready to make the move. Would he come east to help her pack up her things and get them disposed of?

Well, he could hardly refuse. So he arranged to take time off from work and within a month, he was back at the house he'd grown up in. His mother seemed almost normal, though quite a bit older than when he'd last seen her, several years ago on her final trip to Chicago. But then she would suddenly get . . . vague. It reminded Jeff, heartbreakingly, of the signs of dementia that had preceded Chad's death. It was apparent to both of them that he wouldn't move back to take care of her. But she was a tough cookie—she'd have had to be, to have survived marriage to his dad—and so when she said, "I'll be all right," he chose, perhaps selfishly, to believe her.

In the meantime, prompted by the reunion invitation, he'd been thinking about maybe getting together with some of the people he'd gone to school with. Well, one person, actually: Eric Talen.

Back in high school, Eric had been the perfect combination of brains and brawn. He'd played varsity football, and had been a star on the baseball team. But unlike run-of-the-mill high school jocks, he'd excelled academically, too, doing almost as well as Jeff. Moreover, he was a genuinely nice guy, and he'd always been nice to Jeff, or at least so he remembered. It wasn't that Jeff had had a crush on Eric. Bruce Chaffee had been a lot cuter, and Jeff had nurtured an obsession for Ken Washington for a while, until he found out that Ken had been complaining about how "that fag Jeff" had been making eyes at him. Eric, though, had been a gentleman. A gentleman and a scholar. And a baseball star.

Eric Talen it was, then, and Jeff was amazed and gratified that Eric's name was in the local phone directory. Jeff had heard a long time ago from a mutual friend that Eric had gotten married, but apparently he hadn't left town.

"Hey, Jeff. How've you been?" There was no tone of surprise there, despite the decades. It was almost as if he'd been expecting the phone call.

47

"Not bad. And yourself?"

They decided to go out for a beer at the local bar, a place that had been around ever since they'd tried to get of-age guys to buy them six-packs. Eric was, in fact, gorgeous. He'd aged well, into full-fledged handsomeness. There was a minimum of awkwardness. Eric, it turned out, had indeed gotten married. It had only lasted a few years, though. No kids. And Eric, when Jeff told him about his relationship with Chad, reacted sympathetically, no judgment. Yeah, Eric Talen was a gentleman, a *mensch*.

"Hey," he said, when the bar was about to close. "Want to go for a walk?"

Their steps in the moonless, star-filled night led them, as if by common consent, to their old high school.

"Man, I used to hate it here," Jeff said.

"Yeah?" Again, Eric didn't sound surprised.

"Well, not hate it. Not exactly. Not always. But gym class was always so damn . . . and whenever softball season rolled around . . ."

"It's a long time to hold onto something like that."

"Oh, I'm over it now."

"Are you? Want to go for a walk on the ball field?"

Jeff hesitated. "That would be okay?"

"Jesus, it's three o'clock in the morning. Who's going to mind?"

The softball diamond was smaller than Jeff had remembered it. "Here's where I used to stand, here in right field," he said. "Hoping the ball wouldn't come my way." He thought back to those days, feeling the anxiety in the pit of his stomach once again. How many boys had stood there in right field since then, how many of them fearful, how many boys like him?

They stood in silence, side by side. There was nothing but the sound of an occasional distant passing car, a barking dog somewhere. *If this were some damn clichéd gay short story,* Jeff thought, *Eric would turn to me now and tell me he always had a crush on me in high school.*

"Jeff?"

"Yeah?"

"Oh . . . nothing."

Because it wasn't some clichéd short story. And then Eric reached for Jeff's hand.

They kissed there, long and hard, in the middle of right field.

"Wow," said Eric. "Wow. I didn't expect to do that."

"Well, life is weird, huh?" It seemed like such an inadequate thing to say. "Hey, you have somewhere we can go? I feel really exposed out here. And I can't invite you back to my mother's. There's no telling when she'll be awake."

"Yeah, old people are like that. Sure, my place."

Eric's place was an ordinary suburban house, his bed an ordinary suburban Beautyrest. There was no question of what was going to happen; Eric had led Jeff directly into the bedroom, then started taking off his clothes.

"So when we were back in school, you knew I was gay?" Jeff wasn't quite ready to get down to it.

"God, I don't know. I guess I didn't have that word for it. I suspected you were one of the guys who'd blow the boys on the team."

One of the guys? Who the hell were they?

"No, not me, I was a virgin back then. Too uptight."

"Hmmf." Eric was standing there, naked except for his socks. He still had an athlete's finely knit body, though the years had added a few pounds. Added fur, too. He was pleasingly hairy, even a bit on his shoulders, and the thatch on his chest had gone nicely salt-and-pepper. His dick was hard already, and really kind of small, which turned Jeff on. Uncut, too, which, back in the day, had been pretty unusual for boys

49

of their class. He didn't remember that from the locker room. Maybe he'd never noticed.

"Aren't you going to take your clothes off?"

Jeff found himself wondering how often Eric had done this since his marriage ended. Before, even. He kicked off his loafers, unbuckled his pants, stepped out of his boxers, pulled off his socks. Naked from the waist down.

"Hey, nice cock. Nice and thick."

"Thanks. So you were . . . back in school . . . you were?"

"I don't know, I guess I was bisexual. I guess I still am." He reached for Jeff's almost-hard dick, which instantly sprang to full stiffness. Jeff bent over, rubbed his face against Eric's hairy pec, took the hard little nipple in his mouth, chewed down gently. Eric grabbed him, guided them both into the unmade bed.

Sometimes, Jeff thought, *life was indeed like a short story, only better. Sometimes the Cubs did win.*

Eric was good at giving head. Clearly, he'd done this at least a few times before. But when Jeff put his hands on Eric's shoulders, Eric pushed them away, then shoved Jeff's body back. It was then that Jeff noticed Eric was watching himself in the full-length mirror on the wall.

Jeff felt himself getting too close too fast, so he extricated his cock from Eric's mouth and scooted around to return the favor, sucking on his friend's small, stiff dick. Eric's cock might not have been a record breaker, but he had big balls, nice, loose, hanging low. He moved his mouth off Eric's shaft and down between his hairy thighs, licking at the sac. Eric shifted himself around and spread his legs, giving Jeff full access. But when Jeff took what he thought was a hint and slid his tongue farther down, aiming for Eric's asshole, there was another shift, Eric moving his crotch away. The guy wasn't a bottom, then. What was he?

"I want to put some sexy clothes on for you," Eric said. He was an exhibitionist, then. Okay.

Eric got up from the bed, fumbled around in a dresser drawer, and tossed a jockstrap to Jeff. He got back in bed, on his back, legs in the air. Jeff gazed longingly down at Eric's hairy crack, then slipped the jock on over Eric's feet. Nice feet, too. Eric must have noticed Jeff's glance; as he wriggled into the jockstrap, he lowered his feet around Jeff's hard cock. Fuck, that felt nice. Jeff reached down to stroke Eric's feet, but as he did, Eric took them away, and flung his body around until he was lying facedown, his hairy ass in the air. So he *was* a bottom. But when Jeff parted the furry, muscular cheeks and plunged his tongue into the warm hole, Eric moaned for just a second, then skittered off again. Jeff tried rubbing his fingers on the puckered flesh, but Jeff reached down and pushed them away. Fuck, what was this? It wasn't that Eric was a pushy bottom. He was just all over the map.

Right when Jeff was about to give up on the whole thing, Eric pushed back into him, rubbing his ass crack against Jeff's crotch. So he wanted to get fucked, after all? Well, yeah, okay. Eric reached around, grabbed Jeff's hard, thick dick, and rubbed the damp head right up against his asshole.

"There's lube in the drawer of the bedside table."

There was, and a few condoms as well, all of them, unfortunately, colored. Jeff grabbed a garish red one, ripped the package open with his teeth, and unrolled it onto his hard-on.

It was pretty easy to get inside Eric's ass; clearly, he'd been fucked before. What wasn't clear to Jeff was just what he was supposed to do. Eric kept tossing around, rearranging their bodies. Jeff hoped to hell he could keep hard and stay inside. He tried to grab onto one part or another of Eric's body—for the sake of leverage if not affection—but Eric kept pushing his hands away. Then Jeff did slip out. Eric rolled over on his back, and stroking his own hairy, muscular chest, waited for Jeff to reenter him. When Jeff hesitated, a little nonplussed, Eric reached around and stuffed the cock into himself, then grabbed Jeff's waist and kept the hard-on tight inside.

Jeff, meanwhile, took hold of the jockstrap. Under the elastic pouch, Eric's cock had gone soft. Not an unusual thing when someone was getting fucked, of course, and if Eric hadn't been enjoying himself, he no doubt would have simply shoved Jeff away. Still, *something* was wrong, not going well.

And then Jeff got it: The star athlete of his high school had grown up to be truly lousy at sex. He was still inside Eric's hot, soft ass, despite the continued twistings and turnings. But now he was wishing he'd simply let himself come down Eric's throat when he'd had the chance.

"Fuck, it feels good, but I can't take too much more of your thick cock."

All right, whatever. Jeff pulled his dick out, still a discomfortingly bright red, but not as hard as it had been.

"Listen, Jeff, I've got an early day tomorrow," Eric said. "Mind going and washing up?"

Standing over the bathroom sink, a wet washcloth in his hand, Jeff looked at himself in the mirror. He looked bemused. Well, that was that. He could always jack off later, in his boyhood bedroom.

The good-byes were said expeditiously. There were promises about getting together later in the week, promises that were quite unlikely to be kept. Eric already had pajama bottoms on; apparently, he didn't sleep in the raw. He still looked yummy, even while he was closing his front door.

On the way back to the house he had grown up in, riding in the rented white Chevrolet, with a brief detour past the pitch-dark sports field, Jeff saw himself again as a skinny, gawky kid, wanting, wanting.

His mother was awake when he came in, sitting, staring at a wall. She didn't ask where he had been.

When he got back to Chicago, he rummaged around in the closet, found the old baseball uniform he'd brought home for playing with Chad, and gave it back to the Salvation Army.

Glory Days

Shannon L. Yarbrough

―――

"Why do they call it Busch Stadium?" I asked.

"Because if it was Cock Stadium, they'd have to change the shape of the field," my buddy Randy said with a laugh.

This round of one-liners and punch lines between us was as rehearsed as a Laurel and Hardy routine by now. They were jokes we shared with each other at the open of every baseball season.

"You're right. It's V-shaped!"

"Dude, it's a diamond, or a square, however you look at it. The old stadium was a circle though."

"Don't you mean a hole?"

"And a tight one at that!"

I laughed so hard I choked on my beer. It was early April and Randy and I were tailgating outside the new stadium in downtown St. Louis, with a crowd of fans all painted in red. We were eagerly anticipating the first game of the season the following day in the Cardinals' new home.

Most of my gay friends thought Randy was odd, but none of them liked baseball or any kind of sport for that matter. Randy did though, and I think that's why we got along so well. Living in St. Louis gave us access to football, hockey, and baseball right in our hometown; and Randy and I had season tickets for all of it. Baseball was our favorite.

Randy was your typical middle-aged jock living his glory days. He'd played every sport in high school, but had not played anything since. His hair was now thinning from wearing a helmet or cap through all four years. His arms and legs were still large and defined from having been on the wrestling team and from running track back then. Hitting the gym four times a week these days kept the beer gut down and kept his pecs tight. I thought Randy was hot.

He was probably heterosexual in high school, or questioning. He had not yet slept with a guy but stole quick glances at his pals in the locker room, and he banged every chick they set him up with just because she'd put out. When I first met him several years ago, he claimed he was bisexual but I don't remember him ever taking a girl home. He'd let one blow him in a bathroom stall now and then when we were hanging out at a sports bar, but he had confessed to me that guys do it better. He was usually uncomfortable in gay bars so we never hung out together there. Guys coming up to him to talk or buy him a drink made him nervous.

I liked having a gay, or bi, friend whose sex life was fairly anonymous. All of my other friends shared their bedtime stories outright, or I overheard their stories across the bar or in line at the urinal all the time. Randy didn't gossip. He never asked me about my bed partners either, even as lacking as they were these days. I'm glad I didn't have to make things up like I did when I was with my other friends. I didn't want to seem like I wasn't getting laid, but Randy didn't care. Be it baseball or football, his mind was always on the game.

"Where's your girlfriend?" My friends would ask, teasing me when I met them out at a club.

They made fun of me for hanging out with Randy all the time, so I started hanging out with them less and less. I just ignored their sneers. I think they were jealous because they all thought Randy was hot too. Randy never asked about them. With him, there was never any drama. Sure, I pictured him naked from time to time or admired his butt when we'd be standing in line for beer. But I never thought about wanting to sleep with him. I assumed Randy felt the same way about me, too.

"So what do you think the odds are that the Cards will get to the World Series this year?" Randy asked.

"Man, wouldn't that be awesome with the new stadium and all!"

The Cardinals had not won the World Series since 1982. They'd played twice in the finals since then, losing to Minnesota in 1987 four to three and to the Red Sox just two years ago four to zero. If they won this year, it would be the perfect ending to their first year in the new stadium.

The new stadium has more of a traditional baseball stadium feel to it, like Wrigley Field. With a mixture of red brick and steel, it is a much better fit into the downtown St. Louis scenario, reminiscent of the old warehouses nearby that would soon be knocked down to make room for a Cardinals shopping village, more parking spaces, and a baseball hall of fame.

The kick-off game to the season the next day was against the Milwaukee Brewers, preceded by the grand opening of the stadium complete with tours, live music, and lots of speeches by game officials. Randy and I decided to take a tour of the stadium. It seats forty-seven thousand fans and has a perfect view of the St. Louis Arch and downtown skyline, which can be seen from every seat. The view is framed by the brand new high tech scoreboards on each side, one for home games and one for away games.

"Excuse me, where's a restroom?" I asked the tour guide.

"We just passed it about four field entrances back. Go

ahead and just catch up with us when you're done. We won't be too far ahead," the tour guide said.

"Thanks. See you in a few," I told Randy. He had already gone, but I can never seem to piss when everyone else is going.

The restroom was spotless, just waiting to be tainted with paper towels and spilt beer. It was neat to think I might be the first fan using this very restroom, but I'm sure construction workers had already been in here and christened it. Like any gay man would, I checked out each stall, eager to find some bathroom graffiti and wishing I had a pen to leave some of my own. The stalls were spotless. I stopped in the last one to do my business.

I was almost done when I heard a metal banging sound right behind my feet. I looked over my shoulder and noticed the metal tissue holder had fallen off the side of the stall and landed on the floor. It had left a perfect round hole in the wall leading to the next stall, apparently where it was supposed to line up with the tissue holder for the adjoining stall. I guess I now knew how glory holes were created.

I knelt to pick up the metal box, hoping I could hang it back on the wall somehow and then hurry back to the tour. When I leaned back up, I got quite a surprise. There was a rock hard fat cock sticking through the hole in the wall. I laughed a bit to myself, thinking someone had just read my mind. It'd been years since I had shared in any bathroom trade. I hesitated for a moment or two, but had never been one to turn down a nice cock. I rubbed my hands together quickly to warm them up a bit and then reached for the throbbing rod, gripping it soothingly as a pitcher does his glove. I squeezed it gently, feeling the rush of blood beneath the silky skin layering this nice piece of meat, and then knelt to take it between my lips.

ι teased the massive mushroom head with my tongue, before gliding the shaft down my throat until the stall wall touched my nose. The body on the other side of the wall began to buck back and forth, fucking my mouth through the hole in the wall. I gripped the base of his rod as if I were going to pull him through the wall and began to jack him off. I kept my jaw wrapped tightly around the cock and sucked as hard as I could.

A faint grunt from over the wall told me he was about to come. I released my wet warm grip on the cock and continued to stroke him, keeping close so I could lavish his load across my face. His ejaculate was immense and stung me on the cheek like a bullet. I gave his dick a few more strokes, milking it for every drop, and then reached for some tissue to wipe my face. The cock disappeared back through the hole and I heard the sound of a zipper. I expected to see an inviting mouth at the hole in the wall, waiting to receive my own cock. Instead, I heard the unlocking of the stall door and my mystery man heading out the door.

I came out of my stall to wash my hands and check my face in the mirror. The last thing I wanted was for Randy to see me with sperm on my face. I decided not to pursue the guy I had just sucked off, not even to get a look at his face. Why spoil the mystery and intrigue? Besides, it was probably some married guy who wouldn't give me the time of day otherwise, who sought out blow jobs from gay guys because his wife wouldn't do it for him. I decided not to tell Randy what had happened either.

The Cards won the game the next day eight to three. Randy and I didn't miss a game the whole season. Randy even caught a fly ball in the stands when the Cardinals were up against the Mets for the championship. We hung around outside the locker room after the game to see if he could get the batter to sign the ball. The player was a twenty-four-year-old rookie named Edward and this was his first season.

"Hi guys. Oh, you are the lucky one who caught that, huh," Edward said, taking the ball from Randy.

To have played such an intense game, Edward looked like he had just stepped off his baseball card, all shiny and clean. I love a fresh man straight from the showers, but something told me I probably wouldn't have minded his sweaty body that had gone into the showers either. He had scorching blue eyes and sandy blond hair. He was very tan and lean, with a cute baby face and dimples. His smile glistened like a brand new jersey. He personalized the ball for Randy and then invited us to a local bar for the victory celebration. Most of the team would be there and he agreed to introduce us. Randy and I squealed with excitement like teenage fans of a boy band.

The last game of the championship was the following day. If the Cards won, they'd be headed to the World Series against the Detroit Tigers. If the Cardinals won this series, they'd have the most World Series Championship wins in the National League. Randy was running late, and called to tell me to meet him at the stadium. When he arrived, he was grinning ear to ear.

"What gives?" I asked.

Randy was quiet. He giggled and just looked at the empty field with a glazed look on his face. I knew that look anywhere. He'd gotten laid.

"Hello!" I yelled in his ear and snapped my fingers in front of his face. He shook his head, coming out of his daydream.

"Oh! Man, you won't believe what happened last night after you left!"

"At the bar?"

"Yeah. Sorta."

"Well, tell me! What'd I miss?"

"After you left, I stayed at the bar with Edward till they closed down. We were walking to the parking lot together, and he asked me if I wanted to come back to his place. I didn't think much about it, so I said okay."

"What? Are you serious?"

"Yeah, man. I fucked him."

"You gotta be lying. I don't believe you," I laughed. I actually did believe him and was trying to hide my jealousy.

"And get this, he wanted you to come along."

"A three-way?"

"Yeah, man. You missed out."

"Why didn't you call me?"

"I tried. Your cell phone was turned off."

"My one chance to have sex with a baseball player, and I missed it. And not just any player either—the Cards!"

"And you could have had sex with me," Randy joked.

"Oh, shut up!"

The Cardinals won the game that day. Randy and I were stoked and bought our series tickets for the first home game right away. This would be the third series meeting between the Tigers and the Cardinals. St. Louis won the first in 1934, and Detroit won the second in1968; each went the full seven games. A few nights later, the Cardinals won the first game, but lost the second playing at Detroit's home stadium. Then, they won the third game, the first of the series in our new stadium. Randy and I were afraid this was going to be quite a tug-o-war, and might end up going the full seven games again.

Randy had said Edward wanted to hang out again, possibly after the series was over. Since he had already been with Randy, I had no hopes of being included in the next round and wasn't even sure if I wanted to be included. Who was I fooling? Turn down sex with a Cardinals player? Turn down sex with Randy? I'd play it all off like it was no big deal, but the truth is I'd be in heaven. Two of my fantasies would be playing out before me right at the same time!

We were all on the edge of our seats in the fourth game when Detroit tied the score right in the ninth inning. Luckily, a home run put the Cards back on top right at the end, giving them the fourth game win. Rain delayed the fifth game one night and the city was filled with tense momentum. The fifth game, right here in our hometown in the new stadium, was the perfect set up for the Cards to win the World Series again. Everyone in the city was wearing red and ready to play ball, including Randy and I, who had seats right behind home plate. But we'd have to wait one more night.

Randy and I had been staying in a hotel room downtown within walking distance of the stadium during the home games. After the fifth game was definitely rained out, we were running back to the hotel when Randy's cell phone rang. It was Edward and he wanted to know if Randy wanted to get a beer. Randy asked if it was okay if I tagged along. I hated being a third wheel, but I thought it'd be cool to hang out with one of the players and at least talk about the series. Edward had other plans in mind.

We hurried back to the room to dry off and change clothes. Edward agreed to meet us in the hotel bar in about an hour. We figured it would be a little bit more private because all the sports bars nearby would be packed with fans. We were wrong. The hotel bar was just as packed, but Edward suggested that we just stay put because it'd take too long to drive around in the rain and with all the traffic. Luckily, he had come to the bar incognito just in case it was packed with fans. He was wearing plain clothes and a long trench coat, glasses, and a ball cap with no team logo on it. We wouldn't have recognized him, but he walked right up when he saw us sitting at a pub table.

I was surprised that Edward seemed just as interested in carrying on a conversation with me as he did with Randy. He was very respectful, and although we did talk about the World Series a little, it didn't end up being the main topic of conversation. Edward bought us all three rounds of shots in between drinking beer. He only drank about two because of the game the following day, but Randy and I each had four. The bar announced last call just a few minutes before midnight and Edward picked up our tab.

"You should let us pay you back," I said.

"If we win the series tomorrow night, you guys can treat me next time," Edward said.

"It's a deal. You guys are definitely going to win. You have to," Randy said.

"I sure hope so. Are you guys going to call it a night?" Edward said.

Randy and I looked at each other and shrugged, speechless and buzzing.

"We're up for anything," Randy said, hoping Edward might take the subtle hint.

"I think I know a way you guys could pay me back tonight after all," Edward said wide-eyed.

Randy and I just smiled at him and nodded.

Up in our hotel room, he wasted no time getting undressed. Edward had a nice lean and solid build, with just a dash of hair down his chest and legs. He was the first of the three of us to be completely naked, and then he sat on the bed and watched Randy and I slowly undressing. Unintentionally, Randy and I had our backs to each other as we peeled off our clothes. Neither of us had seen each other completely naked, much less shared a major league baseball player in bed as we were about to do. We turned, and for a brief minute admired each other's physique.

Sure, I had seen Randy shirtless plenty of times in the summer and at the gym. He had very dark skin and huge arms and pecs. His pecs were covered with a nice blanket of black trimmed hair. Like Edward, I was a bit leaner. No matter how hard I worked out at the gym, I never seemed to build any muscle. I had never seen Randy below the waist, or at least that's what I thought. When our eyes glanced down to admire each other's package, I immediately recognized Randy's fat cock from the bathroom stall at the stadium. There was no time to confront him about it. By now, Edward had dropped to his knees and wrapped his hands around each of our cocks to pull us in closer.

He took turns sucking one of us while jacking the other off. I stared down at him and admired his skills. He was just as good at this as he was on the field. He smiled up at me with his eyes, his mouth filled with my rod. He fondled my balls while turning to service Randy's thick cock. With no hesitation, Randy pulled me to him to kiss and neck. I pinched his nipples while Edward continued sucking us down below.

Kissing Randy was unlike with any guy I'd kissed before. Most guys I met at the bar kissed softly and gently. Randy's kiss was hard on the mouth and sloppy, the way you think a man should kiss. He licked my lips and sucked my tongue, totally in control. It excited me. I dropped to my knees to join Edward on Randy's cock. We stroked it with our mouths down each side. I swallowed his thick meat, accustomed to its feel in my mouth already, while Edward sucked on Randy's balls.

I had yet to touch Edward's cock and was dying to get my hands on it. I reached for it while we shared a kiss over Randy's dick. Edward's cock was a lot like mine, a long skinny pencil dick with not a lot of mass. But guys always wanted me to fuck them with it. I wanted Edward to fuck me. Edward stood up bringing his cock even with Randy's. They kissed while I serviced them both, unable to stuff both of them in my mouth because Randy's cock was so broad, but that didn't keep me from trying. I glanced up through their rock-hard poles to see Edward nibbling on one of Randy's nipples. He cupped the top of my head with his hand and pulled me back away from their cocks to look up at them.

"I think you need to get up on that bed," Edward said to me.

"Yes sir," I said, looking up at him. He didn't have to ask me twice.

In most of my bedroom situations, I had always been a top. Guys loved my long skinny dick because it didn't hurt much going in but I was good at using it to hit all the right spots. I could make almost any guy come without him even having to touch himself while I fucked him. I had bottomed before, but couldn't remember how long ago it had been. I was ready for Edward to break me back in if he wanted to.

Randy sat in a chair by the bed stroking his cock while watching us. Edward pushed me down on my back and straddled my waist, pinning me beneath him. He was no bigger than me so I knew I could easily wrestle him off me and overcome him, but I enjoyed letting him be in charge. He held my arms down on each side and forced his tongue into my mouth. I wanted to massage his shoulders or grab the back of his head, and I pretended to try to free my arms but he only held them down tighter. He pulled up from my face and just looked at me with his heavily sexed eyes.

"You know I'm going to fuck you," he said in a whisper.

I closed my eyes and nodded.

Edward moved from sitting across my waist to down between my legs. He let go of my arms and pushed my legs up into the air. I wrapped my hands behind my knees to hold my legs up for him, exposing my ass to his face. He spit hard into his hand, like a baseball player should, and rubbed his fingers in his palm. He reached for my tight hole and began to massage it with a finger or two, slowly easing them inside me to relax the silky flesh. I flexed my sphincter muscle attempting to pull his fingers deeper into me. Edward knelt to take my ball sac into his mouth, fondling each of my swelling balls with his tongue. He soon eased his mouth down to my ass, replacing his fingers with his tongue. He buried deep into me, lathering my hole with his warm spit.

I turned my head to look at Randy, who was still sitting in the chair next to the bed and stroking his cock. His eyes were glued on Edward and me. I nodded for him to come over and join us. He got up and knelt over me, planting the big mushroom head of his rod right at my mouth. I opened my lips and took it in willingly, letting Randy fuck my face. With his knees above each of my shoulders, I was pinned to the bed again with a cock down my throat and a tongue in my crack. A night at the World Series didn't get any better than this.

Edward and Randy traded kisses over me while Randy continued fucking my mouth and Edward fucked my ass with his fingers and tongue. In between my moans, I heard Edward ask Randy if he should fuck me now. Randy told him to go ahead. Just as I had imagined, Edward didn't hurt much going in, especially after he had toyed with my ass using his fingers to loosen me up. It was when the tip of his long slender cock tapped my prostate that I buckled beneath Randy like a wild horse.

Unable to move from the weight of Randy's legs pinned on each side of my head, I jolted from the extreme sensation of Edward's deep thrust, and I forced Randy's cock farther down my throat. I felt myself gag briefly, but was unable to pull away to catch my breath since Randy's cock was so thick. Luckily, Randy pulled his dick out of my mouth, which gave me a chance to recover. In the meantime, Edward had been sliding his long cock in and out of me nice and slow. Each time his cock hit that certain spot, my chest heaved beneath Randy and I let out a quick moan of pleasure. This excited Randy. He slapped my face with his cock and began to talk dirty.

"You like Ed's cock in you? Does that feel good? You like Ed fucking you?"

I never had a chance to respond. Randy shoved his cock back in my mouth. He gripped his large hands around the back of my head and force-fed me his massive rod. Edward had picked up speed too and was now plowing my ass with his bat, his balls slapping hard against my ass. I could feel my own load pulsing through my groin. My heavy breathing intensified, letting them know I was about to come.

I shot so hard that it hurt. My load sprayed across Randy's back. Edward reached down and milked my writhing cock for more. I attempted to pull his hands away from my convulsing dick, now twitching with sensitivity, but Edward held both of my arms away with one hand while he continued to service me with his other. I twisted beneath Randy like a patient tied to a hospital bed. Randy was close. He pulled his cock quickly from my mouth and sprayed a warm load of jizz across my face and the bed. I licked at it with my tongue.

At about the same time, Edward pulled his cock out of me. He gripped it in his hand along with my limp cock and began to jack us off using my come for lube. I felt his load land across my stomach and probably onto Randy's back as well. Randy and Edward collapsed on top of me in a heap of sweat and juice, the sound of our breathing was the only thing breaking the silence.

"I hope I didn't wear you out too hard for tomorrow night's game," I said to Edward.

"Nah. I needed this work out. Hell, it might even improve my game."

And I guess it did. With over forty-six thousand fans in attendance, the Cardinals beat Detroit and won the series the following night. The score had been two to two all the way until the eighth inning, when Edward scored a home run and began paving the way for the Cardinals to take the win. One more home run at the bottom of the ninth was all it took. Randy was so excited he grabbed my ball cap off my head and threw it in the air.

"Man, this is so awesome! I knew the Cardinals could do it. What a perfect end to the first season in the new stadium, huh?"

"Yeah. I can't wait to congratulate Edward," I said.

"Did you have fun last night?" Randy asked.

"Oh yeah, it was hot. What about you?"

"Dude, I haven't had sex like that since my glory days."

"Or what about *glory* holes?" I asked him with a smirk.

At a loss for words, Randy punched me on the shoulder like a teenage school kid. I punched him back. He was silent for a moment and just looked at me. A silly grin grew across his face and we began to laugh. We'd both scored and hit a home run.

Juego De Pelota

Charlie Vazquez

José was a bronze god.

A life-sized statue forged by Vulcan—and come to life—he radiated athletic and masculine magic. Many consider men to be the less graceful of the sexes, but José was a man capable of dreamlike flight: he was perfect to my younger eyes. I first noticed him in an idyllic (rather than familiar) light on a summer afternoon, when all the neighborhood toughs took time away from spray-painting and joint-smoking and finger-fucking to play *un juego de pelota* in the parking lot at the end of our street. Sometimes they would wave at me—with sweaty Yankees caps in hand—and it always made me happy to be noticed by my imaginary big brothers.

Black, fat, thin, white, and brown; they all looked out for me. Their combined horrible reputations equaled an honest man to my worshipping eyes and I revered them while they were at their happiest—playing ball. On a heavy August day—the day I would learn of manhood—I leaned forward on a metal fence with all my weight and watched the sweaty boys swinging, running, sliding, and cursing in Spanish.

Coño, carajo, puñeta . . .

I wasn't yet aware of why I'd spend endless hours waiting for José to take flight and land on a base, in a cloud of victorious brown dust, though that realization would soon dawn

68

a new life for me. I watched in amazement as everybody lobbied to get my idol on their team. I wanted so badly to play—to be close to them and *be* like them—but I wasn't athletic. I was just an observer of athletics; a voyeur still cocooned, watching boys stealing bases and bleeding and spitting like lunatics.

A strange monster's egg is hatching in me was what I thought at the time.

I realized that I was feeding my surfacing desire through the drama of athleticism; a timeworn, ancient tantalizer for the silent lover of men. Watching the game on TV wasn't the same. The skill of televised men was admirable, but watching two teams of shirtless street criminals putting their differences aside to hone their speed, strategy, and prowess was more rousing. Where television only gave one sonic and visual transmission with which to reconstruct reality, the real experience featured the heat of the summer sun, the icy taste of cold drinks, and masculine scents twisting on the air.

I had recently left the imaginary world of young boys to attempt my sexual awakening with real young girls, and failed quickly. I found myself back in a boy's world—a world of older boys and young men living in all extremes of hard reality—yet I was, at first, more observant and less participating. The dark and wet spots of perspiration fascinated me. The games I was seeking had nothing to do with bats and balls and bases, yet the ironies shared by sports and sex became known to me when someone made a funny comparison between baseballs and testicles.

José was my key into this new and smelly world.

My earliest memories of him are scattered at best, but he seems to have been in my life for as long as I can remember. José wasn't a "book-smart" guy but he surpassed that because he was a god of the *physical* realm and that equated to survival. He was a soldier fighting all the artificial bullshit in life, a soul that lived for running and eating and fucking and sweating. He was a simple country boy from the island.

I witnessed José's personal transformations, one by one. I remember when he told me he wanted to be a cop; the following year I saw him handcuffed and shoved into the back of a squad car at least twice. José had been locked up a few times (he was barely twenty at the time) and that made me admire him in a way that I didn't look up to play-by-the-rules kinds of guys. I also remember watching him slip into the world of shy women. One day he held the hand of his sister while they walked to the store, and soon afterward the hands of girls who blushed when he tried to kiss them.

José lived in my building. Our sisters braided doll hair together and our mothers were known to gossip, to exchange *bochinche* while sorting through *plátanos* at the bodega on the corner. José took me under his wing, but I perceived it as simply seeing more of him. I think he sensed my loneliness; perhaps he'd been able to see into the future in his mind's eye and realized I was headed for trouble. I was a fatherless galleon tossed atop dangerous waves, headed for an alien land. José seemed to think that baseball was a way to help me with that, since it helped him forget the woes of his own troubled life.

I remember the first time he snuck up on me from behind and locked my neck in the crook of his arm. He wrestled me to the ground with my face burrowed into the summertime stink of his black armpit hair. He was trying to teach me to always remain alert, was what he said: "I could've been a man with a switchblade running down the street with your wallet and keys." Part of me protested the rough play, but the part of me that would later fantasize about it was just awakening. It was a hellish, painful limbo.

José and the boys conned me into a game one day.

Loosely knowing the rules of baseball, I learned more as I went along. Despite my many mistakes, the thoughtful delinquents corrected me instead of ridiculing me—as baseball is practically *holy* in the world of Latino men. Even if you didn't play baseball—as I surely didn't—you had watched countless games on TV with yawning grandfathers, swearing fathers, and funny uncles. The mixed group of Latino youths and men I first learned to play hardball with congregated to forget unemployment, funerals, angry wives, whining girlfriends, and money owed. Yelling was commonplace yet fistfights were rare.

José yelled for me to run when I cracked a lucky ball over the head of the second baseman during the third inning, but Pablo (the tattooed jailbird outfielder), picked it up and hurled it to the first baseman before I could slide in. I ran for it anyway, feeling my defeat before it happened, and found myself at the first baseman's feet. Looking up before standing, I caught an accidental glimpse through his shorts of his hairy thighs and sex organs—they hung low from his body like ripened tropical fruit on a tall tree. He gave me a hand to get up with and I felt sick; the sweat on the air was a nauseating spell of suspended uncertainty. After the game was over and my team won—thanks to José—we went our ways and José walked me back to our building. I was flattered to carry his mitt and bat for him.

José's family was in Puerto Rico at the time and he invited me up to their second-floor apartment. I didn't suspect anything unusual as our voices echoed in the cavernous tiled hallways and painted metal stairwell. Once inside that all changed. José turned the television on to a game in progress and hushed to concentrate on it. In the hallway leading to the bathroom he ripped off his soaked muscle tee, and though I'd seen his bronze torso before, it seemed to glow in a new light. I saw him through new eyes, since I was a late-bloomer, sexually speaking. My expiring youthful curiosities started to realize my soon-to-be adult impulses, as my hormones transformed my body, brain, and spirit. The seeds of what would become my lust were already planted and the first sprouts (or spurts) of my desire were about to see the light of their first day! Tiny lightning bolts tickled my skin all over my body.

I asked him if I could pee first, since my family's apartment was all the way upstairs, on the sixth floor. I wasn't sure why I was there to begin with, yet his gravity kept me in a tight orbit around him. As if he hadn't heard me, he went into the bathroom and pulled off his sweaty shorts and underwear, the long pendulum of his penis nodding left and right as he balanced on one foot and then the other. As he turned the noisy jets of his showerhead to a full, steaming blast he said, "Come in and go pee, I can't wait no more."

I waited—for what I couldn't figure out—frozen in my tracks like discovered prey. Being so close to a naked man seemed like the most dangerous thing I could be doing. As much as I thought to run, or at least go to my own apartment, I couldn't. My courage pulled me forward and past José, who stared at me blankly as he disappeared into the steamy cell of the shower. I reached the toilet and lifted the seat; the release felt the best it ever had. I tried to slip out. Just as I was about to close the bathroom door behind me, José called to me, "Come here, I have to tell you something."

I stood still in place and answered, "I can hear you from here."

José's head popped out of parted shower curtains, his shiny black hair dripping water on the chipped tiles. "Come here . . . come *here!* I can't say it loud." I inched forward and met him face to face. José had a strange smile on his face at that moment, as though he'd succeeded in roping me in—to what I was still clueless about. Steam poured out from behind him and washed over me. *Why isn't he saying anything and what's the strange look on his face all about?* I conjured all my might to appear as though I wasn't terrified, but to say I was terrified was a *huge* understatement: I was mortified.

After an eternal quiet spell, he asked me softly, "Have you ever seen your *jugo de pelotas?*" He cradled his dripping nuts in his free hand and lifted them to emphasize his question. I had never seen a man's genitals in such proximity before, though I remember marveling over photos of them. At that time in my life, pornography had both scared and fascinated me. José transformed to complete menace before me, his sexuality nearly knocking me off my feet and dragging me away to a place from which I could never return.

Juego y jugo. I remember thinking about the similarity of *juego de pelota* (ball game) and *jugo de pelota* (semen). I had read about ejaculation; yet I was eighteen and had never seen my own "juice of the balls" as José had referred to it in Spanish. My limited and forced sexual play with girls never took me that far, yet I answered, "Of course I have." I hardly sounded convincing and began backing off, facing him.

José was intent on something I still could not fully understand. I did however sense that he was reaching a strange breaching of my trust. "Come here," he demanded again, smelling my virginity like the scent of blood on the air. I appeared before him like a dumbstruck rag doll. He put a wet hand on my shoulder and said, "You need to learn how to be a man . . . for the ladies."

"What are you talking about, José?"

"Since you don't have a father, someone needs to teach you . . ."

"Don't be stupid, José . . ."

I doubted his goodwill and felt the stabs of exploitation seize me. At that time of my life, sex had been a dark stranger that had only existed in the windows of Manhattan porn stores and in the bragging of foul-mouthed youths. I had always been fascinated by death as well. The two seemed to merge before me for the first time. I tried to control the shaking of my knees as I began to cave in to his offer. *What could he possibly mean?*

José then said, "Men take showers together all the time, like in professional sports. Come in, I'll show you how I learned. *Don't worry . . .* "

The gaping canyon between José's knowing and my unknowing was one of the biggest rifts I had ever felt between myself and someone I'd thought I'd known so well. I felt as though I didn't know him at all, suddenly. I reached to my core for courage and knew that he wouldn't harm me. Life would continue to throw such challenges my way and I remembered that this was *José* and not some random lunatic. My fear vanished like a fireball gone out. I shed my shirt and shorts and pulled off my filthy socks. José did not watch me undress; he instead receded into the shower's misty cascades. Part of me never entered the shower, only the new "me" did.

When I entered the stall, he was leaning against the tile wall with his soaped-up manhood in his hand. He held it like a pistol and that's when I made the connection between cocks and weapons, bats and balls. "I'll show you fast," he said, acknowledging my arrival, as though he were behind me, setting me up to slam a home run into outer space. José slicked himself to rock-hardness and quickened then slowed the strokes that squeaked with each pass of his hand, the brown marble of his forearm tensing with each slow and tight caress.

I was hard and realized that I'd been watching him for several minutes. He said nothing while he moaned with each long stroke. I marveled at the size of his cock. It seemed to breathe in its own strange way, an organism attached to him, yet with its own consciousness and need. His masturbating seemed to both relax and tense his whole body.

"When you fuck the first time, it feels even better," he said with a shaky voice. He showed me how his hand could satisfy his cock with all of its various swipes and grips and shapes. He went on, "You'll feel really good until you can't control it and then you'll shoot your *jugo de pelotas.*"

Relaxation took hold of me. I imitated his technique with heavy insecurity and blossoming joy. While he brought himself closer to orgasm—a concept he already understood—I zigzagged to find my way to a place I didn't yet know. I continued to mock his techniques, my own moaning finally finding the will to express itself, my soul, in a tailspin. He came closer and said, "Don't tell anyone about this."

"Of *course* not, José."

He slicked his Herculean hands with soap and turned me around, his chest barely touching my back under the waterfall. He cupped his soapy hands under my balls and said, "You need to know what I'm going to show you. These are your *pelotas* . . . always watch them with your life. You'll need them to be a father . . ." His slicked hands slid up to my excitement. He slowly worked it up and down while explaining his approach. "Sometimes you'll like it loose; other times you'll want it tight." As he said *tight* he gripped my cock so hard I thought it would squish between his fingers like a soft banana. The waves of terror I had first felt had collapsed into an overwhelming storm of satisfaction.

His hold of me seemed to last for eternities—until I could not see, until thunder and lightning were born at my core and went out and in every direction—possessing me like a crazed spirit. I lost control of my body in Jose's grip, one of his hands stroking me to madness, his other arm across my chest, keeping me upright. Dragged across a universe of sensation, I was a convulsing and ecstatic maniac in front of him. But he knew what he was doing. His free hand found my mouth to muffle it, when I felt the flash of God's might rise in my core to explode and surround me in the form of his grunting and my gasping combined. I was lifted up and down at the same time, drawn and quartered by my fear, fantasy, freedom, and fixation. José awakened a monster in me that will never rest.

While watching the boys playing a game of hardball a few weeks later, he waved at me and I noticed he was still the same guy—though I was forever changed. When he saw me walking down the avenue one night, he chased me, cradled my head in a headlock, and asked how my mother was doing. But we never again discussed the slippery summer afternoon that I slid out of his Olympic grip in his shower, the day so many mysteries were solved and heartaches begun. We never discussed that day:, the day I collapsed to catch my stolen breath in the pond of soapy come-speckled bathwater that surrounded his godlike feet; the day I held my aching genitals close to my body, in a fetal position in the water, while he stepped out of the shower to dry off.

The day I became a man, after *un juego de pelota*.

Island Ball

Neil Plakcy

When Randy Blair stepped out of the closet a week after signing a twelve million dollar, three-year deal with the Las Vegas Kings, a new Major League Baseball expansion team, the story was on everyone's lips—especially here in Honolulu, where the Kings were just about to play an exhibition game.

Randy's handsome face, bulked-up arms, and slim waist were everywhere as I drove to my job as a homicide detective one fine spring morning. Within an hour, I was temporarily reassigned as Randy's bodyguard and sent to meet his flight.

At the airport, I badged my way in and introduced myself to the gate agent. Randy was among the first off the plane, and I recognized him easily.

For starters, there weren't many guys in baseball as handsome as he was: close-cropped blond hair, a face that resembled Brad Pitt's, chest and biceps bursting out of a royal blue polo shirt that exactly matched his eyes; narrow waist, slim hips, thighs and calves honed by running bases.

I stepped up and introduced myself. Up close, I could see the toll that the last week had taken on him—bags under his eyes, chin unshaven, worry lines around his mouth. He looked me up and down, then shook his head. "How do we get out of here?"

"Follow me."

Okay, so we weren't going to be best buds. That was fine with me. Who could blame the guy for being a jerk: handsome, rich, successful, and now hounded by the press. It would make being around him a lot easier if I didn't have to worry about lusting after his tight ass or wanting to kiss his pouty lips.

The gate agent led us through a locked door, into the bowels of the airport, eventually depositing us at a side entrance where a black limousine waited. Randy Blair climbed into the back and slammed the door behind him, leaving me to sit up front. The driver announced that Randy's luggage was already in the trunk, and we took off.

I saw Randy pull out a BlackBerry and start punching keys, and I settled back for the ride to the Mandarin Oriental in Kahala. If I could convince Randy Blair to stay in his room except for his time on the field, this would be an easy job.

No such luck. "I'm going to hit the hotel pool for a while, then take a nap," he said, leaning forward. "Get me a dinner reservation at Roy's for nine. After that I want to go to a place called Surf Boyz." Surf Boyz was Honolulu's newest, hottest gay bar, a multilevel place with three dance floors and five bars. It would be hell to keep track of him. "Who knows, maybe I'll get lucky."

I called a guy I knew who'd dated a waiter at Roy's for a while, and got Randy the reservation he wanted. Then I called the Mandarin Oriental and asked for a VIP check in. The clerk gave me Randy's room number and arranged for someone to meet the limo and escort us there.

Randy's suite had an ocean view, and while he stalked into the bedroom to change, I stood admiring the surf, wanting to be out on my board more every minute. I was going to be a glorified babysitter, and worse, the chief of police would instantly hear of anything I did wrong. It was clearly a no-win situation.

"What the hell is this shit?"

Randy stalked out of the bedroom, buck naked, brandishing a bottle of Longboard Lager, a microbrew I was actually pretty fond of.

"Beer," I said. "Maybe you've heard of it?"

Oops. Probably shouldn't mouth off to a guy who had the ability to get me fired with a single phone call.

"Somebody screwed up my instructions. I only drink Corona. I want a six-pack here, now. And don't forget the lime."

He turned to stalk back into the bedroom, giving me a prime view of that gorgeous ass—two round white globes dusted with a few pale blond hairs. "I'm your bodyguard, not your secretary," I said. "You want room service to bring you a beer, pick up the phone."

He turned to stare at me, and I saw his dick had begun to stiffen. Hmm, being an asshole made him hard. Interesting.

I smiled blandly, and I could see he wanted to say something, but instead he turned and went back into the bedroom, returning a moment later in a skimpy Speedo. "Let's move," he said, heading toward the door of the suite.

The rest of the afternoon passed smoothly. Randy swam laps for a while, then a couple of giggling teenaged girls asked for his autograph, which he was surprisingly gracious about providing. Then he took a long nap. I was sitting in the living room of the suite reading a mystery novel when he woke up and came out of the bedroom, stretching and yawning, naked once again.

"I hope you won't be uncomfortable in a gay club," he said, smirking, and I realized that he didn't seem to know I was gay. It was a surprise; since I'd come out so spectacularly, it seemed that everybody who cared knew that I was the "gay cop." *So that's why he'd been so antagonistic,* I thought.

"I'm fine with a range of sexual orientations."

His dick was limp again, though impressive in its length and girth, nestled in a blond bush. His six-pack abs rippled as he walked. I noticed he was carrying another Longboard Lager, and this one had been opened. As I watched, he took a long pull from it. "It isn't bad," he admitted, seeing my gaze. "For a local brew."

"Glad you like it," I said.

I'd secured a table by the window for him at Roy's, and I held back as the maitre d' escorted him there. "Come on," he said, when he reached the table. "I hate to eat alone."

I sat down across from him. In the flickering candle light, he looked even more impossibly handsome. The shadows highlighted his cheekbones, the strong line of his jaw. His blue eyes caught the light and glittered.

Outside, the velvety darkness glittered with occasional pinpricks of light. A gentle breeze blew in the scent of jacaranda blossoms. It was the most romantic of settings. If only I'd been there with a boyfriend rather than a handsome jerk.

"What's your name again—Como?" he asked, after we'd ordered.

"Kimo," I said. I spelled it for him. "Hawaiian for James. A pretty common name in the islands."

"More than I needed to know," he said.

Fine. We were quiet for a few minutes, and then our drinks arrived—a dirty martini for him, a Coke for me. "You don't drink?" he asked.

"Not on duty."

He nodded. After a minute he said, "Listen, I'm sorry for being a prick. It's been a tough couple of weeks."

"I can imagine."

He frowned. Little did he know.

I steered the conversation to baseball. How he'd played in his most recent game, what he thought of the Racers, and so on. We ate, we talked. Every now and then I'd steal a glance at his handsome face in profile, and almost unconsciously lick my lips in the hope that I might be able to kiss his. Dumb hope. Though once when his leg accidentally brushed against mine I became hard almost immediately. Then he shifted again without seeming to have noticed.

It was exquisite torture, sitting across from a handsome, sexy man at a romantic restaurant, knowing there was no hope of romance. His light blue button-down shirt was open at the collar, exposing a triangle of lightly tanned flesh and the barest hint of chest hair. The flickering candlelight cast shadows over his face, highlighting the strong jawline, the angle of a cheekbone.

The longer dinner wore on, the more in lust I fell. Randy became every baseball hero I'd worshipped as a kid, every handsome man I'd spotted across a crowded room and longed to touch. By the time we finished a pair of chocolate mousse cake slices studded with macadamia nuts and set in a pool of coconut puree, I was feeling a serious case of blue balls approaching.

He paid the bill with an American Express black card, and when we stood up I had to turn my back to him to arrange my throbbing hard-on so that it wouldn't be obvious to every person we passed on the way out. I'd already notified the manager of Surf Boyz that Randy was coming, and we were ushered right in to the VIP area.

He had another dirty martini, then announced that he wanted to dance. I followed him to the floor, figuring to stand in the shadows. But on the way, guys kept calling out to me. "Hey, Kimo. Looking good, Kimo." I spotted my friend Gunter, who came up and gave me a big kiss.

"I'm working," I said, shouting to be heard over the music. I nodded toward Randy Blair.

"A suspect?"

"A baseball player."

Meanwhile, Randy was standing around looking lost. For once, no one was paying attention to him, and he didn't seem to like it. In the dark club, it was hard to see how handsome he was, and the gay men of Waikiki didn't seem to be big baseball fans.

I kept an eye on Randy as I was talking to Gunter. Finally, Randy stalked over to me and said, "I want to dance."

"Go ahead."

"With you."

I looked at Gunter and shrugged, then followed Randy to the dance floor.

The guy had some moves on him. His hips swiveled while the top of his body gently rocked and his legs executed a complicated choreography. He grabbed my hand, pulled me close, then swung me out. I struggled to keep up with him, tingling every time his hand touched mine.

Fortunately I had to focus on dancing, or I think I'd have come in my pants the third or fourth time I felt his hand on the small of my back, then stray down to briefly caress my butt.

After an hour he pulled my head close to his. "Gotta take a leak," he said. He started toward the bathroom, and I had to go along. I knew that a bathroom would be an excellent place to ambush somebody.

I followed him into the men's room and took the urinal next to his. We both pulled our dicks out and started to pee noisily. I'd already seen the size of his trouser snake, so I kept my eyes on the wall, but I could feel his gaze straying down toward my crotch. Almost unconsciously, I pressed my pants back, letting my dick hang out as far as it would go.

We both finished at the same time, and zipped up. As we turned to leave, though, he grabbed the back of my head with his hand and pulled my lips to his. I was startled at first, but it doesn't take me long to react to the feeling of a sexy guy's mouth on mine. Those thick, pouty lips of his pressed against mine, tasting of olives, and his tongue pushed past my teeth as if he were trying to swallow me whole.

He smelled of soap and sweat and a spicy, lime-tinged cologne. He kept one hand behind my head, while the other reached around to encircle my upper waist. Our upper bodies pressed against each other, and I wrapped my arms around his Oxford-cloth-covered back and pressed my crotch against his. I was so overcome with lust I forgot where I was, until an old queen pushed past us on his way to the urinal and said, "Get a room."

"I'm ready to go back to the hotel," Randy said, as we washed our hands. Our eyes met in the mirror, his sparkling blue in the overhead light. A deep hunger rose in my stomach and I wasn't sure I could hold out that long.

I called the limo driver, and he met us outside. This time, when I held the door open for Randy, he said, "Aren't you getting in?" and moved across the back seat.

What the hell, I thought. *And I was getting paid for this gig?*

I hopped into the back seat with him, and as soon as I had the door closed he had his hand on my crotch and his mouth on mine. We made out furiously on the back seat of the limo, pulling each other's shirts open and massaging each other's crotch. I'd been with a bunch of guys by that time in my life, but it was rare to find one whose passion matched my own. Randy's lust seemed to drive my own to new heights.

"Why didn't you tell me you were gay?" he said, when we stopped to take a breath.

I flopped back against the seat of the limo, catching my breath and waiting for my heart to return to its normal rhythm. "I thought you'd be able to tell."

"I can sure as hell tell now," he said, leaning over to bite my lower lip. He swung over me, planting one knee on either side of me, and I could feel his hard dick jammed against my stomach. My own strained up toward the sexy ass that hovered over it. I thought we might both melt into a pool of lust right there on the limo seat.

We were both a disheveled mess by the time we pulled up at the hotel. I squirmed away from him and said, "Button your shirt," closing mine up before I opened the door. "You don't know who's out there with a camera."

"What the hell do I care?"

"I care," I said. "You think this is what the chief of police had in mind when he asked me to take care of you?"

"I know what I have in mind, as soon as we get upstairs."

I glared at him, and he buttoned his shirt and smoothed his hair. I got out of the limo first, pushing my stiff dick aside so it wouldn't tent my pants too obviously. Then I held the door for him and followed him at a discreet distance through the lobby.

I loved the way he sauntered, a pure jock posture, as if he knew that everyone in the lobby was admiring his strut, knew how successful he was, how much money he made, wanting to be him or fuck him.

Once we got inside his suite, though, there was no longer any distance between us. He grabbed me in a big bear hug, and wrapped his hands around my ass, pulling me toward him. We mashed our lips together and kissed, both our hearts racing as we connected. I was overwhelmed again by his spicy lime cologne, by the feel of his shirt beneath my fingers, the warmth of his skin where we touched.

His five o'clock shadow rubbed roughly against my cheek as I kissed the line of his jaw. I felt his hard-on jammed against me as I unbuttoned his shirt and began kissing and licking my way to his nipples, first one, then the other.

"Man, you're driving me wild," he said, as he shucked his shirt and massaged the sides of my head.

I pulled off my shirt and unbuckled my pants, unzipping them and dropping them to the floor as he did the same. Fortunately, I was wearing deck shoes without socks so I could kick them off, but Randy was wearing sneakers and thick white tube socks, and his pants hung up on his shoes.

I kneeled to the floor in my boxers, passing his crotch encased in white briefs along the way. He tried to pull them down but I grabbed his hand. "Wait," I said. He fell backward on the sofa, stretching his right foot out to me.

I untied his right sneaker and pulled it off, then began massaging his foot through his sock. He groaned softly. Then I pulled the sock off and started to kiss and suck on each of his toes. Big toe first, rough and callused, hard as a stubby dick. Then each toe in sequence. He squirmed and moaned, urging me to his dick instead, but I took my time. When I'd finished sucking the little toe of his right foot, I applied myself to his left, repeating the process.

Then I slid his pants off and lifted my head to his crotch. His dick was rock-hard, tenting the white cotton fabric, and there was a round wet spot at the head where he was leaking precome. I licked my tongue up the length of his shaft through the fabric, and he shivered and moaned. Then, without removing his briefs, I started sucking him. After only a moment or two, I felt his body stiffen and then he ejaculated behind the fabric that separated us.

"Man, that was awesome," he said, relaxing his body against the cushions.

My own dick was hard, tenting my boxers and leaking precome against a pattern of palm trees and hula dancers.

I tugged Randy's come-soaked shorts away from his crotch, put my hand into the cream, and then rubbed it up from his crotch toward his chest. He groaned. "Dude, you are so hot."

"This is only the beginning," I said. I peeled Randy's shorts the rest of the way down and dropped my boxers. Then I turned him so he was lying on his back on the sofa, and lay down on top of him, rubbing my body against his, my dick against his thigh, the come on his chest mixing with mine, getting lost in the black hairs that ran all the way from my crotch to my pecs.

I felt myself coming and leaned down to kiss him as my body stiffened, closing my eyes as my tongue found his and my body erupted in passion. I slumped against him, sucking on his lower lip, and he rubbed my back with the hand that had earned him twelve million. I could see he was worth it.

We lay like that for a while, until I pulled off and our bodies stuck together, come and sweat mingling with body hair. "Yuck," he said. "We need to hit the shower." He pushed me off him and stood up. I slumped back on the sofa.

"You coming?"

"Been there, done that," I said, grinning.

"I'm a professional athlete," he said. "I never shower alone."

I couldn't resist the wicked smile on his face, so I dragged my sorry ass off the sofa and followed him into the lavish marble bathroom.

If anything, Randy's reflection in the full-length mirror across from the shower was even sexier, knowing that I'd made him sweat, that it was my come mixed with his that caked the wiry blond hairs of his bush. He turned the water on full blast, unwrapped a bar of fancy lavender soap, and beckoned me to join him. I was happy to oblige.

We alternated soaping each other, and I got to explore every single muscle group in Randy's finely toned body.

Man, it didn't get much better than that. Hot sex with a world-class athlete, then an invigorating hot shower, the scent of lavender rising around us as we rubbed our soapy bodies together.

Randy dropped the soap. "Oops," he said. "You'd better pick that up."

When I bent over, he stuck his finger up my ass. "You know what they say about us faggots," he said. "Don't drop your soap in the locker room."

I wondered how many times he had heard that phrase since he'd come out of the closet, and I wanted nothing more than to be his protector, to beat the shit out of any guy who dared make a nasty crack at the man who could make me feel so good.

I stood back up, and his finger slipped out of my ass. But he made up for it by sticking his tongue in my mouth. We kissed under the cascading hot water until it had washed away every trace of soap. Randy stuck his close-cropped blond head back under the tap for a minute, then said, "I'm ready for bed. How about you?"

"With you, stud?" I said, worried for a minute that I was sounding like someone in a bad porn movie. "In a heartbeat. Just let me wash my hair. I think you must have massaged your come into it."

He stepped out of the shower and grabbed a towel. "I'll be waiting for you," he said. Through the clear glass door of the shower I watched him towel off, and only turned to the shampoo after he'd left the room, naked as usual.

When I got to the bed, though, he was sacked out, fast asleep and snoring lightly.

I looked around for my clothes. *I probably should go across the hall to my own room,* I thought. But how many chances would I get to share a bed with a handsome, sexy baseball player? Not many, in this life. So I slipped into the bed next to Randy, and he threw a leg over me and pulled me close.

I woke up alone, to rosy fingers of light creeping in through the sliding glass doors that overlooked the ocean. I looked around for a minute at the 400-thread count sheets, the cloud-soft pillows, the elegant furniture, and gorgeous painting of Diamond Head on the wall. It took me a minute to realize that the night before hadn't been just an amazing dream.

I found Randy in the living room of the suite, his head toward the balcony, doing push-ups. "Join me," he said.

I flopped down on the floor next to him, then joined his rhythm. I didn't know how many push-ups he'd done, but I stopped at thirty and watched him do another twenty. Then he rolled over and started doing sit-ups.

"Don't just sit there—make yourself useful," he said. "Sit on my feet."

I did as I was told, plopping my naked ass onto his ankles and feet. He clasped his hands behind his head and began his sit-ups, those glorious abs rippling. With every movement his dick began to stiffen, until he was fully hard, but nothing stopped his rhythm. I counted for him, and when he got to fifty his dick finally subsided. When he got to one hundred, he quit. Then we ran a mile around the hotel before showering and dressing.

In the limo on the way to the stadium, he said, "Sorry about crashing last night." He looked out the window. "I haven't been sleeping all that well since I made the big move." Without looking at me, he took my hand and squeezed it. "Thanks. I needed the rest."

I squeezed back.

I sat up in the stands and watched as the Kings practiced. It was a glorious day, with sunshine, blue skies, and temps in the low seventies. The first exhibition game was the next day, so Randy and the rest of the players were under strict instructions not to get out and raise any hell. In the limo back to the hotel, he said to me, "You know a quiet place we can get some dinner?"

I knew just the place, a Japanese restaurant perched on a cliff on the windward side of the island. He gave the limo driver the evening off and I drove us up there in my truck, relishing the chance to be just a pair of guys out on a romantic date.

We shared platters of sushi, drank just a bit of sake, and spent a long time talking. I told him about my coming-out experience, and he told me some of the responses he'd been getting. Our feet danced with each other under the table, and occasionally we even clasped hands. If there'd been even a chance that our romance could blossom, it would have been perfect. But I knew Randy was leaving as soon as the last ball was hit, and that gave the evening a bittersweet tinge— even though with luck we would spend most of the next week together.

That night, I followed him up to his suite, but he stopped outside the door. "Listen, I have this superstition," he said. "Ever since high school."

"No sex before the big game?"

He nodded. "Are you cool with that?"

I kissed his cheek. "Absolutely. You only play every other day, right?"

"And every other night, we play," he said.

I slept on the couch, joined Randy for a brief workout the next morning, and then delivered him to the stadium. I was invited to watch the game from the owner's box with the chief of police, the owners of the two teams, and a bunch of other dignitaries.

At the end of the third inning, the chief's cell phone rang.

Irritated, he picked it up and barked at the caller. Halfway through the call, he put the phone aside and whispered something to the owner of the Kings, then nodded. He caught my eye and nodded for me to follow him to the back of the suite. "There's been a phone threat," he said in an undertone as we walked. "They've decided to pull Randy off the field. I want you to meet him down in the locker room and keep him there until the game's over."

"He's not going to be happy about that," I said.

"I think we'd all rather have him unhappy than dead," the chief said. "Go."

I went. There was a uniform outside the locker room door, who said he'd be guarding the room to make sure no one got in until the game was over. I walked inside to find Randy pounding the door of a locker with his million-dollar fist.

"Whoa, whoa," I said, grabbing his arm. He hit me, a solid punch to the gut.

I swung his arm around and pinned it against his back, leaning my face against his neck. "I know you're pissed off," I said. "But if you hurt yourself, you're out of the game, and the assholes have won."

He started to shake, and I realized he was crying. I turned him around and kissed him. "Don't cry, baby," I said. "You've got to be strong."

"I'm tired, Kimo," he said. "I'm ready to give up."

"You can't. You don't have to. Lean on me."

He wrapped his arms around my back and hugged me fiercely, and we kissed some more, our tongues dueling with each other. I felt myself getting hard as our bodies pressed together. I reached up under his uniform jersey and pulled it off, then began kissing and licking my way across his chest. I had him pinned against a locker with my hands, and I felt his chest rising and falling in a steady rhythm.

I untied his pants and let them slide to the floor. He was wearing a jock with a cup, which I found incredibly sexy.

"I want to fuck you, Kimo," he said. "I want to fuck you so bad."

"Fortunately, I was a Boy Scout when I was a kid," I said, pulling my wallet out of my pocket. I kept a condom in the back. "Always prepared."

While he pulled the jock off to the side and unwrapped the condom, I pulled my pants and boxers down and leaned against an inclined sit-up board. Randy squatted behind me, spit into my asshole, then slicked his index finger up in his mouth and began to finger-fuck me.

"Yeah, you've got a tight asshole," he said. "You're going to love me filling you up with my big bat."

I squirmed under his digital assault. We were in the locker room, for god's sake, and I was about to be fucked by a handsome, sexy ballplayer. Could it get any better than that?

Then he stuck his dick up my ass. It hurt for a minute, but then he found the sweet spot and started fucking me, and I realized, yeah, it could get better, and it just had. He was pulling on my shoulders, moving my body back and forth as his hips pistoned his dick into me. I wanted to yell out with pleasure but I worried that any excess noise might cause the uniform outside the door to burst in on us.

I felt Randy's blond pubes tickling my ass as his slippery dick slid in and out of me. He left one hand on my shoulder and reached around with the other to jerk me off. It wasn't long before we were both whimpering and catching our breath and then ejaculating madly. He pulled his dick out of me and flipped me over so I was lying on my back on the inclined board, and lowered himself over me.

We kissed deeply, our bodies pressed against each other, sweat and come mingling. "Man, you are some hot fuck," Randy said.

"Back at you, stud," I said. "They don't call you Randy for nothing."

He laughed loudly. "Man, that felt good," he said. "I haven't laughed in a long time."

I pushed him off me. "Come on, let's hit the shower," I said. "And this time, stud, if you drop the soap, you're the one who'd better watch out."

They caught the jerk who'd been threatening Randy that night, and the rest of the exhibition series went off without a hitch. And as promised, when Randy didn't play during the day, he and I played at night. I could see why he was paid as much as he was; he sure knew how to handle bats and balls.

Robert Strozier's Toilet

Shane Allison

━━━━

Here I sit broken hearted, came to shit, but only farted.
—Anonymous

My stall is coated in a rainbow of blue, black, and green graffiti of gay propositions: CALL THIS NUMBER FOR ASS; WHERE'S THE ACTION; SUCK DICK NOW; as well as a plethora of names, e-mails, and phone numbers sprawled across fiberglass walls. I scribble TAP FOOT FOR BLOW JOB above my tissue dispenser. I couldn't possibly go to class today. Not with this hard-on from hell twitching in my jeans. I've already been in here for a good four hours now when I promised myself half an hour at the most. I should have run all my errands first before coming here. I haven't gotten a thing done on my list and I've only attended one class. I got word that it was the newest cruise spot on campus. Don't know why. This place is filthy. Smells like wet red clay, but I've been in worse tea rooms. Heard this place gets a lot of jocks: football, baseball, and basketball players on the down-low between classes and practice. Seems like that's all I've been doing today is lending my lips out to every dick that has been in here, and this pierced punk next to me is about to be number six.

I gaze through the sand dollar-sized glory hole to watch Pierced Punk stroke his thickness. I ball up what's left of my tissue and throw it between my thighs into the toilet of pissy

93

water. I skim the rough hole in the partition between our naked bodies, signaling Pierced Punk to work his inches within it. I can hardly wait to wrap my lips around his cock. I watch him stand up off his toilet, his uncut dick wet. He presses his pubic pelvis against the wall, shoving his hulking inches through the partition's hole. I rope my fingers around Pierced Punk's dick. As I run my thumb across his piss slit, tasting a tinge of precome, I slide a hand between my legs and start to whack my own boner that throbs in my palm.

"Suck me," Pierced Punk says from the other side of my stall. His dick hangs over the lip of the glory hole.

It tastes bitter of pee as I tongue the head, peeling back a tender sheath. A thick buildup of dick cheese is unveiled.

"Suck that dick," Pierced Punk demands, talking dirtier than a porn star. In spite of his smegma, I throw my lips to his sliver of flesh anyway. Drool trickles down the shaft into a bush of musky crotch hair.

As I suckle his dick, the door to the men's room opens. I bolt off my knees in dismay. Someone enters. I gawk through the gutted metal plate on the right side of me as he stands at the urinal and pulls his dick from his jockstrap. He looks familiar, like I have seen him around campus before. I watch as hot gold skirts from his slit. There's nothing I love more than hearing a guy take a leak. The sound of gold streams of piss makes me hard, wishing I was his human urinal. Sounds as if he's been holding it in all day. His thumb caresses a blushed cock head as he holds his dick steady in the mouth of the urinal. As I watch him, I beat off at the sight of urine being sprayed from the prettiest dick I've ever witnessed on a white boy.

I look down to notice that Pierced Punk is poking at my lower leg with a pen with tissue curled around it. I unroll it and read: WHAT UP WITH THAT GUY NEXT TO YOU? HE'S

TAKIN' A PISS. I return the flimsy piece of tissue back through the glory hole.

The cruiser stands in front of my stall with his dick hanging out of the cup of his jock. He's Hispanic with spikes of dirty-blond highlights and a cute, boyish face looking like a younger Jose Canseco. He's got these raging red lips I would give anything to kiss. I can make out his well-trimmed pitch goatee as I peek through the slit of my stall's door. It is then that I realize who the stranger is. Brian Miller. The Brian Miller who led the baseball team with nine wins, thirty-seven strikeouts, and twenty-seven home runs last year. He's the number one pitcher in the ACC and was voted Tallahassee Regional Most Star Player, and now here he is in front of me with a dick that defies all gravity. I didn't even know he was into guys. It just goes to show that you never know. Round here everybody calls him Bri or B.

I slide the latch that holds the door closed, watching it swing in, hitting my thigh. As I lean back, the cold plumbing of the commode presses uncomfortably into my back. I gap my thighs apart so he can get a good look at my dick. His is hard and hung with its twin set of low-hangers in an egg-size sac of rosy goose-bumped skin. He lifts his T-shirt up over his belly, past his nipples, running his freckled hand across a pubic bush. I look through the glory hole to find Pierced Punk playing with his balls.

"Let's see your ass," I whisper. He turns around, grips the lip of the sink, and bends over to show me his ass, which is strong and heavy. Each cheek has a pleasing growth of fur. My dick twitches as dirty thoughts of planting it square between them dance in my head.

Pierced Punk opens the door to his stall, stepping out of his Joe Boxers and jeans that are bunched around his calves. He reaches around and pulls off his T-shirt.

Pierced Punk stands stark naked in front of Bri and takes his dick in his hand. Bri returns the gesture, clutching Pierced Punk's dick in his palm.

"You got a nice dick," I tell him.

"Thanks." Bri smiles modestly.

I would like it even better if it was in my mouth, I thought.

Bri walks over and stands in the doorway of my stall, jacking off as Pierced Punk sits his bare ass on the lip of the sink behind him.

I lean into Bri and tip his dick up to my lips, taking it into my mouth. I watch Pierced Punk whacking off while staring hungrily at the player's butt. I suck him slowly 'cause I don't want to run the risk of my mouth giving out before he gets off. I ease my *fuck you* finger between the cheeks of his ass as I suck his dick, lubing it with spit. Beads of sweat form on my forehead as I sluggishly slide up and down again upon his shaft, devouring countless inches.

"Deep throat it," Pierced Punk whispers, running his own cock along Bri's left cheek. I grip his ass as his pink mushroom head tickles my tonsils. I force my finger deeper into the ripe recesses of his asshole.

Pierced Punk starts to kiss along the nape of his neck. My chin grazes the knuckles of Pierced Punk as he cups Bri's balls.

"Fuck his face," Pierced Punk orders.

He pulls and pushes his dick in and out of my mouth.

"Kiss me," he murmurs, as he fondles Bri's nipples.

I look up as Bri and Pierced Punk's lips meet with tongues intertwining like French lovers.

"Spit on it," Bri demands.

I suck him frantically as if it's the last cock I'll ever have the pleasure of pleasing.

I wash his dick over with spit.

"Suck his dick, man," says Pierced Punk.

Pierced Punk's demand turns me on as I pump my dick simultaneously to sucking Bri. I can feel he's about to let loose a load, like he hasn't had an orgasm in weeks. I gladly accept as he pumps his juices in my mouth. I slide my *fuck you* finger out of him and spit his jizz onto the dingy tile. Bri sits his ass on the freezing floor beneath him.

"Go lock the door, man," he tells Pierced Punk. I peel my jeans off my legs, hanging them, with my shirt, on a hook screwed behind my stall's door. Pierced Punk stands on the right side of Bri as I stand on the left, our dicks milling over his chest.

"I wantcha to pee on me," Bri says.

We both ignore him at first and say nothing as we keep beating our dicks. Bri can't take his eyes off our privates. He stands up on his knees and lunges hungrily at them, licking the heads.

"Pee on me," he murmurs.

Pierced Punk and I look at each most bewildered.

"You want me to what on you?" I ask.

Pierced Punk looks down at Bri fondling his dick.

"I like to get pissed on."

Is he serious? I think.

Both our dicks are servile with droplets of precome.

It tickles when he runs his hand across my pubic patch; Bri is freaking me out with all this pee on me shit. My dick is softening at the thought of his unorthodox demand. I can't believe he wants us to pee on 'im.

"C'mon, baby, piss on me," he begs, waving Pierced Punk's dick in his face. Pierced Punk waits for me to make a move.

I have only fantasized of piss play. Never actually attempted it. Bri slides along the wall to the floor with thighs ajar and dick at full salute. He looks up at me with a puppy dog kind of innocence and says, "Piss on me."

"Go 'head," says Pierced Punk.

Bri slides his tongue beneath the spigot of my dick head, awaiting piss. Pierced Punk runs the tip of his dick across Bri's lips, but he pulls away.

"Pee on me while I jack off," he says.

Pierced Punk and I rub our dicks full with urine against his face.

"You want it?" I reach around, cupping the back of Bri's head. He scoots up to my dick, anxious to be treated like a human urinal.

"Wanna be pissed on?" asks Pierced Punk, smearing his dick across Bri's sweaty brow.

"Do it. Pee on me!" His mouth is agape.

Droplets start from my dick and then a strong stream of gold spatters upon his face. Pierced Punk stands a few feet away and begins urinating on Bri, drenching his face in pee.

"More," he begs. My pee comes long and steady. Bri shuts his eyes as I run my dick like a garden hose across his handsome mug. Pierced Punk's dick hisses as pee puddles in Bri's crotch. It runs down his stubbled cheeks. The aroma of urine and ass hovers like a thick fog. Bri wraps his lips around my dick in hopes of controlling its relentless stream.

Piss trickles down Bri's chest. I start to run on empty, and so does Pierced Punk. I dangle the last drops between Bri's glutes. He turns around and settles into the yellow pool we have made.

"Damn! Wish I could taste it," he says. "But I'll settle for eatin' ya'll's instead."

We back our asses into Bri's piss-soaked face. Pierced Punk and I jack our dicks steadily as Bri gives our assholes equal attention. I'm close to coming as this all-star player burrows through me.

"Show me your ass lips," he says.

I try to relax as his tongue circles my core. Bri's face is wet against my ass.

"I'm about to come!" I yell.

"Let's see you shoot it," Pierced Punk says.

Bri rams his finger in my butt. I press a few drops of pink liquid soap into my hand for lubricant. Pierced Punk leans back onto Bri's face as he chokes his chicken. He watches us both to see who comes first.

Syrupy come squirts from me. Pierced Punk swerves over the sink and shoots off into it seconds after, as Bri keeps at his butt. I look in the mirror to catch Pierced Punk's facial expression. Bri falls back against the wall. Pierced Punk steps over his body, which reeks of piss, into his stall, and unrolls a handful of toilet paper from the dispenser. He wipes away what is left of come and throws the balled-up tissue into the stainless steel trash can under the hand dryer.

"You better try to clean yourself off, man," I say to Bri.

"I'm good," he says. "Just make sure ya'll lock the door behind you when you leave." Pierced Punk and I finish getting dressed and grab our things. "Do you know who that is?" I say.

"Who?" Pierced Punk says.

"Brian Miller."

"I don't follow football," he says. We wander off into separate directions of the field. I head off to catch the last forty-five minutes of an anthropology lecture. I sit in the last row hoping I don't smell like piss. I can't concentrate much knowing what I know about Mr. Twenty-seven Home runs and how much money . . . or dick he would be willing to give up to keep his secret.

Summertime

Curtis C. Comer

━━━━━

The hot July sun bore down on Main Street like a pile of heavy blankets, making it difficult to move. The house I shared with my parents and two younger brothers didn't have air conditioning, and I was sitting on the front porch, hoping for the random breeze to blow, when my best friend, Alex, appeared on the steps.

"I'm going to Schwartz's," he announced, slapping my bare foot, which was propped on the arm of the porch swing. "Wanna come?"

"It's too hot," I protested, not stirring.

"Schwartz's is air conditioned," he countered.

"We've still got to *walk* there," I argued.

"Yada, yada, yada," he replied, forcing a smile from me. It was this response, something he had picked up from watching *Seinfeld,* that Alex used to get out of arguments or uncomfortable conversations. It didn't matter if he was talking to a classmate or a teacher. In fact, "yada, yada, yada" had gotten Alex sent to detention more than once. I liked the sassiness of it and how, with one little non-word, Alex was able to say so much.

Alex was my age, but taller, with curly, blond-streaked hair, blue eyes, a broad nose, and skin that was always tan in the summer.

"I gotta ask my mom," I said, getting up slowly.

Alex shrugged and sat down on the swing I'd just vacated and I stepped into our living room, careful not to slam the screen door behind me, an infraction that caused hysterics in my mother. I headed to the kitchen, where I knew she would be.

Though Alex and I had been best friends through most of grade school, Mom didn't particularly care for him. The consensus around our small town was that Alex's family was poor white trash. Though our family was by no means wealthy, there was talk in town that Alex's dad was a drunk and a wife beater. I never pressed Alex for any details, keeping my curiosity to myself. One day when he appeared at school with a black eye my curiosity was answered in typical Alex fashion.

"Yada, yada, yada."

I found my mom seated at the kitchen table smoking a cigarette, a pile of bills in front of her. I could hear my brothers playing in the back yard.

"Can I go to Schwartz's with Alex?" I asked, trying not to sound desperate.

"What for?" she asked, not looking up from the bills in front of her.

"To play pinball," I replied, wishing it were Dad I was asking.

My father, a soft-spoken man who spent his days working at the local power plant, seemed to feel sorry for Alex and hoped that I could set a good example for him.

"Do you have any money?" Mom asked, stubbing out her cigarette in an ashtray.

"I still have money from mowing lawns," I replied, knowing that I was getting her permission.

"Okay," she said, looking up at me. "But don't forget that you've got a game tonight."

I assured her that I wouldn't forget and rushed out of the

house. I had only agreed to play baseball that summer because Alex had convinced me to. Alex was a fanatic about baseball, and as the best pitcher on our team would talk for hours about his dream of making it to the major leagues one day. I, on the other hand, was not the most athletically inclined kid and didn't really care much for baseball. I only played to be with Alex. We played for a team called Don's Dairy Queen, named after our sponsor, and played against other local teams with names like Bob's IGA and Fred's Café.

Our team was a fairly good one and had so far won four out of six games that season. Though I was sometimes ridiculed by teammates for my lack of skill, it was enough for me to just be there with Alex, and to watch him in action on the mound. One afternoon, during a day game, I even got to see Alex in his jockstrap as he changed from his uniform. He caught me staring, and I could feel my face flush as I quickly looked away, hoping he didn't notice my pup tent.

"Yada, yada, yada," was all he said, pulling on a pair of blue cotton gym shorts.

Fortunately, he never brought it up later.

Mom's permission granted, I bolted from the house and slapped Alex's arm as I ran down the steps three at a time.

"Come on!" I called, glancing back over my shoulder. Alex quickly caught up to me and we meandered down hot, deserted Main Street toward Schwartz's.

It wasn't just the stifling heat that caused the death-like stillness in our small town; Plainsville, Kansas, had been dying a slow, protracted death since Route 66 had been closed, its traffic diverted miles south to a new interstate and away from Main Street. What remained was one high school, a Dairy Queen, a bar, Schwartz's Drug Store and Arcade, three churches, and two gas stations, one at either end of town, to catch you coming or going. Even our town's sign, proudly boasting a population of six hundred, was rusted and fading.

When we got to Schwartz's, a large sign on the window stopped us in our tracks, announcing that Schwartz's was closed and out of business. A hastily written addendum informed customers that prescriptions could be filled at the new Wal-Mart out on the interstate.

"Yada, yada, yada," said Alex, his face grim.

I couldn't have said anything more eloquent to sum up our frustration, and kicked a pebble against the brick façade of the building.

"I can't wait to get out of this town," I said, looking up as a pickup passed.

"Want to go down to the river?" he asked, looking around at the deserted street.

"Sure," I replied, shrugging. I knew that my mom would be pissed, since I didn't ask permission, but I didn't care.

The river was a twenty-minute walk from Main Street, and heat seemed to rise from the asphalt as quickly as the sun sent it down. By the time we got to the river, we were sweating and out of breath. Fortunately, there were few people in sight, so we picked a spot in the shade of a small, two-lane bridge that spanned the river and stripped down to our underwear. Somehow, seeing Alex in his wet, white briefs aroused me more that seeing him in his jockstrap, so I waded further out into deeper water, intent on hiding the evidence of my arousal from him.

"Be careful, doofus," he warned. "The current's pretty strong out there in the middle."

I was turning to reply that I was fine when I slipped on a large, flat stone; before I knew it I was being pulled downstream by the current. Not a good swimmer, panic seized me as the current pulled me beneath the water, and my arms flailed helplessly. Suddenly, I could feel Alex's hands grab me and begin pulling me back into the shallow water and onto the embankment under the bridge. I stood up next to him, shivering, and wrapped my arms around him. He put his arms around me in a tight embrace, and we stood there silent for a moment.

"Doofus," he finally said, his breath hot on my face.

"You . . . you saved me," I managed, looking up into his eyes.

"Yada, yada, yada," he said, tenderly, meeting my gaze.

I had the urge to kiss him on the mouth, but a voice from the other side of the river caused us to jump, and we immediately broke our embrace.

"Is your friend okay?" asked a woman, concern on her face.

"Yeah," replied Alex. "Just a little shook up."

Convinced that I wasn't dying, the woman waved and disappeared.

"Alex . . ." I began, frustrated.

"Come on," he said, turning back toward the riverbank where we had left our clothes. "We should get back."

Reluctantly, I followed, careful to watch my footing. We dressed in silence, pulling our shorts on over our wet briefs, and neither of us said much during the walk home.

In front of my house, it was Alex who broke the silence.

"Do you think your dad will give me a ride to the game?" he asked, looking down at the sidewalk.

"Sure," I replied, still not wanting him to go.

"Cool," he said, turning.

"Alex . . ." I said, unsure of what I wanted to say.

"What?" he asked, turning his blue eyes on me.

"You're . . . you're my best friend," I blurted, instantly feeling stupid.

"Shut up," he said, but I could see by his smile that he appreciated the compliment.

I ran into the house and upstairs, quickly stripping off my wet underwear, not wanting Mom to know that I'd been to the river without permission. I quickly changed into my baseball uniform and combed my hair, which had dried into a tangled mess. There was a short knock at my bedroom door, and Mom appeared, attired in the nurse's uniform she wore at her job at the local nursing home.

"I thought I heard you come in," she said, eyeing me suspiciously. "How was pinball?"

"Schwartz's is out of business," I replied, still combing my hair. "So we just walked around."

Mom just stood there looking at me, her hands on her hips, but if she suspected that I was lying she chose not to pursue the matter.

"Dinner's almost ready," she said. "I've got to work the night shift and your father will be home soon."

"I'll be right down," I said, relieved that she hadn't pressed for details.

As I descended the stairs, I could hear my dad coming in the front door and quickly intercepted him to tell him that Alex needed a ride to the game.

"Billy, your father just got home from work," said my mom, who had appeared in the door, wiping her hands on a dishtowel. "Let him rest a minute."

"Sure, we can pick up Alex," he replied, tousling my hair. "But, first I gotta shower and eat."

Twenty minutes later, seated around our dining room table for a meatloaf meal, Dad and Mom discussed the closing of Schwartz's and how it would hurt our town; my little brother, Mitchell, complained that the weather was too hot for him to eat.

"It *is* hot," my mom agreed. "Maybe we could go to that new Wal-Mart and look at air conditioners."

"Those things aren't cheap," my dad replied.

"You work for the power plant, for god's sake," said Mom.

"Yeah, I *work* there," laughed Dad, nudging me and winking. "I don't *own* the damn place."

"I just think we should look," said Mom.

"I'll *think* about it," replied Dad, using the tone that meant case closed.

After dinner, we all piled into the blue Suburban that Dad drove in place of his truck when it was a family outing. Alex was waiting at the end of his driveway when we pulled up. He opened the door nearest to me and I scooted over to accommodate him, displacing one of my brothers, who crawled over the seat to sit between my parents, all the while protesting loudly.

"Hey Alex," said my dad, looking in the rearview mirror.

"Hi, Mr. and Mrs. Hayes," replied Alex.

"Put on your seatbelt, Alex," instructed Mom, looking over her shoulder.

As he dutifully complied with her request, I couldn't help but smile. While I knew that she didn't exactly approve of Alex, this little act of kindness, however small, gave me hope that she might be warming up to him. Maybe she was beginning to realize that Alex was merely a kid stuck in a bad situation. Whatever the case, I felt happy as we sped to the baseball field.

Dad pulled onto the gravel lot beside the field and parked among the assorted vehicles.

"You guys have a good game," he said as we piled out of the car. "We'll be rooting for you."

"Be careful," said Mom, kissing my cheek. She turned and ran her hand through Alex's messy hair. "You need a haircut, young man," she said, only half-seriously.

As we strode to the dugout I was grateful that, even though it was still hot, the sun was beginning to move toward the horizon. Unfortunately, Coach Weaver looked pissed and was flipping frantically through papers on his clipboard. A corpulent, balding man with only a swatch of blond hair covering his sunburned scalp, Coach Weaver was fond of telling everyone who would listen the story of how he almost made it to the major leagues until a knee surgery put him out of commission. For us, his players, this meant that he would push us hard, almost as if a punishment for his unfortunate turn of fate. As we neared the dugout, it was evident what was causing the coach's foul mood: Jeff, a tall blond kid who played shortstop for our team, had a plaster cast on his right arm. He smiled up at us weakly as we entered the dugout.

"Jesus, what happened to *you?*" asked Alex, laughing.

"I fell out of a tree," replied Jeff, a smirk on his face.

"Christ," snapped the coach, turning on Jeff. "You think this is *funny?*"

Jeff fell silent and hung his head, staring at his cleats.

Knowing all too well that the coach would never place me at shortstop, I looked around at my assembled teammates. Coach Weaver would never take Alex from the pitcher's mound, and Brian, our catcher, had been placed in his position merely because of his large size.

"Listen up," barked the coach, reading from his clipboard. "Miller, you'll take shortstop. Jackson, you move to centerfield, and Hayes," he said, pointing at me, "you'll be in left field."

"Ah, *man,*" I heard Kyle say under his breath.

I knew what he and most of the team were thinking: Billy can't bat. He's going to lose the game for us. While his attitude pissed me off, I understood. Usually, I was content to be the bench warmer—there was no pressure to perform, and yet I was still part of the team. "You'll do okay," said Alex, nudging me.

Our team took the field and Alex effortlessly struck out the first two batters. Fortunately, no hits made it to left field before the third out was bagged at first base.

Our team hustled back to the dugout for our turn at bat. Kyle, the best hitter on our team, was up first and slammed one out of the park, bouncing it off the hood of a red pickup parked behind centerfield. Jimmy was up next, and after a ball and a strike sent the ball deep into centerfield, making it to first base safely. Mark popped one over the pitcher's head, but it was retrieved by the second baseman, who tagged Jimmy then beat Mark to first. Alex got a hit and made it to second base, but Brian struck out, ending the first inning with a score of 1–0.

At the top of the second, the other team managed to score two points before it was, once again, our turn at bat. Ronnie was up first and managed to get to first base. Les hit one deep into left field, allowing Ronnie to make it to third base and him to second. Pete was walked, and the bases were loaded.

"You're up, Hayes!" barked Coach Weaver.

I swallowed hard and made my way up to the plate, gripping the bat nervously.

"You can do it, Billy!" I heard Dad yell from the bleachers.

Unnerved by the chatter from the other team and not wanting to let down my own team, I swung recklessly at the first pitch.

"Strike!" announced the umpire.

"Watch the ball, Hayes!" Coach Weaver yelled from the dugout.

The next two pitches were way outside and I had the good sense, despite being horribly nervous, not to swing. I held my breath as the pitcher wound up for his next throw. It was as if everything was moving in slow motion, but somehow I swung my bat and connected with the ball, sending it deep into centerfield.

"Run!" I heard the coach yell.

I dropped the bat and ran as fast as I could. Ronnie and Les made it to home, Pete was on second, and I was at first. Kyle stepped up to the plate and sent the ball flying out of the park once again, allowing three more runs. Back in the dugout, I was ecstatic, and Alex playfully slugged my arm to show his approval. I wish I could say that the rest of the game was like that but, unfortunately, that was my best performance at bat that night, getting struck out and walked two times each. Nonetheless, we won, and after dropping Mom off at the nursing home, Dad offered to take me, my brothers, and Alex to Dairy Queen for ice cream.

Afterward, as we pulled up in front of Alex's house, I could see him tense up.

"Is your dad home?" I asked.

He nodded and wordlessly got out of the car.

An hour later, my dad passed out on the sofa and my brothers asleep in the bedroom they shared, I was lying on my bed trying to read, wearing only briefs because of the heat. Even the open window offered no comfort, as no breeze was stirring. Suddenly, the sound of something hitting my screen caused me to go to the window. Peering out into the stillness of the night, I could hear a dog barking nearby, and the sound of a distant train, but saw no one. I was about to return to my bed, when I saw Alex standing forlornly on the lawn. I waved and motioned him to the back of the house, quietly making my way down the stairs, glad that Dad had left the television blaring. I sneaked through the kitchen and opened the back door where Alex, bruised and bloody, was waiting. His bottom lip was cracked and swollen, and it was clear that he would probably have a black eye by the next day. I didn't say anything; I knew what had happened.

"Yada, yada, yada," he said, weakly, as if reading my mind.

I quietly led him up the stairs and to my room, closing the door behind me. I could see marks on his arm where his father had hit him with something, and without saying a word, pulled off his T-shirt as he lifted his arms. Deep welts crisscrossed his back, and I led him to the edge of my bed, where I pulled off his gym shorts and told him to lie down. Reaching into my bedside table, I pulled out a bottle of baby oil and told him to roll over. Squirting some of the oil in my hands, I slowly began to massage his injured back, and could feel him wince now and then. Responding to my gentle nudge, Alex rolled over onto his back, and I began massaging his smooth, tanned chest. I could see that he had an erection and swallowed hard, my heart pounding. Gently, I reached down, pulled off his briefs, and massaged his erection, my hands slick with the oil.

"Take yours off," he whispered.

I obliged, exposing my own erection, and climbed onto the bed, where Alex climbed on top of me and began rubbing his oily body on mine. I kissed his cracked lips, and moaned as he squirted more baby oil into his hand and smeared it on my erection. The combination of the slick oil and Alex's weight on top of me was too much, and I came quickly. Not yet finished himself, Alex knelt at the headboard and allowed me to take his stiffness into my mouth. When he came, he moaned softly and I swallowed the gooey load. We soon fell fast asleep, holding each other.

I awakened a little later to the sound of Alex dressing.

"Gotta go," he said, whispering.

"Stay here," I replied. "Don't go back there." Alex shook his head and playfully slugged me.

"I'll see you later," he said, closing my bedroom door behind him.

The next morning, my mom woke me up, her face serious.

"What's wrong?" I asked, afraid that she knew what had happened.

"This note was on the door when I got home from work this morning," she said, handing me a piece of paper.

I took the folded paper, afraid of what its contents might have betrayed to my parents. Looking at Mom, however, I sensed sadness, not anger, and I unfolded the paper.

It was a note from Alex, in his untidy handwriting, explaining that his mother had decided to leave her husband, and take Alex to live in California with her parents. Alex had only grudgingly gotten her to consent to stop by so he could leave the note; she was in such a hurry to get out of town. He assured me that he would call when he could and signed his name. I fell into Mom's arms and sobbed, and she held me until I was done.

The remainder of the season was crap without Alex as pitcher. I only stayed on as a favor to my dad, who assured me that it was the right thing to do for the team. It was my last season to play baseball, and the call from Alex never came. Eventually, he faded from all but the most guarded of my memories, though I never completely forgot him.

It wasn't until many years later that I heard Alex's name on television; it seemed that he had finally made it to a major league team like he always dreamed. Though in a relationship, I was curious to reconnect, and wrote him a letter. He responded immediately, and it was as if that summer so many years ago had only been yesterday.

Though time and experiences have placed us on different paths, there are always tickets waiting for me at the box office when I visit California, and he still knows how to get me with one little non-word.

Home Run at Madgecull Park

Lew Bull

The sun's intense rays beat down on me as I sat alone in the empty stands at Madgecull Park Stadium. I had sneaked into the grounds to watch the Rangers baseball team practice prior to their first game of the season. I had never been a fan of theirs until I saw a couple of photos of some of the players in our local newspaper; then my whole attitude toward the team changed.

I had always been a sports fan, and no more so than if the sportsmen were encased in either a tight outfit which revealed their muscular definitions or in some flattering uniform. I enjoyed watching those muscular football players skidding and sliding around the field in their skin-tight pants, but it was only when I saw the photo of a couple of Rangers baseball players in tight-fitting pants that my interest in baseball superseded that of football. Although the newspaper article and photos covered four new team members, it was two of them whose appearance attracted my attention. Joe Banducci and Kyle Kaplinski were the two men who smiled back at me as I gazed down at their photos. I read all about them and made it my business to get to know them better, if that was at all possible. But who was I? A mere mortal like so many others who had an interest in baseball and made an effort to attend as many of the Rangers' games this coming season as possible.

As the perspiration trickled down my face in the blazing heat, I watched as the Rangers team sat on the baseball diamond below, being spoken to by a man whom I assumed to be the coach or his assistant. My eyes swept over the men until they focused on both Joe and Kyle, who were not sitting together. Both men appeared relaxed and tanned. I watched their every movement and even noticed on one occasion how Joe appeared to be scratching his balls. I watched and wondered whether his balls were like a baseball, firm and large, and whether they were snugly encased in a tight jockstrap under his equally tight-fitting off-white baseball pants. I felt a twinge within my groin and immediately switched my attention to Kyle. Both men were young and extremely good-looking, with Joe appearing Hispanic and more tanned than Kyle and perhaps a little more muscular as well, but whatever, both appealed to me.

After some time of me sweating and them listening to their coach, they rose from their sitting positions and readied themselves for a practice game. I noticed that Joe and Kyle had been placed in opposing teams and Kyle positioned himself as the fielding team's pitcher. Immediately a smile crossed my face as I wondered whether Kyle was in fact a "pitcher," in a sexual sense.

The first batsman positioned and readied himself to face the first ball from Kyle. He took a few practice swings while Kyle's body tensed, ready to pitch the first ball. The ball sailed through the air with speed, a *clunk* was heard as connection between ball and bat was made, and I watched as it flew toward the outer field. I saw the disgruntled look on Kyle's face as the batter managed to make his way as far as second base.

The process of fielding and batting changed at regular intervals and I even watched as Joe hit a magnificent home run off one of Kyle's disappointing pitches. I could hear Kyle muttering to himself as the ball sailed majestically into the grandstand and Joe's team cheered.

After what seemed like half an hour, the teams took a break and I heard Kyle say, "Hey guys, I need a break—I need to take a piss." As he started walking away from the rest of the group on the diamond, the tanned Joe ran after him shouting, "Hey Kyle, wait for me, I need one too." The two of them headed toward the nearby tunnel that led to the change rooms and I rose from my seat as I watched them disappear. The rest of the players who were left on the field all headed for the dugout to cool off, while I rushed from the grandstand and headed toward the same change rooms that Joe and Kyle were headed for.

When I eventually entered the change rooms, it was very quiet, with only a musty smell abounding. On entering, there was a large open room with wooden benches around the walls and a set of lockers in the middle. A few catchers' mitts were lying around on the benches and I picked one up, slid my hand into its cold interior, and thought of Joe and Kyle. I could feel myself being aroused as my hand began to feel warm and comfortable inside the mitt. I then took it off and replaced it on the bench. I walked quietly around the lockers but there was no one in the room. Off this room was a door that led down a passage to the showers and toilets. I went quietly through the doorway, past the showers, and into the toilet area. Before I entered, I paused at the entrance because at the urinal stood Kyle and the tanned Joe. Both had their cocks in their hands and I could see that they were stroking themselves.

I heard Kyle say, "I need that cock down my throat, Joe."

I could feel my own cock getting harder and thicker as I watched them. Unconsciously, my hand went down to my running shorts and I started rubbing myself. Joe turned to face Kyle and for the first time I saw his gigantic weapon pointing straight toward Kyle. As I saw his huge, uncut dick, resembling a long baseball bat, thicker at the end than at the handle, I shivered with excitement. Kyle knelt in front of Joe at the urinal, pulled his tight pants right down to his knees, and began to lick the folds of Joe's foreskin.

As Kyle's tongue entered the folds and licked over the piss slit, Joe gave a low moan. His dark eyes were on Kyle, who was about to take this meat down his throat. Kyle licked the underneath of the stem and carried on down, wetting Joe's cock until he reached his balls. Slowly, he took one ball into his warm mouth and gently rolled his tongue around it. Then he moved on to the other one; all the time Joe was groaning in satisfaction. Kyle released that ball and then began to work his way up Joe's shaft with his tongue, licking and kissing. Although Kyle was facing the entrance to the toilet area, his eyes were closed as he enjoyed this meal and didn't see me enter through the doorway. As I did so, his mouth engulfed Joe's dick and he began to swallow it whole, forcing the foreskin to roll back to reveal Joe's cock head. I watched as he went slowly down the shaft and then paused—*obviously trying to relax the back of his throat,* I thought—and once he had done that, he continued on down.

Joe said "Oh fuck!" in a loud groan and began to thrust his pelvis toward Kyle's face. As he did so, Kyle took his right hand from Joe's butt and started frantically stroking his own cock while I did likewise inside my shorts. Neither of these two hot men had seen or heard me yet, but I felt I had to make my presence known because I wanted to be part of this action.

I went quietly up behind Joe, whose head was thrown back in ecstasy, and put my arms around his chest, feeling two hard nipples protruding through his shirt. He turned his head in fright and I clamped onto his nipples with my thumb and forefingers. This obviously set him off because he started groaning louder and pumping harder into Kyle's loving mouth. At that moment, Kyle opened his eyes and saw me, but it didn't stop him from continuing to take those ten inches into the depths of his throat. While I pinched Joe's nipples, my cock was rubbing against the crack of his ass, trying to get out of my running shorts.

Joe suddenly pulled his cock out of Kyle's mouth and said, "Cool it guys, before I blow my load."

With his hands on either side of Kyle's head, he gently lifted him to his feet and began to kiss him, letting their tongues explore each other's mouth. For a moment I thought they regarded me as an intruder, but as Kyle freed his mouth from Joe's, he said, "Come with me. There's a room off the shower room," and proceeded to lead the way.

I watched their tight asses strut before me as Kyle led us into a small room, which had a table in the middle of it and a shelf on which some towels were piled. As I was the last into the room, I closed the door behind me and watched as Kyle, with his back to me, pulled his pants down to his feet and then bent over to undo his shoes. As he did so, the cheeks of his ass parted and I saw this delicious pink manhole. Joe also saw it and gently rubbed a finger over and around it. Kyle stayed bent over as Joe did this and quietly moaned with satisfaction. Was I about to see my "pitcher" become a "catcher"?

I pushed my running shorts down over my hips, down to my feet, and stepped out of them. My cock was like a periscope looking for something to attack. I walked around to Kyle's head and stood in front of him, my cock inches away from his face. How I wanted that hot, young mouth around it, especially after I'd seen the way he had handled Joe. He opened his mouth and I felt his warm breath on my cock followed by the warmth of his mouth and tongue. This sent shivers through my body as he worked on my dick.

In the meantime, Joe had gotten rid of his baseball pants and had his tongue up Kyle's asshole. Every time Joe's tongue pushed into that pink opening, Kyle's sensations of pleasure were carried through his body to my dick. Joe then stood up, lubricated a finger in his mouth, and slowly inserted his finger into Kyle's hole. Kyle was writhing in pleasure and was working even harder on my dick. When two fingers were inserted, Kyle started pounding his own dick and mine slipped out of his mouth. I looked at it and admired how swollen the head was. Kyle saw the precome oozing from my cock and gently licked it off with his tongue, then proceeded to swallow my erection once again.

Joe slowly withdrew his fingers, pulled a condom from a pocket in his pants, slid it down his thick, long rod, and aimed it at Kyle's pink target. Kyle felt this huge cock pressing at his entrance, stopped stroking his own cock, and slowly pushed back onto Joe's pile driver. Initially there was some resistance, but as Kyle relaxed, he slid onto the massive pole with an "Aaagh!"

Joe's face was a picture of total pleasure, having reached first base by having his ten inches rammed into Kyle's beautifully tight ass. They remained motionless for a while, allowing Kyle to get used to the size of Joe's cock. Then Joe started slowly to withdraw the shaft until the head was about to pop out, and then slowly drive it all the way back in again. Every time he did this, Kyle gasped with pleasure and sucked my dick. Watching Joe's huge pole drive into Kyle's tight ass and feeling Kyle's hungry mouth working on my cock was beginning to get me worked up. Joe's chest was heaving and I slid my hands under his shirt, running them over his chest and pinching his nipples. He let out a loud groan and started pumping Kyle harder, and as he pounded Kyle's ass, Kyle's mouth moved faster and harder on my cock. I wasn't going to be able to last much longer. I suddenly felt a dizzy excitement.

"I'm coming," I gasped and my balls exploded, shooting my heavy load down Kyle's throat. I groaned with delight and fucked Kyle's face as Joe fucked his ass. He was breathing heavily as he sucked me dry and then I heard a muffled sound of ecstasy from Kyle as he shot his load onto the floor. He hadn't, in fact, touched his cock while Joe was ramming him because he was holding onto my hips. As Kyle shot his load, his ass muscles clenched tightly around Joe's cock causing Joe to gasp and speed up his fucking. With his cock tightly imbedded in Kyle's ass and me pinching his nipples, Joe cried out and sent his load flying into Kyle. "Oh shit! Ohhh Fuck!"

He pumped hard, slapping his heavy balls against Kyle's ass as he sent one load after another into Kyle.

Eventually his eruption subsided and he lay across Kyle's back, kissing his neck while I kissed Joe. As Kyle straightened himself up, all three of our faces were close to one another's and we just laughed.

"I hope you didn't mind me joining in with you two guys," I said.

"Mind!" exclaimed the two of them in unison. "Next time you're in the middle," said Joe.

As Joe's limp cock slid from Kyle's ass and he removed the condom, I noticed his cock still continued to throb and I thought to myself, *I can't wait. I need that cock now. I want Joe Banducci inside me.* I moved to Joe and grabbed his cock, squeezed it hard around its fatness and looked lustfully into his eyes. It throbbed in my hand and I could feel it beginning to grow again. I went down on him and wrapped my lips around his pulsing shaft. As I licked it I could taste the salty-sweet come that was left on his cock and as I sucked on his cock head I drained what was still in his shaft. While I was busy licking his shaft, Kyle came face-to-face with me on the other side of Joe's cock and also started licking up and down. Our tongues touched and as my tongue ventured into his mouth, I could taste the leftover come that I had earlier shot into his mouth and throat. Kyle's mouth then went to Joe's balls, and he burrowed his nose in Joe's crotch as he gently licked and rolled his balls around his mouth. I busied myself trying to take Joe's long pole deep into my mouth. I had never before taken anything as big as this down my throat, but I was determined not to let an opportunity like this go to waste. At one stage, I thought I had a baseball bat down my throat and would gag, but I relaxed and slowly let it slide in. I've never felt such an exhilarating feeling before as Joe slowly started thrusting his pelvis forward and backward. While he fucked my face, I thought of how Kyle had taken Joe's cock down his throat and I convinced myself that they had done this before. While I was thinking of this, Kyle's face reappeared next to Joe's cock and as Joe's shaft withdrew from my mouth, so Kyle's lips and tongue wrapped around the side of it. And as Joe drove his shaft into my mouth, so Kyle's mouth met mine.

I felt Kyle's hand wrap around my stiff cock and start stroking it. I reciprocated while we both knelt on either side of Joe's cock as though we were worshipping this ten-inch idol. Throughout the whole time Joe had been groaning in blissful satisfaction, until he eventually pulled away from us. He looked down at me with a wry smile on his beautiful face, and holding his stiff shaft, he said, "Do you want this?" My lips were wet and saliva dribbled from my mouth.

"You bet," I said. "You can hit a home run with me anytime."

Kyle got to his feet and walked to the towels. He grabbed a few and threw them on the table in the center of the room. He came back, took me by the hand, and gently eased me onto the table so my legs were hanging over the edge. He then walked around the table behind me, and putting his large hands onto my shoulders pulled me back into a lying position. I lay there looking up, face-to-face with his cock, which dangled seductively over my nose and mouth. All this time, Joe had silently watched, and when I was on my back with my legs over the edge of the table, he moved between my thighs and lowered his mouth to lick and salivate around my balls.

A warm feeling tingled inside me as Joe's warm tongue moved over my dick until his mouth engulfed it. It felt so warm and fulfilled inside his glorious mouth and I closed my eyes, a feeling of ecstasy running through my body. As I did so, I felt Kyle's cock gently touch my lips. I automatically opened my mouth and proceeded to swallow his engorged pole. Kyle's hands massaged my nipples and moved down over my taut stomach. I felt my legs being lifted as Joe's tongue moved between them toward my butt hole, and felt the tip of his tongue darting in and out. I could feel myself shuddering with pleasure as I was worked over at both ends of my body.

I moved my head away from Kyle's dick and told Joe that there were some condoms in the back pocket of my running shorts. While he crossed to where my shorts lay, Kyle stretched across my body and took my throbbing cock in his mouth as I took his again. While we were in a sixty-nine position, I felt two wet fingers being inserted into my butt hole one at a time. Just then I felt my legs being lifted into the air and Kyle released his grip on my cock and raised himself from my body. I looked up and saw Joe standing between my legs. He moved in closer and I felt his huge cock rub against me. He then gently lowered my legs onto each of his shoulders, freeing his hands to guide his hard baseball bat cock into my waiting hole. As he prepared to enter me, Kyle's hands rubbed over my hardening nipples, which felt great. I relaxed and prepared for Joe's entry.

Slowly he began to push his barge pole into me. There was an initial sharp pain as he entered me and I grimaced. He stopped where he was to allow me to get used to his huge size. Once he felt me relax, he continued his journey. Oh, it felt so good. I had never taken anyone so big before, and to feel his cock tightly squeezed into me sent dizzying spells through my head and body, and I knew that Joe had hit my base. Joe began to get his rhythm going, but all the time he was careful not to hurt me. At last I got used to his enormous size inside me, and began to meet each of his thrusts as his thick cock rubbed against my prostate. This turned both of us on and he started pumping faster and deeper.

While Joe had been entering me, Kyle stood and watched in awe while he rubbed my nipples between his thumbs and forefingers. I lay there on my back playing with my cock and balls, feeling ecstatic while Joe's cock pounded away at me.

Suddenly, Kyle left us and walked over to where my shorts lay. "I hope you don't mind!" he said, taking a condom from the back pocket. Of course I didn't mind, but I wasn't quite sure what his plan was. He opened the packet and rolled the condom onto his erect cock. Once he had done this, he walked back to us and stood behind Joe. I suddenly realized what was going to happen—he was going to be Joe's pitcher while Joe was fucking me. The thought sent a spasm of excitement through my body. My two favorite baseball players playing pitcher to each other.

Joe paused briefly to allow Kyle to enter him. As he pushed onto Kyle's cock, I thought he was going to slip out of me so I tensed my muscles and gripped his huge dick with my ass. When Kyle started fucking Joe, it felt as if Joe's cock was going even deeper into me. Kyle put his arms around Joe and held onto my legs that were still over Joe's shoulders. When he did this, it felt as if he was pulling me farther onto Joe's dick. Every time Joe pummeled my ass, I could feel Kyle beating Joe's ass. My hand feverishly worked on my own dick and I could feel myself getting closer to exploding.

"I'm not going to be able to hold on much longer," I groaned.

As I said that, Joe quickened his pace and the result was that his movement was getting Kyle equally closer to shooting his load. I gasped and started shooting my hot come all over my stomach. My ass muscles clamped tightly on Joe's cock and I pushed myself onto his solid dick until the only thing that wasn't inside me was his balls. He rubbed my come over my stomach with his hands and pumped his cock into me at the same time. He was breathing heavily and I knew he was going to come.

"Aaargh!" he shouted as he pounded my ass. "Oh yes! Oh yes!"

I could feel his dick throbbing inside me as his warm come filled up the condom. As he came, he started a chain reaction and Kyle pumped his hot come into Joe, grunting as he did so. Both my baseball stars were hitting home runs at the same time.

Once our bodies began to relax, Kyle kissed the back of Joe's neck and slowly withdrew his cock. Joe began to pull out of me but I didn't want this to end. I held onto him for a moment hoping that he wouldn't remove his beautiful big dick. As he withdrew, my whole body relaxed and I closed my eyes. This had been fantastic; me being with the two best-looking players from the Rangers. I felt someone kiss my limp, spent cock. I opened my eyes and saw it was Joe. He looked at me and said, "I like this, you little fucker."

Kyle came around and kissed me on the lips. "Come, let's get out of here," he said.

We made our way past the showers and out of the change rooms. As we headed down the tunnel toward the daylight, with Kyle and Joe walking on either side of me, Joe said, "By the way, do you play baseball?"

"No, but I've always been a fan of yours," I replied, smiling like a contented cat that's just drunk a saucer of milk and knowing that what I had said wasn't entirely true. After all, it was only thanks to the newspaper photos that I had gotten to see Joe and Kyle in the first place.

"Well," said Kyle with a glint in his eye, "we practice here every day, so if you'd like to come and watch and maybe play with us, just pitch up."

"Oh, I'll pitch up, even if it's not to play baseball," I said, laughing.

As we neared the exit to the tunnel, Joe gave my ass a gentle slap followed by a squeeze and said, "Keep this in shape because both Kyle and I need to practice quite often, and it's only the start of the season."

I smiled at the advice, and watched as my two newfound friends went out into the sunlight at Madgecull Park to mingle with their teammates and continue the real matter at hand—playing baseball.

Locker Room Heat

John Simpson

———

It had been a very hot summer at spring training as the team got ready for the regular season, and hitting the showers after a day of playing hard in the sun never felt so good.

As usual the guys were fooling around with one another, flicking towels at a bare ass that just happened to be a viable target and so on. It was the usual stuff that happens in locker rooms all across the nation. Jocks especially like to roughhouse in the locker room, and I participated many times in tackling that perfect jockstrap-framed ass with the tip of my towel, resulting in a howl of pain from one of my hot teammates.

Where it got really hot was in the showers, watching these athletes soap up their hard nude bodies. I was careful to take only quick looks at the other guys. One of the most gorgeous members of the team was Scott Rippenale. He was our main pitcher, standing six feet four and weighing a solid one ninety-five. That, combined with the coal black hair and piercing blue eyes, a six-pack, and a marble-like ass with a nice-sized cock, made me weak in the knees every time I saw him naked.

Scott had caught me looking at him in the showers a couple of times and I was worried my secret would be found out. I tried extra hard today not to look at him, but gave in to my baser instincts and took one look as I turned away from the shower wall. There I found Scott staring right back, and he actually smiled. His dick seemed to be a bit longer than usual, and I wondered if he was slightly horny today. I smiled back and quickly turned back to the wall of the shower. A moment later I left the shower room and grabbed my towel, far more nervous than usual.

Scott's locker was directly behind mine, so unless I turned around I could not see what he was doing. As I was drying off, I felt a tap on my shoulder and looked to see Scott standing there.

"Hey Scott, what's up?"

"I think I may have pulled a shoulder muscle on the mound today, and I was wondering if you would mind staying behind and help me work on getting it right? I figured maybe a massage and the whirlpool would do the trick. What do ya say?"

How could I say no with this man of beauty standing naked in front of me, gently toweling off his hair?

"Of course, Scott, be happy too," I said with a smile.

I suddenly became aware that I too was naked, and found that my cock was reacting to the thought of massaging Scott. I quickly turned around to put my shorts on.

"Don't bother putting any more clothes on, Jerry, you'll probably get wet helping me in and out of the whirlpool," Scott said, smiling.

Out of a roster of forty men, there were no rumors about anyone being gay, including myself. I just could not even begin to believe this was anything more than it seemed. The locker room emptied out, leaving just Scott and me alone in the room that smelled like used, wet jocks.

"Come on Jerry, let's get started. I only have an hour or so," I heard come over the lockers from the sports injury area of the locker room. As I rounded the last row of lockers, I found a sight that almost stopped my heart. There, lying on the massage table without so much as a towel covering his beautiful ass that I had lusted after for so long, was Scott.

"I hope you don't mind my laying here naked; it's that I'm still hot from playing today and this feels cooling."

"Nah, I don't mind at all, Scott, just relax."

"Somehow I didn't think you'd mind."

As I pondered the meaning of that statement, I began the shoulder massage that Scott had requested. As I dug deep into his muscle groups, I continued to stare at that gorgeous ass. Some guys just get all the luck in that department.

"That feels terrific, Jerry, I really needed this. If you don't mind, go ahead and work my back and butt muscles if you can. I seem to be tight all over."

I could hardly believe my ears. I was going to get to work on his ass. As my hands worked their way down toward the two mounds of flesh-covered muscle, I grew a tent in my shorts. By the time I was working his ass I was fully hard. Scott turned and looked back at me and directly at my shorts. He smiled and said, "I thought you were queer, Jerry. I caught you looking at my ass and dick one too many times in the showers for you to be straight. All guys look, but usually once is enough. But don't worry, I'm not gonna tell the team. You're safe."

I didn't know what to do as I stopped the massage and backed away from the table. I began to panic and felt like running away. But just as I thought I would pass out, Scott turned over on the table and smiled as I looked down at his dick, which was just as hard as mine before it had gone limp from fear.

"I always wondered what it would be like to have a guy suck on my cock. How about getting down there and giving me some good head, Jerry?"

"Scott, are you serious? You've never had a guy blow you

and now all of a sudden you want head from me? What about your wife?"

"Yes Jerry, I have wanted to get head from a guy, but it's not like I can just go out to a bar, now can I? Everyone who watches baseball knows who I am, which is why a teammate is perfect. Now are you gay, and are you going to blow me?"

I was once again rock-hard and stood up from the bench, dropping my shorts, letting my own cock have some freedom. I walked back over to the table, grabbed Scott's hard cock, and jacked him a little bit. I played with his balls as I stroked my own cock. I studied the length and girth of Scott's cock, and admired the way the veins stuck out when he was this hard.

"You've got a beautiful cock, Scott, just incredible."

"Thanks buddy, but I really wish you would give the head of my dick the attention it deserves with that tongue of yours."

I couldn't resist any longer and dove down onto Scott's prick, taking his whole joint all the way down my throat. Scott moaned out loud, so loud I feared someone might hear us. I gave more than just the head of his cock attention. His cock tasted fucking great and I became determined to give him the best head he had ever had. As I moved up and down on his cock, sucking every inch of his meat, I jacked my own cock with my one hand. I could not believe that I was giving head to the best-looking teammate I had, one who was famous in every corner of the world.

"My balls, my balls, suck 'em good for me."

As requested, I released his swollen cock from my mouth and began to lick and suck gently on his two large nuts. This drove him as wild as the cock sucking. I alternated between licking his balls and the shaft of his cock until I decided to give him a treat I was fairly certain he had never had before.

I let go of his balls and lifted his legs up and back, exposing his asshole. Before Scott could protest I drove my tongue
deep into his ass, which made him groan and move his entire
body almost off the table.

"Damn! Man, that feels fucking fantastic dude, eat my
ass!"

"No problem, just relax and enjoy," I said.

I spent the next five minutes or so listening to him moan
as I munched away on his fine ass, tickling his asshole with
the tip of my tongue. I kissed and licked each mound of flesh
surrounding his hole until he begged me to stop or he would
come.

"Man, that is one of the best things I have experienced
sexually, dude. Do you do that to all the guys you date?"

"No, only to guys with fine asses, like you. I have been in
love with your ass since I joined the team. This is a dream
come true for me."

"Well, I need to cool off a bit, so let's get into the whirlpool tub," Scott said. "And bring that lotion so you can continue to massage my shoulder while I'm in the tub."

I grabbed the bottle of hand lotion that the coach kept
around for dry skin and followed Scott's naked body over to
the tub, which was already on and bubbling away. I watched
with lust as Scott climbed into the six-man tub and motioned
me in with him. Since I was already naked, I put the lotion
on the shelf next to the tub and climbed in.

I moved over toward Scott and reached down into the
water to check his cock out. It had indeed gone flaccid.

"In a minute you can do something about the condition
of my dick. I want to fuck you Jerry, right up your smooth
ass. You cool with that?"

"Yeah, I'm good with that. I'm the first guy you've
fucked, too?"

"Yep, I figure might as well go all the way after you just ate my ass out like a pro."

Scott stood up, turned around, reached over to the shelf where he had a small travel case, and opened it up. He found a rubber and took it out. He grabbed the lotion and turned back to me.

"Now since you are my first guy fuck, do you take it like a woman or what?"

"No Scott, you got to use plenty of lotion and ease your cock up my ass. I'll let you know if you need to go slower and then I will tell you when you can fuck away. It's not like you got a little dick."

"Okay, let's do it. How about standing up and leaning over the railing there. That should expose your ass good and be at the right level to take my cock."

I did as he said and bent over the railing, which was warm since it led down into the water. I felt a finger roughly greasing up my hole, using a lot of lotion as I had instructed. I heard him rip open the rubber packet and turned my head to watch him unroll the entire rubber onto his cock. He then lubed up the rubber and moved in for my ass. As I felt the pressure on my asshole from the head of his dick, I urged him to go easy at first. Scott did as I asked and I felt the head slip into my ass, with about two inches following.

"Now give it a couple seconds to adjust and then insert the rest slowly."

Scott paused, then finally I felt the entire penis of this gorgeous man buried in my ass. We both moaned in unison.

"Okay, I'm fine, fuck at your own pace," I said.

With that okay, Scott began to fuck me soundly. I might have been his first male ass, but I was for sure not his first fuck. He varied speed and length of insertion, adjusting my ass position to suit his needs.

"Damn this feels fucking great, dude! You're so tight, like my wife's ass only better."

Just as he found his speed and force and I was beginning to fade into that place where I go mentally when I'm being fucked well, I looked up and saw another of our teammates watching us. I stood up in horror just as Scott saw Randy also.

"Hey Randy, this isn't what it looks like," Scott said.

"Well, unless you're taking his rectal temperature with your cock, it looks like you're fucking the shit out of his tight little ass, and I've been watching for five minutes at least!"

"Look Randy, it will cause major shit if you tell anybody, please think about it," I said.

"Tell anybody, hell I want to join in. I want your lips wrapped around my cock as good ole Scott there pounds your ass, boy. Okay or not?"

I turned around to look at Scott, and he said, "Sure. Why not." Randy came over, stripped, and walked up a step so that his cock was at my face level when I was bent over.

"Go ahead, Jerry, blow Randy so I can watch a little and get hard again and get back to pounding your sweet ass."

I did as I was told; I bent over and watched as Randy brought up his cock as I opened my mouth. Randy shoved his cock in and I began to suck him. It didn't take long before Scott was rigid once again, and pushed his cock back into my ass with only long stroke. I now had an average-sized cock fucking my mouth and a big fat one fucking my ass. I had to admit this was beyond anything I had ever dreamed was possible. Two baseball players, teammates of mine, were giving me a double-ended fuck that had my cock standing straight up. I was afraid to touch it, as I knew it would take very little to make me come.

"Let's take the action out of the tub and onto a locker room bench," said Randy.

Scott had no objection so the three of us, naked, walked through the locker room with roaring erections. Scott told me to lie down on the bench that was right in front of his locker, which I did. Everyone got positioned and the fucking and sucking resumed, this time without hot water and steam. As Scott rode my ass, my cock rubbed against the bench. At first it was uncomfortable for me to bend my head up to take Randy's cock while being ass-fucked at the same time. This problem was solved when Scott flipped me over on my back and continued fucking me. This position allowed Randy to drive his cock down and into my mouth and throat. My ass was getting a little sore from the pounding Scott was giving me and when Randy asked if he could switch with Scott, I readily agreed.

I was in almost a sexual haze at what was happening. Here were two of my teammates, who were close friends, giving me the fucking of my life, in the locker room, at the ballpark. Randy quickly inserted his now covered cock into my ass as Scott bared his dick and began to probe my mouth and throat with his horse meat. Randy fucked at a quicker pace than Scott, but did not have the impact that Scott's pecker had. Now I had two men fucking both ends of me, moaning with pure lust, as I did my best not to come from the pure sexuality of it all. Scott was pushing the entire length of his prick down my throat and left it there a couple of times for a few seconds, cutting off my air. When I began to choke, he would remove it and slap my face with his dick.

Randy bent my legs all the way over, so that he was drilling my ass almost down at a straight angle as Scott began to pump my mouth again. As I continued to be fucked, I heard Scott ask Randy if they wanted to switch again or come in their current positions. Randy merely grunted and it was plain he had no intention of giving up my ass, which he was drilling as if for oil.

"Fine with me. Jerry, where do you want my load?" Scott asked as he withdrew his member from my mouth. By that time I was so hot I didn't care.

"When you get ready to blow, pull out and I will keep my mouth open and you can shoot your hot load into my mouth and down my throat," I replied.

"Sounds good to me guy," Scott said as he resumed his face-fucking.

"I'm coming in your tight gay ass Jerry unless you have a problem with that," Randy said. I couldn't answer him with a throat full of cock so I let him know it was okay with my eyes.

Scott suddenly pulled his dick out of my mouth and said, "Take my load dude 'cause here it comes!" As promised, I opened my mouth wide and stared up at his massive cock. I watched with ecstasy as stream after stream of white hot come flew out of Scott's cock into my mouth and all over my face. I had to swallow at least four times before Scott stopped coming. As if to finish it off, Scott pushed his cock once again down my throat.

"Suck out every drop, Jerry, do me right now."

I did as I was told and received a little more come as my reward. Randy was next to shoot as he tensed up and increased the pounding of my ass with maximum force. His face contorted and he began grunting and breathing out hard as his cock unloaded into the rubber. As he was coming, I reached down, gave my cock a few hard strokes, and began shooting all over my face, as my legs were so far back my cock was in line with my own mouth. As I came, my ass muscles automatically tightened giving Randy an extra squeeze that made him spurt at least one extra time.

When Randy was spent, he slowly withdrew from my battered ass and let my legs down. I noticed the rubber was full with a large load at the tip. Both men collapsed on their backs so they could recover and catch their breaths. I reached over to Scott's locker and grabbed his towel, wiping the remaining come that hadn't gone down my throat off my face and mouth.

Scott was the first to speak. "Man, that was some fucking fantastic sex dude, thanks for taking care of my dick for me. I wouldn't mind a repeat sometime."

Randy peeled off the rubber and commented that I had a fine tight ass that was made for his cock. He also promised that he would be in it again in the not-too-distant future.

Three very happy and sexually satisfied friends headed off to the communal shower room for the second time that afternoon to get clean once again. All three of us had smiles on our faces, thinking about future road trips for out-of-town games. My only problem was that two married men were now fucking me! Well, maybe we would win the World Series this year, and it would be due to me keeping two of our biggest stars sexually satisfied. After all, I once promised the coach I would do anything to help the team win the championship!

Bat-and-Ball Wager

Jay Starre

The moment he walked into the locker room, Wade regretted the wager he'd made with Terrence. Scattered throughout the room, hunky jocks were in various states of nudity: bare cocks, balls, and asses paraded around before being hidden under jockstraps and baseball uniforms. Wade bit back a groan of nasty need as his dick swelled in his jeans and his blue eyes darted from naked butt to flopping dick to bouncing ball sac. Fuck! To Wade, nothing was hotter than a locker room packed with jocks, and nothing more frustrating than realizing he could do nothing to satisfy his burning lust.

"I bet you can't keep that hungry dick of yours out of mouth or ass for the next week of our play-off series," Terrence had dared with a sneering laugh. This was two days ago, as they'd both collapsed in the darkened stands after a hasty bout of heavy ass-fucking.

Two days, and Wade was so horned up he thought his balls would explode from backed-up juice. Wade caught Terrence's eye from across the packed locker room. Wade smirked and shook his head; so far he'd managed his half of the wager.

Terrence offered a wink and a toothy smile before deliberately raising one foot up onto the bench in front of him, then bending over as if searching for something in his locker.

Naturally, the baseball player's bare ass gaped open in that position. Wade was left gawking at a smooth crack, a tempting hole pouting deep in the valley's center.

Wade groaned aloud this time. His mind reeled, memories of their recent fuck bombarding him as he stared at that muscular white ass presented so casually and so provocatively.

It had happened as it usually did. After a sweaty, tense ball game, the dark-haired Terrence had caught his teammate's eyes and nodded, wandering off into the emptying stands to wait for their inevitable rendezvous. Their sex games had started during spring training, and continued, sporadic and unplanned but hot as hell whenever they occurred.

It had been an evening game, the sun setting during the eighth inning and twilight descending in the ninth. The cheers of the crowd deafened Wade and his teammates as the home team achieved victory against an opponent that was considered stronger. Those cheers died away quickly as the spectators deserted the ball field and headed to the local bars or victory parties elsewhere.

Wade found Terrence, his white grin flashing in the near darkness of the littered stands between a pair of plastered walls in a walkway that led to the spectator washrooms. Hidden from the bright field lights, with an eerie quiet settling over the vacated stands, Terrence was already leaning against one of the walls with his hands and feet wide apart, his ass waiting.

Wade moved in, dragging Terrence's striped uniform pants to his knees and exposing his chunky butt. Terrence uttered a quiet laugh as he wriggled that bare butt nastily and urged Wade to fuck him good.

"Drill my butt. Shove that big bat of yours up my hungry hole. I'm your catcher tonight and you're gonna pitch me a real good fuck!"

Wade grinned at Terrence's dirty talk. The stocky ballplayer was always coming up with something kinky and nasty to say, or do. Wade's dick, a lengthy rod of curved greed, slammed up into the deep valley of Terrence's full butt. The knobbed crown slipped around in the sweaty crevice only long enough to find the crinkled anal slot. Once targeted, that hole was immediately stuffed.

"Fuuuuuckkkkkkkk . . ." Terrence exhaled in a drawn-out moan as dick drove deep into his guts.

It had been quick and savage, the risk of being discovered spurring the two on as Terrence squirmed over Wade's pounding cock, his palms planted flat on the wall, his own cock stiff but hidden within the cup and strap of his baseball jock. The black-haired baseball player was all hole as the blond Wade rammed him furiously. Wade appreciated that about Terrence; his ability to give it up and give it up good.

Sweaty, clinging, hot—Terrence's asshole was all that, and willing too. It opened up to Wade's dick yet massaged and trapped it with eager anal muscles at the same time. That jock hole was made for jock dick.

"I'm gonna blow," Wade gasped into Terrence's ear as he whipped his pounding cock out of the slippery ass channel and blew good on his word.

Leaning into the sweaty jock and pressing his pulsing shaft against one muscular butt cheek, Wade shot his load all over that writhing ass. One heart-pounding minute of pure ecstasy as Wade's sticky load squirted out in big gobs, then a hasty shuffle to dress as they heard some chattering fans approaching from beyond the wall.

Terrence turned and grinned as he snapped his fly shut, Wade's load trickling down his ass cheeks inside his uniform. With a nasty chuckle, he'd made that dare. "I bet you can't keep that hungry dick of yours out of mouth or ass for the next week of our play-off series."

Wade had laughed in his face. "You're the one always wiggling your ass in front of me. I can last without a fuck longer than you."

They'd made a hasty escape just as a group of rowdy fans rounded the corner. The wager had been cemented later over a couple of beers and now two days later Wade was stuck with it. Terrence had added a stiffener to the wager, forbidding jerking off to relieve any pent-up desire.

Wade's thoughts returned to the locker room, and Terrence's white ass waving at him from across the busy change room. He could barely tear his eyes from that fetching can, his dick throbbing now at full mast inside his jeans. Beyond even that tempting butt, Terrence was very sexy. Short, packed with stocky muscle from head to toe, buzzed jet-black hair, surprisingly pale eyes under jet-black brows, easy to laugh and a bit of a joker, Terrence was popular with his teammates and not too full of himself.

Wade pondered Terrence's reasons for making that wager as his eyes finally abandoned that alluring butt and he found his own locker. While he undressed, he tried to think of something other than ass and hole and dick and balls so his cock would soften and he wouldn't have to worry about hiding the offending boner from his teammates.

It was too late for that when one of those teammates caught sight of the still-swollen tool as Wade attempted to stuff it into his cup and strap.

"Nice bone, bud. Excited about the game?" The words were spoken in a low, sultry whisper that only Wade would have heard.

Wade turned to the jock beside him. Of all the luck, it had to be Adolfo! The dusky-skinned baseball player normally changed beside Terrence, but today had moved to Wade's area of the locker room.

Facing the smiling jock, Wade laughed nervously while he

hastily completed the task of shoving stiff cock into jockstrap. Their eyes met briefly, bright blue into honey-amber. Wade was momentarily transfixed by that smiling face. Adolfo was incredibly handsome, with broad, placid features, those amazing soft brown eyes, and a pursed mouth with red lips. Wade had imagined those red lips wrapping around his cock a dozen times since the beginning of the season.

That was it! Terrence had realized Wade had the secret hots for Adolfo, and was trying to head off any nasty shenanigans between the two of them by making that stupid wager!

Wade shook his head and looked away, his thoughts whirling. No, Terrence didn't strike him as the jealous type, but as his eyes strayed over Adolfo's shoulder, he caught Terrence staring back, the look on his face contemplative.

Was that it? Suddenly Wade wanted to fuck Adolfo more than anything, to shove his cock between those pink lips and pump and pump. He wanted to hear Adolfo gurgling over dick, flopping around under him, slurping, moaning, and loving it.

Wade was going crazy!

He laughed to himself, a little hysterically. Terrence was right! He couldn't survive the brutal play-off series with his stiff cock unsatisfied. He would fuck a hole in the wall if he had to, but he had to fuck someone or something!

He gritted his teeth and pulled himself together. He was tough. He could handle it. He'd prove Terrence wrong, the little fucker! With that renewed resolve, Wade deliberately waved over Adolfo's shoulder at Terrence and gave him a big grin. He also leaned in close to "accidentally" bump into the half-naked outfielder then beam at Adolfo in apology while he was sure Terrence was watching.

That would teach the little fucker!

The game that followed was a test of Wade's inner strength. Regardless of the resolve he'd made in the locker room, the testosterone raging through his system could not be denied. The afternoon was pristine, a few puffy clouds mitigating the early September heat. A gusting breeze added a challenging element to hitting and catching, which should have focussed Wade's sex-starved thoughts.

Instead, Wade saw everything through a blur of sexual innuendo. Gripping the bat in his hands as he prepared to hit, he actually imagined that bat was his own stiff cock, huge and hard and ready to pound the ball right out of the playing field.

But then, the pitcher lifted one leg as he wound up for the pitch, and all Wade could think of was how hot that butt and crack was and how he'd love to shove his dick deep up it and fuck and fuck!

Wade smacked the ball way out into left field, one of his best hits in weeks. But as he propelled his legs around the bases with a pounding heart and racing lungs, the opposing players were all sexual objects, naked in his mind, with hard cocks and big nut sacs full of steamy loads.

Amazingly, he ran so fast around the bases—and the outfielder fumbled his throw to third base—that Wade slid into home amid wailing cheers from the stands.

More crazy thoughts were to follow. Playing shortstop, Wade was right on top of a sliding player as he hoped to achieve second base. He tagged the poor dude out, but was left gawking at the player's sprawled ass at his feet.

I want to rip off that uniform and fuck that spread ass in the dirt right now in front of both teams and all these fans! Fuck, I'm nuts!

Wade barely collected himself and got back to the game. To make matters worse, Terrence was always nearby, playing first base or batting just before him, and wiggling that cute ass provocatively or bending over for no reason in front of Wade to show it off. The stocky jock made certain to bump into Wade innumerable times and push his butt into Wade's crotch or thigh.

Adolfo was almost as bad, for some unknown reason. He grinned at Wade every time he caught him looking, pursing those full pink lips and winking. He sidled up to Wade in the dugout and pressed close as if merely excited about the game.

And it was an exciting game. It was close, although after every inning they were a run or two ahead of the other team, a bunch of hotheads from South Carolina. The dugout was a steamy, swearing mass of cheering, jeering baseball players oozing sweat and pheromones. Wade imagined he smelled come in the air, but that might have been the steady oozing of precome out of his own stiff dick under his uniform.

They won, and Wade was more exhausted than he could ever remember after a game. In the locker room it got worse. Even though his limbs were so weak from a hard-played game they felt like lead, he felt a vibrating inner energy of sexual frustration that just wouldn't allow him to relax. The victorious players shouted and joked as they stripped off their sweat-soaked uniforms and paraded around, swinging dicks and balls everywhere.

In the showers, Wade could barely stand it. Both Terrence and Adolfo were there, the steaming water cascading down a pair of hot jock bodies in the prime of perfection. But did Terrence have to rub that soapy hand so deep in his ass crack and take so long to do it while Wade was forced to grit his teeth and watch? Did Adolfo usually stand there under the gushing showerhead with his mouth gaping wide open, his red lips battered by the gushing water, his eyes closed, and his hands absently fondling his balls and dick?

Wade fled the showers only to enter the charged change room again. Did all his teammates usually dawdle so long before dressing, naked or half-naked, displaying taut butt globes, fat cocks, tight pecs, bulging biceps, or seed-full nad sacs?

Adolfo returned to his new locker beside Wade, fresh, clean, and naked. Terrence made a detour to pass by and clamp a friendly hand on both of their shoulders. "What a game! You guys were awesome. Great home run, Wade. You're a wonder with your bat!"

The smirk was intended, and the hand lingering on his shoulder was warm and stimulating. Both Terrence and Adolfo were buck naked, their towels casually slung over their shoulders. Their asses were within reach of Wade's twitching hands.

"Yeah, great game, you guys," he mumbled as he turned away to search for his pants. His underwear was tented obscenely with a huge hard-on, and he hated the fact that Terrence would see that and get a secret kick out of Wade's frustration.

A sudden slap on his butt startled Wade as Terrence laughed and waltzed away. The little fucker! After this series was up, he was going to pound that jock's butt for a solid hour of nonstop fucking!

Wade was sure that's exactly what Terrence wanted.

He made it out of the locker room without making a fool of himself by jumping Adolfo, although in his vivid imagination Wade pinned the hot outfielder down on the bench beside him and fucked his mouth with his curved dick bat right there in front of the entire team.

It was a five-game series that grew heated as two of the worst South Carolina hotheads lost their tempers and instigated a minor brawl during the final game. The fans were on their feet and loving it, cheering and booing at the same time. They went nuts when Wade's team walloped the Southerners on that same sunny afternoon.

The reverberating cheers from the stands vibrated through Wade's entire body. His teammates hugging him and thumping his back had him breathless. It was over! He'd done it, to spite Terrence and prove something to himself. Now what, he wondered?

He was miffed at Terrence, who seemed to enjoy the entire celibate game, as cheery and full of jokes as ever. Wade had also grown increasingly attracted to Adolfo, who had never seemed too out of his sight during that frustrating play-off.

An unexpected calm settled over Wade as he returned with the team to the change room. His cock was only half-hard, and his mind was not totally dominated by thoughts of fucking anything in sight. He was still horny, very horny, but now that he'd accomplished that test of his will power, he was prepared to wait a little longer for satisfaction.

He took time to think over whom he would fuck first. Terrence, or Adolfo? Terrence would be pissed off if he spurned him for Adolfo, but Terrence didn't need to know. Maybe he'd fuck Adolfo first, then go for Terrence in a second round. He was probably up for it. His balls were roiling with loads begging for release.

Wade was decidedly distracted as he changed and showered, hardly noticing the others around him who were jubilant with their victory. In fact, he lingered so long in the showers, soaking up the steamy water and letting the pulsing flow massage his aching muscles, that they were deserted when he opened his eyes and looked up.

It was oddly quiet when he turned off the shower. Beyond the doorway, there should have been victory banter, lockers slamming, hooting, and all the usual racket. But there was nothing. How long had he stood in a daze under the shower-head? Half an hour, probably!

He towelled off slowly, still in a quandary about Terrence and Adolfo. He wasn't sure what the big deal was; he could fuck whomever he wanted, if they wanted to get fucked. Wade knew Terrence loved Wade's lengthy bat up his butt, and felt certain Adolfo would welcome that jock pole in either of his two holes, mouth or ass. *So fuck them both, and quit worrying about it,* he was thinking.

It was even quieter when he finally strolled into the change room with his towel in hand. It was so still he could hear an echoing whisper that he would never have heard normally. It came from the other side of a bank of lockers, against the far wall in a cul-de-sac of lockers.

Wade stopped and listened. He couldn't quite understand the words, but he recognized one of the voices, even at that level. Terrence. What was he up to, hidden back there in the corner?

Wade suddenly realized that with their wager over, Terrence could get laid now too. It might not necessarily be with Wade! The blond jock's mouth dropped open with shock as he suspected that's what was going on right now. Terrence was offering his butt up to someone else!

Wade bit back a mixture of snarl and laughter. How could he be mad at Terrence for doing exactly what he'd been planning himself? But still, he'd catch the little fucker in the act and embarrass him at the same time—if Terrence could even be embarrassed.

Quietly making his way through the labyrinth of lockers toward the back of the change room, Wade's swaying cock grew stiffer and stiffer until by the time he rounded the final corner, it stood at full mast and slapped obscenely against his navel.

"What took you so long? At least it looks like you're ready to pound some hole with that stiff pole!"

Terrence stood beside Adolfo, arms draped across each other's shoulders, naked. Both were stroking boners of their own and smirking.

Wade's mouth dropped open. The joke was on him.

Wade recovered from his shock in a nanosecond. Two quick strides brought him in front of the smirking pair. "Down on your knees, Adolfo, with that sweet mouth wide open! And you can get up on that bench and spread your ass for me, Terrence!" Wade growled.

The two jocks were still laughing, but were quick to oblige their demanding teammate. Wade straddled the kneeling outfielder, staring down into his honey-amber orbs as he used one hand to cup the jock's chin and open the wet mouth and the other to feed his drooling knob between those full, red lips.

Adolfo gurgled and slurped. Wade gasped as silky lips massaged his cock head and wet warmth enveloped it. He swayed on his feet for just a moment as he revelled in that warm satisfaction before he went for Terrence.

The stocky second baseman crouched on the bench beside them, his feet wide apart, bent over with his head down around his knees and looking back between them at Wade with a nasty smirk. Ivory-pale ass crack loomed right in Wade's face.

Wade buried his face in that crack. Tongue darted out to attack the hole, stabbing into it, swabbing the puckered ass lips, sucking them inside out with loud slurps that nearly drowned Adolfo's eager suckling and Terrence's moans.

Wade had never been so horned up. Recalling how he'd been manipulated by his two conniving teammates, he was determined now to show them who was boss. He'd fuck them senseless!

Feet planted on either side of Adolfo, Wade's muscular thighs trapped the kneeling outfielder between them. One hand gripped Adolfo's chin while the other fed inch after inch of curved dick between those smacking red lips. Wade fucked Adolfo's mouth relentlessly while he continued to heat up Terrence's hole with a vicious tongue drilling.

Terrence squirmed his ass back into Wade's face, as full of pent-up desire as his teammate after their week of self-imposed celibacy. Wade grinned between the plump ass globes as he drew out the tongue-fucking into a teasing foreplay that had Terrence begging for more.

"It's wet and slippery and hungry for cock! Give it to me, buddy! Pound my poor ass with your big baseball bat," Terrence groaned from between his own thighs as he humped Wade's face and tongue like a slut in heat.

Wade was happy with the status quo for now. He hadn't taken the time to eat out Terrence's steamy hole in the past, usually ramming his cock home with few preliminaries as they engaged in furtive, hasty butt-poundings. Now, he was determined to enjoy himself to the fullest. He had two wet holes, and he'd use them however he wanted.

Wade clamped his thighs tight around Adolfo and fucked down into his gurgling mouth, sliding past tonsils and into tight throat. That was hot! Adolfo's hands clamped over Wade's powerful, hairy ass and remained there, kneading and groping, pushing cock deeper into his own mouth at the same time. He couldn't seem to get enough of Wade's cock!

Terrence was frustrated with that tongue eating him out, his asshole wet, gaping and needing more. He watched from between his own spread thighs as the cock he wanted rode in and out of Adolfo's red lips. Terrence's asshole throbbed and pouted, growing steamier as Wade sucked him inside out with intentional deliberation.

Wade loved the way Terrence squirmed and begged.

d the little fucker right! But he was beginning to cave in the constant pleading. He wanted to fuck Terrence, and fuck him hard.

"All right. Both of you get on that bench on top of each other. I'm gonna fuck both your holes. I know that's what you need, my big baseball bat cock up your butts."

They scrambled to obey the demanding shortstop. Terrence grinned like a fool, thrilled with Wade's rough and dominating attitude. In seconds, the pair of baseball jocks were piled over the wooden bench with their legs on either side and their assholes exposed and waiting.

Wade straddled the bench, nursing his spit-wet boner with one beefy paw as he took aim. One ivory-pale ass and one olive-skinned butt, both spread open and available, both with deep cracks and eager holes! Terrence was on top, his wet hole dribbling Wade's own saliva down the hairless crack. Beneath, Adolfo's tight pucker pursed pink, just like his mouth had.

The blond jock slammed into Terrence's gooey slot first, driving right to the balls in one savage plunge. Terrence squealed, but lifted his butt to swallow all that meat with pure glee. Wade grimaced with the sensation of quivering guts encasing his entire shank. So long denied, he was nearly paralysed with pure pleasure.

Wade's enormous will power kicked in. Just as he'd been determined to win their wager, as tough as it had been, he was now determined to fuck his two teammates relentlessly.

Wade pulled out of Terrence's steamy hole and immediately aimed for Adolfo's puckered slit. Gooey with spit, the purple bat slammed against the tight ring and forced its way beyond. While the powerful outfielder emitted a huge grunt, he managed to raise his butt off the bench, and Terrence along with it. With that move, Adolfo's hole sucked up half of Wade's lengthy bone.

A hot vice encased Wade's dick! He gritted his teeth and leaned into the pair of naked jocks pinned beneath him. With a thrust of his hips, he impaled Adolfo to the balls. Adolfo's sweet mouth and red lips gaped open as he let out another explosive grunt.

"Are you feeling that bat up your butt? Good! You're just gonna get more of the same. I'm gonna fuck a load out of each of you."

Wade was determined to do just that. He wouldn't achieve his own satisfaction until he'd pounded those two jocks' asses so hard that Terrence and Adolfo both blew their wads, merely from the gut-churning pleasure of getting their holes stuffed.

He pumped a few times in and out of Adolfo's clamping ass channel, the pinned outfielder grunting, then pulled out and rammed into Terrence's steamy slot. The difference between the two fuck holes was nasty and exciting.

Terrence raised his white ass and swallowed the cock when it rammed into him. Talented anal muscles opened wide to accept all that curved length in one gulp, then immediately massaged and chewed on it. Terrence knew how to take cock!

Wade revelled in that steamy fuck cauldron for a few pounding thrusts before he whipped out and lowered his aim to slam into Adolfo's tight sphincter. As tight as before, the outfielder's hole seized Wade's poker with relentless heat as Adolfo bucked under both his teammates' weight.

"Fuck me," Adolfo grunted, his amber butt writhing and his body flopping under naked flesh.

Wade obliged him, taking the time to thrust vigorously in and out at least a dozen strokes, stretching the tight channel and rubbing the aching ass lips with each lunge. Adolfo grunted in time, louder and louder.

It was music to Wade's ears. He pulled out of that tight

hole and plowed into Terrence's to hear the dark-haired jock shout out his own pleasure. Slippery and hot, Terrence's spit-lubed slot squished, sucked, and swallowed as Wade rammed it furiously.

The two pinned jocks had their own dicks continually rubbed beneath them, Terrence's against the outfielder's solid ass beneath him, and Adolfo's against the wooden bench under him. Curved cock rammed up their butts relentlessly, broken only by the other taking his turn at bat-swallowing.

Wade remained on the very brink of orgasm. Steamy holes sucked in his drilling cock, massaging and searing it. Yet his will power overcame his aching lust, and he rammed his cock harder and faster while the pair of baseball jocks beneath him grunted, writhed, and steadily grew closer to their own climaxes.

Wade felt it first in Terrence. He knew his teammate well by that time, and had fucked him enough times to know when Terrence was close. Wade increased his pace, thrusting in and out of Terrence's squishy hole in a furious drilling. Terrence moaned and flopped, his thighs wide and his mouth drooling over Adolfo beneath him.

"Give it up. I know you're ready to blow!" Wade snarled in Terrence's ear.

"OHHH GAAWWD!" Terrence wailed. His prostate mashed, his cock rubbed against the sweaty jock under him, that pounding dick in his guts—he was driven over the edge.

Terrence spewed. Goo plastered the pinned pair, oozing out between belly and back. Wade immediately pulled out and slammed into Adolfo's tight ass channel. While Terrence moaned and thrashed between them, Wade plowed Adolfo's clinging hole like there was no tomorrow.

Adolfo grunted beneath all that weight, pinned and fucked. His climax came almost instantly now that cock remained up his ass for more than a few strokes. He actually lifted all three of them up in the air as he sprayed the bench with his sticky come.

Wade had done it, fucked a load out of both his team-mates. Now, he could give in to his own orgasm. Adolfo's clamping fuck hole was enough to do the trick. Wade let himself go, ramming in and out furiously before finally pulling out and leaping up to spray all over both players while laughing at the same time.

"I win! You're both fucked and fucked good," he chortled between gasps as his balls emptied out over the pair.

Naturally, Terrence had to have the last word, even in the face of Wade's amazing stamina.

"I bet you can't do that all over again. I'm sure Adolfo hasn't been fucked enough, and I know I haven't."

Wade collapsed on top of his well-fucked teammates. He couldn't win! Terrence was insatiable, and now it seemed so was Adolfo. Oh well, he might as well enjoy it.

He'd fuck them both all over again, and love every minute of it!

Rain Delay

T. Hitman

———

Whether or not they'd get the game in was the big question that had shaped the day from the start. One line of thunderstorms had already moved through at a sluggish and maddening pace. Another lurked a hundred miles south of McKinsey Field and was sweeping steadily closer, carried on the July jet stream. The window of opportunity to play at least five innings of baseball was a small one, and it inched down with every passing minute. You could smell the storm's charge in the air above the sweet mow of the well-tended ball field grass, the aroma of fried onions and buttery hot dogs, and the summer sweat of glistening bodies as thousands of fans packed into their stadium seats.

The sun shone briefly right before the opening pitch, but by the middle of the third inning, the sky again opened up and the grounds crew was pouring drying agent on the mound and raking it across the infield. Right after the start of the fourth, the drizzle became a hot, driving rain and the umpire in charge called for the tarp.

Baseball fans and players from both teams scurried for cover. In contrast, the grounds crew leaped into action, jogging onto the field dressed in bright red T-shirts and a mix of khaki pants and navy-blue shorts. The dozen-plus guys, mostly college students employed to do a summer dream job, rolled the giant metal cylinder holding the tarp across the infield. The waterproof canvas slid off the massive paper towel roll, then was hastily unfolded into its diamond shape, anchored at one end, and dragged over the bases.

Mark Sheppard had run the grounds crew at McKinsey Field for four summers, and with all the recent soakers, he and the guys had it down to a science. Of course, it helped that he'd hired most of last year's crew. These guys didn't let him or the team down. Well, most of them didn't.

When a baseball game went to a rain delay, time had a way of speeding up, like someone had just stabbed the fast-forward button on a giant remote control. Running out the tarp was always a dangerous mission—if one of the guys slipped, it was possible he'd get trampled flat. Because of the high wind gusts, unfurling the tarp could get you blown halfway up to the nosebleed seats if it took flight. So Shep didn't realize Sparkman's boy Jake had abandoned the grounds crew yet again until the troop of fourteen were gathered safely back in their pen beneath the mezzanine.

Shep took a rapid headcount, saw that one of his guys was missing, and only on instinct did he look out across the infield. No human-shaped mummy contorted the tarp's ground-hugging flatness. No, Shep already knew the missing guy's identity, and he wasn't out there, pinned beneath the canvas.

"Fucker," Shep huffed.

Jake Sparkman only got his job at McKinsey thanks to his dad, one of the team's longtime radio announcers and a former star pitcher. And the useless cocksucker had seized every opportunity to remind Shep of this fact. While most of the grounds crew were working their asses off over the summer break from college for spending money—and mostly, for the chance to live out a tailored version of that dream shared by every guy who owns a baseball glove—Jake was completely unreliable. He'd given Shep plenty of attitude since the start of the season. Worse, he'd done a shitty job the last time they'd secured the tarp.

Shep checked to make sure the outfield's drainage system was engaged, then put Rollins, a senior at one of the local colleges, in charge. The storm had opened up fully and was soaking the ballpark. The humidity had gone from uncomfortable to rotten, but Shep's anger was setting fire to his insides worse than the miserable mugginess in the air. The naked skin of his arms and legs glistened with a glaze of rain and sweat. As he stormed through the garage door and into the inner guts of the stadium, perspiration and rage heated his armpits and toes. It also unleashed a nagging, wet itch behind his balls.

The big concrete and steel room beyond the door housed his heavy lawn equipment along with shovels, rakes, and the spreaders used to chalk the lines. Once, about a month earlier in the season while the rest of the guys had dragged the infield during the seventh-inning stretch, leveling out divots, he'd caught Sparkman smoking in one of the alcoves. The twenty-four-year-old pretty boy had given him lip, invoking the almighty name of his dad, Jack Sparkman. To his surprise, Shep had backed down at the mention.

But he refused to be intimidated today.

"Fuck that," Shep grumbled. Unless Jakey-boy was in First Aid hooked up to an intravenous, his ass was O-U-T, *out!*

The equipment bay, however, sat empty. So was the men's head. No, the object of his wrath wasn't in there, jerking on his dick, either—though it wouldn't have been the first time Shep had walked in on one of his guys doing just that inside the doorless stall. He'd busted more than a few loads in there himself over the past couple of summers. No Jake though, just the raw, heady perfume of men's piss and the ghosts of past ejaculations.

Shep's blood boiled. The itch in his most private of places worsened with every step, triggered by the bounce of his sweating balls in his boxer-briefs. The underside of his dick even tingled, the sensitive nerves egged on by his surge of anger. If he didn't kill Jake Sparkman once he found him, there was a good chance he'd fuck him out of spite, he thought, adding a humorless chuckle.

Shep plodded deeper down the tunnel leading beneath McKinsey's first base grandstand. To his right lurked more of the storage areas for team equipment like batting cages and league-issued baseballs. Farther up were the maintenance doors—electrical, then plumbing. The air near the latter stank of mold and standing water. On the outside, McKinsey was one of baseball's fine old ladies of tradition, but behind doors like this, her veneer was cracked and her pipes leaked.

Beyond, the door to the home team clubhouse loomed, with the one for the visitors several hundred paces deeper. Only a keypad guarded the clubhouse on the outside of the door. Shep punched in his access code and was greeted by the security guard on the inside.

"Hey," Shep said.

"Hey yourself," the guard returned. "Any chance they might finish this thing?"

"The way the shit's coming down, don't be surprised if they call it."

The guard swore under his breath.

"Dude, you seen Sparkman's boy?"

"Jake?" The guard shook his head. "Naw, even being his old man's kid don't get him in here." He aimed an enormous thumb over his shoulder at the door to the actual locker room area of the clubhouse.

"You see him, squawk me on the box, okay?" Shep clapped a hand over the radio clipped to his belt.

"Will do," the guard promised.

Shep turned on the heels of his grass- and dirt-stained sneakers and marched back into the tunnel, where baseball legends had strutted, spit, and scratched their sweaty balls for almost a century. Shep's were now so itchy from the caged heat in his boxer-briefs, he couldn't ignore them any longer. Sweat clung to him everywhere. The hairline of his athletic cut felt almost as swampy as the toes of his socks and the sac of nuts suffering in his shorts. He needed to scratch and to bust a load and to kick Sparkman's ass like it had yet to be kicked.

Shep didn't realize the key to all three of his goals was so close by, separated by one meager, rusting door.

The door to the waterworks sat the slightest degree ajar. On the surface, that wasn't much in the way of a big deal, because very little at McKinsey Field was plumb anymore. Not sure why beyond the fact that his instincts told him to, Shep gripped the door's handle. It was slick to the touch with condensation. He gave the door a push and it groaned open. A musty smell assailed his nostrils.

The room, lit at the center by a pair of naked fluorescents, continued ahead in a rough rectangular shape before arcing to the left and out of sight into a region of shadows that Shep knew, based upon the park's layout, led right up to the wall separating storage from the clubhouse showers and urinals. Shep guided the door back into place with his fingertips to stop it from slamming, and once he knew he was alone, shoved his hand into his pants. His balls had become their own swampland. He scratched at his meaty sac, savored the relief, and then fingered the wet, itchy region between his nuts and his asshole. The sensation was intoxicating, and the fullness of his balls surprised him. He hadn't shot a load in two days, and that one had been milked out courtesy of his own hand.

You're hurting, dude, teased a voice in his thoughts.

A trickle of water and the sound of distant voices pulled him out of his trance toward the darkness at the left side of the vast room. The musty, steamy stink of the men's locker room infused the air, and he realized through slitted eyes that he could just make out a pencil-thin shaft of light, emanating from somewhere in that male-smelling fog.

The clubhouse, Shep thought. *Yet another crack in the mortar of baseball's favorite darling.* Shep reached into the leg pocket of his cargo pants and pulled out the small flashlight he kept there for those unexpected instances requiring such a handy tool. Plumbing and structural maintenance weren't his responsibility, but if the clubhouse's walls were falling down, it wasn't a bad idea for him to report it to those whose it was. He aimed the beam into the shadows, toward that sliver of light.

Shep jumped a step back and choked down a gasp of surprise when the beam connected with a set of wide, white eyes.

Rumors that McKinsey Field was haunted had circulated among the grounds crew, players, and even the management for years. But the eyes glaring back, equally as shocked as Shep's, didn't belong to the ghost of some long-dead Hall of Famer; when his shock passed, Shep recognized the blue irises, the trim goatee ringing the mouth beneath them, even the five lazy fingers clamped in a choke hold around a stiff dick. Beating off was the most work Shep had ever seen Jake Sparkman manage.

Anger, slippery and hot like the itch in his pants, replaced Shep's surprise. He tipped the flashlight down the course of Sparkman's privileged college jock body, from the swell of his cock to the twin bloated balls in a hairless sac dangling beneath it, athletic legs dark with hair to big feet in expensive sneakers. He then quickly went up again to the fucker's handsome, hated face.

"Shep." Sparkman choked out the lone, dry word, in contrast to the very wet rivulets of precome being throttled out of his cock.

"What the fuck are you doing?"

It was, Shep realized, perhaps the stupidest question ever asked of a member of the grounds crew. What Sparkman's son was doing was pretty fuckin' obvious—he was stroking his piece, that's what. But as he gave the flashlight another pass up and down the fucker's body, Shep got a good look at what was really going on. Sparkman was kneeling near the wall in a way that put him in the perfect position to look through the crack.

In the strangulating silence of those tense few seconds between Shep's question and Sparkman's answer of, "Nothing, dude!," a deep, gruff exchange of male voices filtered through the darkness. It originated from the other side of the wall, in what had to be the clubhouse.

Shep hunched down and aimed an eye into the shaft of light. The sound of running water came at him, twice as noticeable. He was staring into the showers and again, to his surprise, at another man's naked dick. Unlike Sparkman's, this one hung only half-hard, swollen to thickness by a bar of soap and the hand that was washing it along with a large, loose set of hairy nuts not a yard distant. Shep recognized the starburst tattoo sprouting out of the thatch of hair on the man's left calf muscle: it was Mike Beckett, the team's flame-throwing right-handed relief pitcher. Standing beside him under the spray was a second set of legs, balls, and a meaty above-average man's cock, this one crowned by lush folds of foreskin. Shep immediately recognized the voice as belonging to utility player Oswaldo Lopez.

It struck him fully what was happening here in the dark, male-stinking corner of the maintenance room: His missing grounds crewmember was rubbing one off while looking through a chink in the wall at some major league dick!

"What the fuck?" Shep repeated.

The fuck, some sane voice in his thoughts declared through the insanity, was that Jack the Flying Sparkman's college boy was a cockgobbler, as simple as that.

"It's not what you think," Jake whispered in a desiccated voice.

Under the jiggling flashlight beam, Shep watched the boy clumsily attempt to yank his shorts back into place, wincing as the head of his steely dick resisted imprisonment. Sparkman tried to stand, his nuts still hanging out of his open fly, his dick pinned behind the button of his shorts; a pair of camouflage cutoffs, Shep noticed. Cammies. Yeah, right . . . like this privileged little puke would have done hard time in the military! They were a fashion statement worn by an arrogant come guzzler who'd walked around the ballpark all summer like he owned it.

Shep reached his free hand out and grabbed Sparkman by the shoulder. Using a level of strength he hadn't planned to, Shep shoved the college boy back down, the squeak of his sneakers on slick concrete a clear indication that his adversary was right where he wanted him.

On his knees.

"Not so fast," Shep threatened.

"Dude, what—?"

"Shut up," Shep said. He released Sparkman but stepped closer, liking the fact that his crotch and the boy's face were now on the same plane. "You've been fucking around all summer. On me, on my crew, and apparently on the team's dudes, too."

"No . . ."

"Yeah, it's not what I think. You already said that. Well,

what I think is that for all your big talk, you're a cockhound who needs to learn some respect."

Shep's dick ached in his pants. He'd never messed around with another dude in spite of the numerous opportunities he'd been presented with over the years. Hell, even a couple of the team's players had come onto him before this, like a certain third baseman from a few seasons back after a night of beers following a perfect home stand. No, Shep wasn't into that. He loved women, and he'd loved a lot of them. But this wasn't about sticking it to another dude. It was all about sticking it to the guy who'd been a serious thorn in his ass all summer, and that idea launched his cock up to its full thickness.

Shep opened his zipper, reached in, and freed his tool and both perspiration-drenched nuts from the prison of his underwear. His own ripeness gusted up to assail his nostrils when Sparkman sighed nervously, stirring their stink into the stagnant air that surrounded them.

"No way, dude," Sparkman protested, though he nonetheless grabbed Shep's rod around its root.

"Yeah way, cocksucker. Now suck my dick or your ass is out of here and every dude on the baseball team knows you've been sneaking down here to check them out when they're showering!"

That threat—and the heady smell emanating from Shep's package—seemed enough to get Sparkman to accept his punishment. The cock in his hand slid forward and vanished into a warm, wet cave whose suckling walls coaxed a grunt of approval from deep within Shep's chest. Shep tossed back his head on instinct, exhaled a breathy sigh, and invaded Sparkman's mouth. For a brief, unbelievable instant, it felt like falling into a bottomless pit.

Shep had measured his dick once before on a dare, so he knew he was packing a thick piece of meat in the eight-inch range. He could have stuck ten down Sparkman's throat and it wouldn't have mattered, he guessed. Sparkman was no newcomer when it came to providing oral relief to a man's dick. That much was obvious.

Shep's balls gonged off Sparkman's furry chin, and the sensation of falling vanished. Shep retrained the flashlight down to see the college boy's mouth clamped around the base of his sweaty cock, all arrogance gone from the fucker's face. Replacing it was the desperate expression of a starving man given the best meal of his life. Jack Sparkman's boy Jake was a true cocksucker, so desperate to taste a man's meat that he didn't care how wet with perspiration, how hairy, how ripe. Hell, that raw male stink probably made it even more of a buffet for him!

After a few stiff sucks, Shep stepped back and yanked his cock from Sparkman's lips. The tight seal broke and a wet, sloppy popping sound shot through the soupy air. "Lick my nuts," Shep ordered.

Sparkman didn't argue this latest call—ironic when you considered how much effort it was to get him to do anything else competently. The warm, wet brush of Sparkman's tongue over Shep's perspiring ball bag incited a mix of excitement and rage. His cock, tick-tocking over the bridge of Spark-man's nose, had stiffened beyond mere hardness. It was as solid as a length of mountain ash, so erect it had become mildly painful. He'd never experienced this kind of boner, not even when he'd banged two of the players' wives on a Fourth of July fuckfest while the team had played on the road.

"Fuck," Shep groaned, hypnotized by the swirling of Sparkman's tongue over the flesh of his nuts. So much so, he barely registered the clinking sound of Sparkman's belt being opened, or his zipper lowering. The fucker was jerking on his tool again, but Shep didn't care. "Yeah, that's right. Clean the stink off my bull balls . . ."

Shep loved having his rocks worked on. Sparkman sucked the left one between his lips. The pressure nearly made Shep squirt. Going on automatic, he grabbed hold of his cock and worked it, using Sparkman's spit, his own sweat, and the copious amount of precome trickling out of his piss hole. The rest of the world felt time zones and light years away. The rain delay, the grounds crew, even the naked, half-stiff cock of the major league stud showering less than a yard away on the other side of the wall, all of it evaporated in his need to rape Sparkman's mouth. To show him who was boss, and who was the cocksucker. To yank that silver spoon out of his mouth and replace it with a wad of whitewash.

Jake Sparkman, who'd strutted around McKinsey Field with an arrogant, entitled attitude all summer, was on his knees licking the stink off another man's balls. That thought, and the proof of it under the jiggling beam of the flashlight, pushed Shep over the edge.

"Aw, fuck," Shep groaned. "Open wide and suck my dick, fucker!"

He hastily shoved his cock back into the college boy's mouth. A second too late, the first spurt splashed Sparkman's goatee, but the five that followed ricocheted off his tonsils before being gulped down. As the world fazed out of focus around him, Shep felt a ribbon of steamy wetness strike his calf, just above the ankle. Sparkman moaned weakly around the cock in his mouth—the fucker was coming and had shot a load across his leg!

Shep clamped down on the urge to howl, nearly impossible considering how intensely the seed was blasting out of his dick. This time, the climax seemed to start way down deep in his toes, not just his dick. He pushed in as far as possible and didn't stop until his balls snagged on Sparkman's chin. Bellowing at the top of his lungs like he wanted to would have alerted the players in the showers. Shit, the few diehard fans still in the grandstands waiting out the rain delay would have heard him. Instead, Shep growled a litany of swears and didn't pull out until his dick was drained and he was satisfied that Sparkman had milked every last drop of juice out of him.

He heard the college boy lick his lips and imagined the smile on his face. The energy that surged through Shep's insides was the equivalent of climaxing a second time, an explosion of pleasure shared by every cell in his body. He tugged on his cock, found it still impossibly stiff even after ejaculating so much batter, and choked up on it the way the famous sluggers on the team did to their bats. And then, mirroring those major league studs, Shep swung, striking Sparkman across the face. Home run!

"Get your loser ass back out there, and the next time I catch you fucking around, your punk ass is fired. You understand me?"

Sparkman jumped to his feet and hitched up his pants in an attempt to hide his guilt. "Yes, sir!"

Shep liked the sound of it. "Do your job, and maybe I'll give you some more of this." He shook his cock before returning it to his boxer-briefs. "Just maybe . . ."

In the muddy darkness, Shep made out the hopeful expression on Sparkman's face. As the college boy turned, nearly tripping over his own big feet on the way out of the room, Shep launched a swift kick at his ass. Sparkman tumbled into a heap across the floor and yelped in surprise.

Doing that had felt almost as good to Shep as the first blow job he'd just received courtesy of the college boy's lips. Almost, but not quite.

"Not so fast," Shep said, because he was ready for another.

Bennington Boomers

Joel A. Nichols

It was spring, spring of 1923, and all of Bennington was covered in mud. It was too warm for April. Henderson's tires got so jammed up skidding down Main Street, he had to hitch his car to two pull horses, and even then the rest of the boys and I had to push! We had a game against Rutland that afternoon—so Andy and I, our uniform trousers caked with mud from helping Henderson, filed out on the gooey field with the other players.

Rutland batted first. From behind the plate I watched Andy wind up and sail them right over home. His arm wasn't like his brother's. But nobody's was. Andy's brother was playing down in Hartford at that point—it was before he went down to play for Robins in Brooklyn, before our hometown boy won a pennant. But as far as we were concerned, Andy pitched magnificently. His shoulders were wide and strong, and you could see his bicep bulge even from where I crouched, behind the batter. He was a lefty, too, just like his brother, and when he threw back his shoulder and arced his arm, this look came over his face. His eyes narrowed until the ball popped out of his hand. Then the lines in his crinkled up forehead disappeared, his green eyes shone above those sharp cheekbones, and all his teeth erupted in a satisfied grin. It was as if he knew the pitch would be perfect, and couldn't help himself but smile. That day he had dirt in his hair, flecks of brown mixed in with the red curling out under his cap, and a line of dried mud streaking down his neck from pushing against the back of the car.

I can't ever remember not being in love with Andy. But I wonder what I actually thought then. I never imagined I'd be able to live with him, like you young people do now, playing house. I never imagined being able to tell anybody how I felt, much less some young person with a tape recorder!

Two of the men from Rutland got hits. One, a short Italian with a very tight rear—ass, you'd say now—that bulged in my face. I remember being able to make out the straps of his supporter, through the red pinstripes in his uniform. Back then the trousers were baggy and you couldn't see in person half of what you can see on TV, but that guy from Rutland with bushy eyebrows . . . I watched him swing and miss twice. He swore both times, then reached under his collar to kiss his cross, and it must have worked because his bat connected with Andy's fastball and popped right over the first baseman's head. He had short little legs, too, but that ass could run, and he made it all the way to second.

Can you imagine? Nowadays I forget my phone number, but I can see that Italian hit a double like it was this morning.

The next batters struck out before the Italian could make it home, every one a victim to my Andy's arm. He kept winking at me, and tugging down the brim of his cap. Every wink jolted me. We Boomers won that game easily, even though I paid more attention to Andy than to the ball. All of us players were covered in mud, and when we lined up to shake hands, I noticed it drying up and flaking off everybody's pants and sleeves. I stood behind Andy while the team from Rutland lined up opposite us. I could smell him from a foot away, his underarms reeking of loam and musk. On the collar of his uniform seeped a ring of sweat and his red curls were getting fuzzy in the heat. Usually some of the guys on the team wanted to sneak somewhere and share a bottle, and I was hoping that Andy wouldn't go with them. As the Rutland players filed past us, I watched the Italian. When he passed Andy, Andy brushed his hand over the guy's hand, then patted him on the rear. I'll tell you I almost burst! My face got hot and it felt like my skin was burning off. I started to breath heavily and my throat closed up. When my hand had tapped the hand of the last Rutland player, I ran over to the water pump and yanked it until some drizzled out the end of the nozzle, splattering into the muddy puddle at my feet. I drank huge mouthfuls of water in between deep breaths.

Andy trotted after me. "You all right?" he said, settling his palm on my shoulder. I felt that spark again as the weight of his calluses spread across my arm.

I shook my head yes, and swallowed another gulp of water. "I feel like running. Race you home?" And he was off, down the road toward our houses, his long legs carrying him through the minefield of puddles and soggy grass just as easily as he had lobbed fastball after fastball. My knees were weak, but I shouted after him and sprinted to catch up.

I had to finish feeding the cows. That was about the time my father's heart was giving out; I remember how he was getting paler and paler every day. He was still doing the morning feeding, with mother's help, but he rarely could stay awake past supper, which we always ate right at five. Here I am, alive at eighty, when my father barely made it past forty . . .

Andy and I had reached the end of my driveway at the same time—his legs were longer but I was a hair quicker— just like we'd always done on the way home from school. He had to help at his farm, too, but only during the morning milking. His parents never expected him home after a game.

"I'll help you with the cows," he said, flashing that mouthful of teeth. "And we'll be able to go down to the river." When we'd graduated from Bennington High last

June, Andy'd snuck a bottle and we'd drunk it, throwing our school books in the river and singing the school song. In the months since, he'd dragged me down there night after night, even when it had snowed. I say dragged, but you can probably tell that I wanted to go. Maybe even more than he did.

"We better get changed up first," I said. "I've got a pair of coveralls for you." My parents were sitting on the porch, my father dozing while my mother darned a legging.

"Did you win?" she said as we walked up.

"Sure did! Beat Rutland 7–3," I said.

"It's that arm of yours, Andy! Your parents must be so proud of you. We certainly are." He blushed and said thanks in a clear voice that mothers liked so much. We went inside and the screen door slapped shut behind us.

Andy followed me into my room, a big closet stuck behind the kitchen, and started unbuttoning his uniform shirt. "I don't think my ma'll ever wash this mud out," he said as he kicked off the pants. I pulled two pairs of coveralls from my chest and laid them across the narrow bed.

My dick had started to stiffen as soon as we walked in the bedroom, curving around inside my jockey strap. The cold metal shell around my balls got very tight as I worked at my buttons. While I was still struggling, Andy stood there and watched me. He was wearing only his strap and a white undershirt. He winked at me again, and reached over and grazed my belly with his hand. My throat tightened up.

He'd gotten harder, too, as we stood there. From the wide elastic waistband, he had a line of silky red hair that ran straight up to his belly button before it branched out like butterfly wings over his chest. Through the threadbare undershirt his nipples were wide and flat underneath the wisps of brown-red hair, and freckles specked both of his shoulders. The front of his cup was heavy, the gray fabric pulling tight around either side of the metal. I could see the lumps of his balls and the pointed tip of his tool trying to peek out. Andy's legs were as covered with curls as his head.

I had a thicket of black hair growing at the bottom of my dick and a spray covering my belly, but my legs below the knee were completely bald. On my thighs, soft black strands grew thicker the closer they got to my crotch. Finally, I tugged at the fly of my uniform trousers and the button popped right off. Andy bent forward to pick it up, his head almost brushing against the hardness still wrapped up in my pants. I took a sharp, startled breath and he giggled.

"Calm down," he said, making a fist and shadow punching me in the shoulder. I blushed as I stepped out of my pants. I undid the last button of my shirt and let it fall on the floor. My fingers shook as I reached down to move my dick so it wasn't pressing so hard against the cup. I was breathing hard, taking shallow little gulps of air. All I could see was Andy, standing half-naked in my room . . . the edges of the room had just disappeared.

"Hey!" he said, grabbing me by the shoulder. "You look like you're going to faint." His fingers curled over the knob of my shoulder and rested on my neck. "Gonna be alright?" As he lifted his arm I caught whiff of him again, sweet and sour. Farm boys didn't have deodorant, then, you see. Light brown hair was plastered in the crack of his armpit. For a second I could smell the difference in our sweat—his was fouler but laced with something spicy. Mine stank milky, and like very wet grass. I took a deep breath through my nose and then couldn't tell the difference.

"Sure," I said. Andy nodded, and stripped off his jockey strap.

He sighed. "Good to be out of that thing." His cock sprang up when it was freed, and I stared at the bright pink tip of it hiding inside its fleshy hood. I stepped out of mine and the metal cup clattered against the floor. I was worried we were making enough noise to make my mother holler in, but she didn't. And we stood there in our undershirts, our cocks sticking straight out at each other. Andy tipped his hips forward and touched his pink tip to mine, which had oozed one little tear of wet. Then he turned and yanked my spare coveralls over his bare legs, and tucked himself down one of the legs. He picked up my baseball and cracked glove from the floor and shoved it in his pocket.

"What are you waiting for? Let's get that hay out."

When we were finished, cow shit and mud caked our pant legs. From the barn, we tracked off toward the river. There was a footpath my grandfather had cut through a half mile of pines growing tight on one another. The sun was finally dropping on our long day and the two of us were beat, from the game and from haying the cows.

Andy hauled my glove and ball out of the deep coverall pocket. There wasn't more than a half hour of light left. The ball was grimy—it was an old one, one I'd thrown around for years. The stitches had started out red and the ball white, but by then the years of oily hands had stained it all beige. Andy tossed me the glove and I massaged my hand into it, flexing my fingers into the crackling leather. He pitched lighter when we were tossing it around like that, but I still needed the glove far more than he did. My pitches flew softly and it was like Andy plucked them right out of the air.

"Tell me about where your brother plays again, the ballpark," I said. He'd taken the train down to Hartford and visited the stadium, an honest-to-goodness stadium like Fenway, where he'd met all the players and watched them practice. I'd wanted to go with him, but my mother and father wouldn't have managed a whole weekend without me.

"I've already told you everything: the rows and rows of seats, the grass they trim with a pair of scissors," he said, slamming a pitch that landed thudding in my glove. I cradled my hand against my chest for a second until the throbbing stopped. "And the boys who wait outside the fence for the players. You really wouldn't believe how big the whole thing is."

I heaved one back at him and it smacked as it connected with his palm, but he barely winced. "There's got to be something you haven't told me about yet. Come on, I might never get to see it."

We lobbed a couple back and forth. Andy said he had to take a leak, and I climbed up next to him on one of the boulders wedged in the riverbank. He stared at my dick as I unthreaded it from my coveralls, and I started to get hard before I could piss. He loosed a clear stream into the river, smiling at my flushed cheeks. "I didn't tell you about the shitters, did I?"

I shook my head no, and finally got a dribble from the end of my stiffening piece.

"It's just a big trough, and all the guys just have to line up. Like at the fair almost. You'd never be able to piss at a game, if all you do is get stiff."

"Shut up," I said, and jiggled my dick so a few drops of piss sprinkled on him. Andy laughed and punched me in the arm. I managed a few dribbles more and shook myself dry.

He hadn't tucked himself back into my spare coveralls, and was lazily pulling on his foreskin, stretching it off the end of his cock with his thumb and forefinger. By then I was standing straight up, jutting out from my hips as I had been earlier. I undid the top of my coveralls and let them fall. I jumped down on the ground, and leaned up against the boulder we'd been standing on. I made a tube of my fist and ran it up and down my shaft, squeezing every time my thumb got near the ridge just below the tip. Andy jumped down too, his own dick jutting out the fly of the coveralls. It bounced as he landed next to me.

We'd done this twice before, both times in the previous week: silently jacked in front of each other, leaning against this boulder. There was still enough sunlight to see that his eyes were pointed at my crotch, watching my hand as it went up and down. He kept rubbing his foreskin with his fingers while he held himself around the root with his other hand. He started to massage his nuts, reaching through the fly. Andy licked his palm and slicked it across the head of his dick.

My balls slapped against my thighs as I worked. A bead of wetness spurted out of my piss hole and I felt it coat me all the way down to the ridge. As I moved my skin back and forth over the wet tip of my cock, it made a *shshsh*ing noise that sounded like leaves before a rainstorm. Andy grabbed himself around the base and slapped it into his palm. I could see more blood flow in, saw him get thicker as a big vein popped along the length of it. My mouth had been hanging open, and I didn't realize until I tried to wet my lips that my tongue was so dry it stuck.

Then Andy moved. He took a step closer to me, let go of his own dick and grabbed onto mine. His fingers pushed mine off, taking over pulling me in the same rhythm. He'd never done it before, and when he did, I could feel every muscle in my body freeze. My pulse pumped loud in my ear, and my vision narrowed so all I could see was him. I scooted closer to him until his furry thighs tickled my hipbone, and reached over for him. His underarm scent was strong, standing so close, and I breathed deeply through my nose.

He felt so hot in my hand. It was heavy—I remember thinking it was like a sock filled with lead. His was thicker than mine, and as I ran my fingers through his coarse hair and ringed my fingers around the base it grew thicker. In Andy's hand, my own flared bigger, too.

Suddenly he bent at the waist and I lost grip on his dick. He fed himself my cock—taking it all the way in his mouth without warning. I heard him moan as I felt his tongue taste my hole and then trail down the length. I started breathing heavy and staggered back against the rock. Andy laid his palm along my thigh, just below my hipbone, steadying me. His mouth was so wet and so hot it didn't feel real, even though I could see his lips wrapped around me in the fading light. Blood pounded in both my ears.

I grasped again for him, in vain. He was still pressing one hand into my leg, but with the other he was beating himself fast and hard. He was leaking, too, because I could hear the wet crackle.

I struggled to say something, trying to match the grunts he was making in the back of his throat, but I couldn't make my dry throat work. He'd kept me in his mouth this whole time, licking me up and down, playing me against the silk of his cheek. I wanted so desperately to touch his soft hardness, to feel the weight of him in my hand, that I flailed again but still couldn't reach. Finally I dug my fingers into his sweaty curls, scraping his scalp with my dirty fingernails. I felt something hot hit my leg, and realized that he was spraying. The white squirted out of him in three and then four and then five jets and my ass clenched and balls tightened as I let loose in his mouth.

Then he released me. More come dribbled out of me, beading from my hole in a gooey string. Andy stood back up with some of my come in the corner of his lips, which he wiped away with the back of his hand. I squeezed myself a couple of times. As I watched Andy tuck himself back into my spare coveralls, I noticed that he still had that streak of mud on his neck I'd noticed after the game.

"Better pull up those pants," he said, winking. "I'll race you back."

Jock Sniffer

Bearmuffin

———

Boomer doesn't fool me. He's a big homophobe or at least he pretends to be. He bashes gays every chance he gets. On TV. On the radio. Sure, he has to apologize afterward, but he doesn't mean it, or at least he wants you to think that. Nobody indulges in more homophobic talk in the locker room than Boomer. Cocksucker. Homo. Fudgepacker. His favorite words. But you know something? It's all bullshit. You see, I know that deep down inside Boomer loves hot man-to-man homo sex. Yeah, I know that for a fact.

Because one day the game is over. The locker room is deserted. I'm going through Boomer's gear looking for his jockstrap. Boomer is square-jawed, six foot tall, and 210 pounds of solid muscle. A handsome, thickly muscled blond with iron girder abs, thick thighs, and glutes of steel. His beautiful, sexy blue eyes are riveting. His chiseled face and dimpled chin are a knockout. He's the hottest stud in baseball today.

I've been checking out Boomer's hot glutes ever since he joined our team. I saw his naked butt when we were suiting up for the game. The straps of his jock hugged his hot butt so fiercely. His sweet asshole looked so tight and rosy. Just like a little mouth waiting for my anxious tongue. I want to rim Boomer. I want to suck that big piece of meat he's packin' inside his jock.

171

So Boomer's jockstrap is lying underneath his jersey. I pick it up. It's drenched with sweat. I put the pouch over my nose. His hot smell just shoots up my nostrils. My cock goes rock-hard. I almost faint. Fuck, he stinks so goddamn good. I'm fuckin' delirious. I fish into my jock, pull out my cock, and fist it. I'm snorting loud, tripping out on Boomer's hot man stink. Then I hear a growling voice say, "Sniff this, sucker!" I look up. Boomer is standing in front of me with a shit-eating grin on his face. He's shaking his fat cock right at me!

I drop the jock. Boomer's magnificent body is dripping with sweat. His muscles pop out like steel plates underneath his smooth, taut skin. I lick my lips. "Fuckin' A!" I say. I grab Boomer and kiss him, driving my tongue all the way down his throat. His hands are all over my cock, squeezing and rubbing it hard. He shoots his rough tongue down my gullet. We start swapping spit. I plop my hands on his tight bubble butt. I'm squeezing it hard. Huge masses of muscle harden underneath my palms.

We haven't showered so we stink real good. His raunchy b.o. wafts to me making my cock bolt with lust. I lift up his muscular arms and start sniffing his deep, dank pits. His pits are filled with dirty blond hair. Sopping wet with sweat. The stench is intoxicating. Boomer's cock twitches against my abs, so I grab it and start stroking it. His cock veins swell inside my hand. I bury my nose in his pits and inhale deeply. The stink hurtles up my nose. Boomer grunts hard. I run my tongue all over his reeking armpits.

Boomer is fisting my cock. It twitches inside his hot, hard hand. I run my tongue all over his broad chest. His nipples are poking through his blond chest hair. My tongue lands right on them. I twist one of them with my hand and start sucking on the other. "Unngh, unngh," I hear Boomer sigh deeply. "Yeah, dude. Suck my tits. Twist 'em good!" So I crank them up, pulling and tugging on them, twisting his rubbery nipples like there's no tomorrow. Boomer throws his head back. He's sighing and moaning. Deep growls boom from the back of his throat. His barrel chest rumbles.

I'm fisting Boomer's cock harder now, running a fingertip over the piss slit. Big drops of precome are oozing out. Boomer is moaning, groaning, trembling. I just know he's gonna shoot. But I won't let him come. Just yet. I reach down and start licking his stomach. My tongue runs down the long fur trail running from his big fat paps down to his mind-boggling six-pack abs. The thick cords of muscle look like steel girders underneath his smooth, tanned skin. When I reach his belly button I stick my tongue in and lick up the sweat inside. His cock is twitching, bobbing up and down before my lips. Tufts of thick, blond hair curl around the root of his mighty cock.

I lick the salty sweat off his pubes. His man meat pulsates lustily against my chin. Boomer's cock is so powerful, so strong. I can't wait for this big, blond butch baseball stud to shove his cock up my ass! I lick Boomer's cock with big, broad tongue strokes. His cock veins throb lustily on my tongue. Then I glide my tongue over his piss slit and dip the tip into the hole. Boomer sighs. A drop of salty precome seeps onto my tongue. My chin rubs against his balls. They look like two baseballs inside his scrotum.

"Suck my balls, stud!" Boomer hisses down at me. I open my mouth and let both balls drop in. His balls are awesome. They taste so raunchy and sweaty. He hums with macho pleasure as I suck hard on his low-danglers. I reach behind him, cupping his butt as I continue to slurp on his meat. His butt is muscular, rock-solid. He's clenching his buttocks together, but I manage to stick a finger inside the crack and start massaging his hole. He goes crazy when I jab his prostate. "AWWWWWWWWWWWWW, FUUUUUUUUU-CKKKKK!"

Boomer jerks back and my finger sinks into his hole right up to my knuckle. I feel his cock bolt against my face. He's gyrating his hips, moaning and groaning as I finger-fuck his hot butt.

Boomer is chanting "Yeah, oh, yeah, stud," over and over while I finger-fuck him. Soon, my finger is slick with his hot, slimy butt juices. I hear a low moan. Then Boomer screams at me, "SUCK MY ASS, DUDE!"

I scoot down between Boomer's magnificent tree trunks and pry his cheeks open. There's his sweet little asshole. It's clenching and spasming. It's waiting for me to lick it. I mash my face between his boulder-like cheeks and thrust my tongue forward. I dig deep into the sweaty puckers. "Yeeeeeaaaaaaaahhhh!" Boomer grunts with a heavy sigh. He reaches down to grab my head and forces my face inside his butt. I probe deeper with my tongue, licking out all the sweat, crud, and funk from his dirty asshole. My tongue is fluttering, swirling, turning into every nook, every cranny of his fantastic bubble butt.

Then Boomer spins around. His cock is bobbing all over the place. He has a wild sneer on his mouth. His eyes flash at me. "Suck that cock!" he screams. I swallow his cock, opening my throat wide. His hot man meat fills up my feverish cock-sucking mouth. "Yeah!" he screams, grabbing my head and pushing me against his groin with all his might. "Suck my cock! SUCK IT!"

I'm sucking Boomer's cock like crazy. My head is a blur over his spasmodic cock. He's face-fucking me, holding me steady over his thick, turgid man meat. His balls are banging against my chin. His stinking pubes scratch my face. His cock balloons like a huge sausage inside my mouth. I'm gagging, choking on his cock. The fat doorknob-sized head is crushing the back of my throat.

Boomer is screaming, howling wildly. "Do it cocksucker,

yeah do it!" I stick my finger up his hole again. He scream.
again. "Yaaaaaaarrrrrrgh, oh yeah, YEAH!" His loud grunts
punctuate my moans as I suck harder and harder on his
cock. Just as I think he's about to come, he turns me around
and hurls me to the floor. "Gonna pork ya, dude!" he howls.
"Yeah, stud!" I say. I'm on all fours. I stick my ass out at
him, wiggling my butt right in his face. "Fuck me with that
big horse dick!" I yell.

Boomer wrenches my cheeks apart and spits on my spasming hole. A shudder goes all through my body when I feel
his hot spit land right on my butt bud. Then Boomer slaps a
hand on each of my haunches and goes in for the kill. His
blunt cock head rubs against my anxious puckers for a moment. Then he slices right into me. A blood-curdling scream
shoots from my mouth. "ARRRRRRGHHHHH NOOOO-
OOOO AWWWWWW FUUUUUUCKKKKK!"

My fists pound the floor. My mouth twists with pain. My
hole clamps shut. Boomer's cock head springs back. Then he
moves forward again with a harsh grunt. He slaps my ass
and this time my hole pops open and his cock shoots right
inside me. He holds his cock head there for a moment. Then
he shoves it all the way up my ass. I scream again. "OH
GOD, NOOOOOOO NOOOOOOOOOOOOOOOOOOO
OOOOO!"

Tears run down my face. Boomer is fucking my hole raw
now. He pumps in and out, his hands right on my butt, holding me steady. Then he slaps my butt sending shooting
sparks of pain that sear my ass. I buck and heave but he
stays right inside me like a cowboy on a bronco. Boomer
reaches under me and grabs my nipples. He digs his fingernails right into the tips. I howl. "YEEEEEEEOOOOWW-
WWWWWW!" I nearly toss Boomer off. Needle-like pain
sears my nips. But he just keeps on squeezing and pinching
them. Boomer pulls my sore nipples out as far as they will

go. I fist my cock, my mouth wide open, gasping as he pumps harder into my hole. I'm beginning to enjoy the wild fuck.

"Yeah, stud!" I cry. "Pump me, dude. FUCK MY FUCKIN' HOLE!" I want Boomer to fuck me for hours. I want him to shoot his hot load inside me. "Shoot, dude!" I gasp. "Shoot your fuckin' wad!"

Boomer screams at me. "Want me to shoot, dude?"

"Yeah, stud," I moan. "Let 'er rip!"

Boomer's lusty cry bounces off the walls. "YEAH! YEAH! YEAH! FUUUUUUUUCCCCKKKIN' A!"

Boomer plunges right inside me, his cock swelling to outrageous proportions. The head crashes against my prostate. His splooge starts to shoot out, burning my asshole, flowing from my butt down my thighs. My cock is ready to explode. A wild scream burns my throat. "YARRRRRGH! FUCKIN' A! YEAH! YEAH YEAAAAAAHHHHHHHHH! I spunk huge wads all over the floor. Boomer pops his cock from my hole.

"Think ya can come again, stud?" Boomer asks. He grins wickedly, scooping up some come from the floor. He runs a come-dribbling finger across his tongue.

"Fuckin' A!" I say.

"'Cause I wanna feel you shoot a big wad up my asshole!"

Boomer hits the floor. He's on his knees doggy-style, wagging his ass back and forth, just waiting for me to stick my ten proud inches of prime grade-A man cock up his stinking jock wazoo.

Then a sudden thought occurs to me. "Ever been porked before, dude?" I ask Boomer.

He whips his head back, snarling. "Fuck no!" Then he grins. "But I want you to doink me, dude." His face is beaming, his eyes sparkling. "You'll be the first!"

So I have a jock virgin on my hands, huh? I realize his hole must be tighter than hell. I spit on a finger and stick it between his cheeks until the tip scrapes against his hot, raw virgin puckers. I hear him gasp when I prod against the anus ring, which feels rubbery and taut against my finger. I push it in and he screams. Damn! I've never felt an asshole this tight before. It looks like I'm going to have to break it in. "Hold on, dude," I say. "Be right back!"

I go to my locker to find my dildo. Fortunately, it's there. You never know when you're going to need it to break in some tight ass jock virgin's man hole. I grab the tube of lube too, and sprint back to Boomer. He's still on all fours. But I noticed he's shaking with anticipation. Or is it fear?

"Whaddya gonna do, dude?" Boomer asks anxiously.

"Relax, stud," I tell him, slapping his hard buttocks. "Just gonna spread those puckers a bit!"

So I lube up the dildo with half the tube and place the head smack against the entrance to his hole. When Boomer feels the hard cold rubber against his hot flesh he groans, "Ah, fuck, dude. What's that?"

I start laughing. "A dildo, you dildo!" I can't resist smacking his butt again. "Now relax, dude or this'll fuckin' hurt!"

I push the dildo inside him but he cries out again. "Nooooooo, please . . . don't do it, dude!"

"Shut up!" I hiss at him. "You big pussy! Take it like a man!" Boomer immediately stops whimpering so I keep pushing the dildo into his ass until I have it halfway up his butt. Boomer is crying now, moaning, getting used to the dildo stretching him wide open. He gasps and shudders, his mouth wide open, wagging his ass back and forth. "C'mon, suck my dick," I tell him. I scoot in front of Boomer and shove my cock between his lips. The dude obediently slurps over my crank like a pro while I shove the dildo farther up his hole.

Boomer is choking, gagging on my cock, which is all the way down his throat. Then, with one mighty push, I force the dildo all the way up his ass.

"Yarrrrrrrrgh!" Boomer screams, pulling away from my cock. I scoot back and start fucking him with the dildo. "Ah, fuck, ah fuck," he moans. "It hurts dude, it fuckin' hurts!" But after a while he begins smiling and he's moaning with pleasure and not from pain. "Oh yeah, yeah, dude! Play with my ass. Fuck my hole!" A few more minutes of that and he's going besonkers.

"Your cock," Boomer pants. "I want your cock up my ass!" I'm only too happy to oblige my hot jock buddy so I yank out the dildo. It flies across the room and lands with a thud ten feet away. I position myself right behind Boomer. I spread his sweaty buttocks apart and see his asshole twitching lustfully, begging for my cock. I spit on his hole, place the head of my cock against his pucker, and ram right into him.

"YEOOOOOOOOOOOWWWWWWW!" Boomer howls, trying to escape, but I grab his haunches and force him against my groin as my cock sinks up to the hilt. "Oh yeah, dude!" Boomer cries. "It feels so fucking good. Pump me, dude! Pump me hard, stud!"

I pump for hours. His asshole is wider but still tight, sucking around my cock like an anxious mouth, holding me firmly inside his ass.

"Yeah, buddy, yeaaaaaaaaaahhh! Oh man, I wanna feel you come inside me. Shoot your load, dude!"

"Ready for my load?" I hiss at him.

"Fuckin' A!" he yells.

I push forward and my cock smashes against his prostate.

"YEAAHHHHHHHHH!" Boomer screams as my cock erupts, flooding his jock ass with prime grade-A jism. As the last spurt coats his love button, Boomer screams, shooting several sticky wads all over the floor.

"C'mon, dude," I say, slapping Boomer's butt. "Victory party at Coach's!" We shower, dress, and hop into Boomer's car. Fuck! You know we'll have an orgy!

The Bird

Erastes

———

I'd had him hanging on my wall for longer than I can remember. It's an early poster, tatty and ripped around the edges. The uniform has changed a few times since I bought that poster. The walls have changed too, from the spaceship wallpaper of my parents' house to the peeling paint of the first apartment I owned to the impeccable interior decor of my much loved loft space in the center of town. But he remains himself, frozen in time, youthful and oh so hot.

Mike "The Bird" Starling.

He was the reason I got into baseball, pro baseball that is. I'd first seen a picture of him in a magazine when I was eleven, when he signed to the major league, and he took my breath away. He'd have been about my age back then and coming up to his prime. I didn't understand why I found him so compelling, not when I was that young, but I sure did now. He's standing proud in the poster, with his bat over his shoulder, and he's smiling at the cameraman like he wants him. His raven-black hair is shining in the sun and his uniform clings to his body, accentuating his wide shoulders, his long powerful legs, and a bulge that clearly calls the eye, obvious for its lack of a protective cup.

For years I'd followed his career, going to his games when I could, reading about them when I couldn't. I saw him rise, shine at the top for a while, then inevitably, as must we all, he began to slide down. Not for him the celebrity life and opening supermarkets. Not for him retirement and approbation of household implements. He was content to play, and only that.

But *he* was the reason I got into the sport. I wanted to meet him, I wanted to play like him. I wanted to *be* him. Later on, when I realized that guys floated my boats and not girls, I *wanted* him.

A lot of work, a helluva lot of work made my baseball dreams come true, and the day I signed my first professional contract I silently thanked The Bird for helping me get where I was. I was known and recognized wherever I went, too. Which is why I got roped into the charity game. It wouldn't do my blossoming career any good at all to have refused to play, so I agreed. I wasn't particularly looking forward to it; there never seemed to be any logic as to whom they invited, and butter-fingered catchers from the lowest leagues were often found attempting to field balls traveling at ninety miles an hour from the scorching pitchers.

Imagine my elation, then, when I got the list of the players involved in the game. *Yes,* I thought, as my eyes scanned down the list. *The usual mix of power hitters and also-rans.* But there were a few veterans too. And there, nearly at the end of the page was the name that made my heart jump. Mike Starling. I was finally going to meet the man I'd been lusting over for as long as I could remember.

I felt as nervous as the first time I'd played for money when I entered the grounds that morning. Kyle, a teammate of mine, had been invited too, and we met up at the conference breakfast.

Typical of him, Kyle took all the junket hype of reporters and agents and razzmatazz in his laconic Texan stride. "Food looks good," he said, heading for the buffet table. I was scanning the room. I mentally tagged about eight guys I knew well, the rest I recognized but didn't know to speak to, and then I found him. There he was. The Bird. Sitting with a woman reporter on the far side of the room. Whatever he was saying was making a hit with the woman, as she was clearly flirting with him. My heart sank, as did the very little hope I had been harboring that he might cast an eye in my direction. I gave myself a mental kick up the ass. *So what, he's not going to be bowled over by your pretty face and cute butt cheeks, Tommy. But he's still Mike Starling and you're in the same room as him. So go and say hi!*

I waited until the reporter had shaken his hand and left him, and then I stepped up and introduced myself.

"Tomas Sprague?" My stomach gave a jolt as he took my hand, and my cock twitched at the warm dark rumble of his voice. "You're doing well." Up close I could see the years on him: there were lines, deep lines in his forehead, and crinkles around his eyes and mouth. It spoke of a face that smiled a lot. And he was smiling at me, and he was still holding my hand. His was warm and callused and I allowed mine to move a little in his, just to raise my hopes a bit. He didn't pull away and the warmth did not go out of his dark brown eyes, and my hope and my cock surged to life. His hair had a fine dusting of gray, but it suited him. I felt like a kid again, crushed under the weight of hero worship. But he put me at my ease and I found him so easy to talk to that I almost forgot to fantasize about what lay beneath that plaid shirt and jeans; what his body would be like, whether he had chest hair, and whether that was going gray, too.

We talked for a while, until my agent appeared and dragged me off for photo calls and interviews. I got through it by allowing myself to finally give in to those fantasies about The Bird, and allowed myself to hope that my final question to him, one he'd left unanswered, meant something more . . .

I'm not going to talk about the game, as it wasn't the main event of the day as far as I was concerned. Once I got into position, the play took over and although I stole a look at The Bird from time to time, especially when he was up at the plate, I did my job and yes we lost, but we tried. Their pitcher was on top of his game and our batting frankly sucked. But it was a charity match and we had a lot of fun, too. It was a great atmosphere and when we headed down the tunnel to the changing rooms, we'd already put the game behind us—aside from some good natured leg-pulling—and were looking forward to the evening to come.

Another excellent reason for a gay man to get into baseball is the changing rooms. Naked men. Wet naked men. Communal showers. Communal baths. Hot tubs. It's gay nirvana. And in spite of the fact that only a tiny fraction of gay players have ever admitted it to the media, they are around, thank the Lord. There's action to be had, that's for sure. There's something about hot running water and tight, toned bodies that I'll never get tired of. Hell, once I get past my best, perhaps I'll continue down the leagues too, just so I can still feast my eyes on all that male beauty.

I decided to get into the tub before anyone else. My cock has a mind of its own and I didn't want to be buck naked with a hard-on wandering around the locker area. Kyle joined me and started reliving the game and when Mike appeared at the edge of tub, naked as the day he was born, I was glad I was clothed by warm, bubbling water.

He was a sight to behold. He was brown all over, no white anywhere. His chest was massive, his arms tightly muscled. He'd looked after himself. Some of the other veterans out on the field had let themselves go, but not Mike. His stomach was still flat, and if the washboard wasn't quite as it was, it was still impressive. He had no hair on his chest, but a dark line started just below his navel and led down to a thick dark, cut cock. I tried not to stare but it was a tough call.

"Room for one more?" he asked, and stepped down into the water. He sat opposite me and didn't join in the conversation. He just sat there, watching me, as if he knew that my cock was waving around underwater, as if he knew that I was getting off just looking at him.

I began to wonder if Kyle was ever going to go, and so I leaned back, rested my arms on the edge of the tub, tipped my head back a little, and closed my eyes. I'd often fallen asleep in the tub—had been ribbed for it many a time—and so I guessed that Kyle would fall for it. He rambled on for a while, some long boring story about what his grandma had said after his first professional outing, and after a few minutes I wondered if my ruse was going to work.

Mike showed no sign of leaving, I was pleased to note, and eventually Kyle said, "Well, I'm startin' to prune up here. Nice to have met ya, Starlin'. When Sleepin' Beauty wakes up, tell him I'll see him tomorrow."

"I'll do that." Mike's voice was a warm rumble, and the splashing that followed indicated that Kyle had finally gone. I opened my eyes slowly to find Mike still smiling at me, his eyes crinkled at the edges. He looked even more delicious when wet, his black hair plastered to his scalp, forming tendrils around his neck. "They've all gone. I had a feeling you weren't asleep." He shifted, and slid along the bench, causing a wave to surge toward me. "As to your earlier question," he said, as he settled himself next to me, "I think you know exactly why I didn't marry." His hand was on my thigh then, kneading and traveling north, answering every question I might have wanted to ask him. "But as you obviously know, it's all right being gay in private, but it's professional suicide in public."

I nodded, but that's all I wanted to do. I didn't want to

talk. Not now. I reached out and pulled him to me, my heart thudding. *It's Mike Starling and he's fucking gay . . .* I didn't know what I'd done to deserve this, but there was no way I was going to waste it on small talk.

A hot tub kiss is something everyone should do. The water adds a dimension of sensuality, makes everything somehow sexier; perhaps it's the effect of having every part of your skin touched at once. The water lapped around us as our mouths met and Mike's arms slid around me. There was that small awkward moment while we adjusted and then he had me, his tongue darting into my mouth, taking control. I'm not a small man, but I felt like he dwarfed me. His arms crushed me in a bear hug and I loved being crushed, although I missed his hand on my thigh.

For a long minute he kissed me and it was a hard, brutal, dominating kiss. He took my mouth by storm, his tongue plundering and claiming. It was all I could do to kiss him back; there's no way I could have stopped that kiss, even if I'd wanted to. Then he broke, and he was as out of breath as I was. "I want you," he growled in my ear. "I want to fill you so full of my dick you'll be tasting me for days."

I still couldn't believe it; it was a dream come true but as horny as I was, and as much as I wanted him to fuck me senseless, I had to be careful.

"Not here," I muttered, groping under the water to find his cock deliciously hard. "Cubicle."

"Sensible Tomas," he chuckled and stood up, leaving me gasping at the fabulous sight of the water cascading down his back and over the firmest, roundest butt I could have imagined. I wanted to bury my face in that crack and rim him until he came from that alone. He stopped at his locker to get a condom and as I locked the door behind us, I turned to him.

Mike reached for me but I dropped to my knees before he could kiss me again. I wanted that cock and I wanted that ass, mostly the ass—I make no excuses for being an ass man. But first, an appetizer. When I licked at the head of his cock he groaned, so I worked him over with my tongue, moving around the head down the shaft, using my teeth gently as I lapped and sucked my way down. While I licked, my hands alternated between massaging his balls, huge and heavy, and his ass cheeks. When the muscles tightened they were like steel. Not bad at all, for a middle-aged guy.

"Suck my balls," he ordered, and he raised one leg up onto the bench to give me better access. I wriggled round, only too happy to fill my mouth with his nuts and swallowed them down, one at a time. While I sucked and licked he wanked himself, a few short strokes at a time, with encouraging grunts of pleasure, the fingers of his other hand tangled in my hair.

I was just considering getting him to turn round so I could pull apart those magnificent ass cheeks and lick his hole until he screamed, when he said, "Enough," and pulled me up from the floor. He handled me as if I were a ninety-pound weakling and I found to my surprise that I loved his rough dominance and impatience. There wasn't enough room for me to get down on my hands and knees so I knelt on the bench, bracing my arms against the cool white tiles.

"Such a pretty ass," he said. He ran his hands down my back and cupped my ass cheeks in his palms. His hands were rough and huge. "Doesn't seem possible it'll take all I've got to give it."

"It wants it though," I muttered. "Fuck me, Mike."

"Say it again," he growled, pushing his fingers between my cheeks and rubbing at my hole, which made me yelp with want.

"Fuck me, now. Please, Mike . . ." I was completely under his control; I never thought I'd be a needy, grabby little bottom.

"As you wish," he said. I heard him put the condom on, then his hands were back on my ass and he was pushing slippery fingers inside my hole. The relief was delicious and I pushed my legs farther apart—I liked my balls to swing when I was fucked. I was glad I had, too. When his cock pushed against my entrance it felt as big as a beer can and I had a momentary panic. I'd never taken anything that size before. "Easy," he said, "breathe out," as if I were a virgin who needed instruction. I pushed back to ease him in and as his thatch pressed against my ass I realized he was in and I felt amazing. "Hot and tight," he said, shifting a little. "Perfect." He moved an inch out and then back, setting off fireworks of pain and pleasure that I thought I'd never have enough of. Inch by inch he worked, pulling out then pushing in, all the time kissing the back of my neck and shoulders, muttering the whole time. I'd never been with a man who talked a lot before and I thought it would be embarrassing, but with Mike it was wonderfully arousing. "Yes," he'd say, "yes, yes, yes," over and over almost as if he were talking to himself. But by his talk I found that he liked to take it slow and to almost pull the head of his cock out of my ass before plunging back again, faster than he'd pulled out.

He reached forward and took hold of my cock and like a kid, I lost it at the touch of his callused hand. I came hard and noisily and I felt like my head was coming off, my come splattering the tiles and wooden bench. He laughed, grabbed me by the hips, and started to slam into me, his cock going farther in me than anyone had been before. We were both gasping for breath when he grunted a final "Oh yeah" and pulled me back to him. He rocked his hips gently a few last times as his orgasm slowed him down.

"I'm getting too old for this shit," he said, giving me a final kiss as he pulled out, leaving my ass feeling emptier than it ever had been. "Next time we need to find a bed." All I

Erastes

could do was grin like a fool. *Next time.* I wondered if I was going to walk like John Wayne from now on. I'd never felt so well fucked.

That night in bed, I smiled up at his poster on the wall, all warm and horny with the memory of a blissful afternoon. Yes, The Bird had been beautiful back then, but I closed my eyes and the image of the poster-perfect Mike was replaced by the mature man I'd been with that afternoon. There was no comparison; experience and maturity were far better than just another twink fuck. My hands tingled as I recalled his skin and the rough feel of his stubble against my cheek. As I drifted off, my fingers curled around my cock and I went to sleep, knowing that one day the young Starling would be watching the older Starling fuck me into the mattress, and that the next hand on my cock would be his.

188

Phenom

Todd Gregory

━━━━━

The arms around me had hit a grand slam tonight.

It didn't matter; we lost the game anyway. But I didn't care. I've never really cared much about baseball. In fact, I'd never been to a game until our local team signed Billy Chastain. As soon as I saw him being interviewed on the local news, I knew I was going to start going to games. It's not that I don't like baseball, I just never cared enough to go. But all it took was one look at Billy Chastain, and I was sold.

The interview had been one of those special pieces. He'd been a high school star, played in college a couple of years, and then one year in the minors, where he'd been a force to be reckoned with—with an amazing batting average and some outstanding play at third base—he'd been called up to the majors for this new season, and everyone was talking about him. I just stared at the television screen.

Sure, he was young, but he was also composed, well spoken, and seemed mature for his age. He was also drop-dead gorgeous. He had thick bluish-black hair, olive skin, and the most amazing green eyes. They showed clips of him fielding and batting, and then came the part that I wished I'd recorded: they showed him lifting weights. In the earlier shots, it was apparent he had a nice build—he seemed tall and lanky, almost a little raw-boned—but once they cut to the shots of him in the weight room, I was sold. His body was ripped as he moved from machine to machine in his white muscle shirt and long shorts, his dark hair damp with sweat. As his workout progressed and his muscles became more and more pumped, more and more defined, I could feel my cock starting to stir in my pants. And then they closed the segment with a shot of him pulling the tank top over his head and wiping his damp face with it. I gasped. His hairless torso was slick with sweat, his abs were perfect, and his pecs round and beautiful, with the most amazing half-dollar sized nipples that I wanted to get my lips around.

I bought tickets and started going to every home game.

Our team sucked, to be frank, and it was soon apparent that there was no World Series or even division pennant in our future that year. But Billy was a great player and everyone was talking about him. He was leading the division in hits and had one of the highest batting averages in all of baseball. He made the cover of *Sports Illustrated* with the headline PHENOM, his beautiful face smiling out at people on newsstands all over the country. There were several shots of him without a shirt on—shots I had scanned into my computer, enlarged, and printed out for framing. I made sure my seats were always behind third base, so I could get as great a view of him as humanly possible in his tight white pants that showed every curve and muscle of his legs—and that amazingly round hard ass I thought about when I closed my eyes and masturbated. Every so often he would look up into the stands and smile, saluting us with a wave.

As much as I wanted to believe the smile and the wave were for me, I knew better.

Tonight's game was the last of the regular season, and our record ensured it was our last game of 2006. The Red Sox were on their way to the play-offs, and we had only taken two games off them all season. We were beaten 10–4. All four runs came from Billy's bat—a grand slam on his first pitch with the bases loaded. The stadium was half-empty, as most of our fans had given up on the team at the midway point of the season. But not me. As long as there was a chance to see Billy swing his bat, I was there. And when he circled the bases he paused briefly at third, looked up to the crowd, and waved at us.

I thought about waiting for the team after the game, seeing if I could get Billy to sign my program, but decided against it. I knew I was more than a little obsessed with him; my friends liked to call me his stalker. They were just giving me shit, but there was a fine line there I was afraid to cross, so instead I went to my car and drove to a little gay bar close to the stadium. It was one of those places you went to meet friends for a beer or a drink; not one of the places you went to do recreational drugs, dance to music played at ear-splitting levels with your shirt off, and look for Mr. Right Now. The bar was pretty empty when I got there; it was usually only crowded during happy hour. The drinks were cheap but strong. A lot of guys met their friends there to get a nice cheap buzz going before they moved on to other bars in their eternal quest for tonight's orgasm. The bartender was a nice-looking man in his mid-forties who popped the top off a bottle of Bud Light when he saw me come in and place it on a napkin at the bar. I grinned my thanks and took a long pull. The television hanging from the ceiling behind the bar was playing a rerun of *Will & Grace* on Lifetime. There were only two other people in the bar, shooting pool in the back area.

I was on my second beer, watching as Grace decided for the thousandth time that her gay best friend was more important to her than any straight man could be—which always struck me as kind of tragic, sad, and twisted rather than uplifting—when the door opened. I didn't turn and look to see who was coming in; I didn't care, and I wasn't looking to get laid. I was on my second and final beer before heading home, and I preferred to be lost in my thoughts about Billy and how he looked in those tight white pants rather than doing the shall-we-go-to-my-place-and-fuck tango with a stranger. It had been a long day, and I was looking forward to sleeping in tomorrow morning.

I took another swig and almost fell off my bar stool when the person who'd walked in stepped up to the bar a couple of stools down from me.

I'd recognize Billy Chastain anywhere.

He was wearing a sleeveless navy blue T-shirt with the words CREW CUT WRESTLING written in yellow across the front and the image of two men wrestling in singlets. His jeans rode low on his hips, and as he leaned forward on the bar to show his ID to the bartender his shirt crept up in the back and the jeans rode down a little farther, exposing the red waistband of his tight gray Calvin Klein underwear. The way he was standing showed off that oh-so-perfectly round ass to anyone who wanted to look at it. My mouth went dry and I took another swig of my beer as the bartender handed him a bottle of Bud Light. He stood back up and took a drink. He saw me out of the corner of his eye and turned to look at me, giving me a friendly nod as he put the bottle back down.

I turned my eyes back to the television screen as fast as I could. Another episode of *Will & Grace* was starting. My heart started pounding as he moved down the bar toward me. "I know it's bad form to say this," he said, in the husky voice I'd heard on television a million times but still made the hair on my arms stand up, "but I really *hate* that show. In the real world, a gay man would have told Grace years earlier, 'You're single because you're a neurotic self-absorbed cunt who's completely unlovable with no redeeming qualities whatsoever. Why would any man want you?'"

I laughed. I'd thought the same thing any number of times. I turned and looked at him, managing to remain calm on the outside while inside I felt like I was going to turn into a pool of jelly at any second. "Will's no better than she is."

He nodded. "He's a lawyer in New York with a nice body, a gorgeous apartment, and he's kind of handsome—and he'd rather hang out with that crazy bitch instead of getting laid, yet he can't figure out why he's single? How the hell did he get through law school if he's that stupid?"

I tapped my beer bottle against his. "Exactly."

He tilted his head to one side and squinted a bit. "You know, you look familiar."

"Do I?" I struggled to keep my voice from squeaking. "Well, I know who you are. Billy Chastain, the phenom."

He laughed. "Yeah, that's me." He took another drink from the beer. "Man, this beer is good. I don't drink while I'm in training, but the season is now officially over, and man, does this taste great." He looked at me again. "I know who you are. You've been to almost all of our home games. You sit up behind third base, right?"

"Guilty as charged."

"Big baseball fan?" He grinned, and I could feel my cock stir in my jeans.

"Not really." I grinned back at him. "More of a big Billy Chastain fan."

"Really?" He stepped closer to me, and put his hand on the inside of my leg. I felt an electric shock that went straight to my balls, and my cock was now achingly hard. He licked his lips. "How big?" He moved his hand into my crotch and lifted his eyebrows, his eyes getting wider. "Nice."

This can't be happening, I thought. *This has to be one of the best wet dreams ever.*

"You got any beer back at your place?" He lightly brushed his shoulder against mine.

"Um, yeah."

He gave my cock a squeeze and I thought I might come right there in my pants. "Mind if we go back there?" He winked at me. "You got a car? I take cabs."

"Yeah."

"You up for it?"

I finished my beer in one gulp. "Sure."

All the way to my apartment, he played with my cock. It was hard for me to focus on driving. We made small talk, me barely able to get out more than two words at a time. I parked and we walked up the flight of stairs to my front door. My hands shook as I unlocked it. Once we were inside with the door closed behind us, he grabbed me and pulled me to him, our bodies pushed tightly together as he tilted his head down, pressing his mouth onto mine. I sucked on his tongue and his hands came down behind me and squeezed my ass. My cock was aching, and I put my hands on his chest. I pinched one of his nipples and he moaned. He tilted his head back as I kept pinching, not letting go of his erect nipple. "Man," he breathed, "that drives me crazy."

I slid my hands down and pulled his shirt up. He raised his arms, his lats spreading like wings as the shirt came up and over his head. He dropped his shirt to the floor and I kissed him at the base of his throat, moving my mouth down to his left nipple. As I sucked on it, I pinched the other. He moaned and started thrusting his crotch forward. A little wet spot appeared on the front of his pants. I didn't let up, sucking and licking and sometimes playing with his nipple with my tongue. He leaned back against the door, his head back, his eyes half-closed. I traced my tongue to the center of his chest, and then slowly slid it down to his navel. I undid his pants. They dropped to his ankles and I put my mouth on his hard cock through the underwear. My mouth played with the head of his cock until he put both hands under my arms and pulled me up to my feet.

Billy smiled and pulled my shirt over my head, tweaking both of my nipples before putting his mouth on my right one. He toyed with it, played with it—I couldn't believe how good it felt—and then he too was sliding his tongue down my torso, undoing my pants and pulling my underwear down. My cock sprang free. He looked up at me and smiled. "That's a beauty, man," he said, before putting his mouth on it.

I moaned as he tongued the underside of my cock and licked my balls. I still couldn't believe it was happening. *Billy Chastain was sucking my cock—no one was going to believe this.*

He stood up and smiled, putting his arms around me and pulling me close to him. He kissed my ear then knelt down, picking me up. I wrapped my legs around his waist and kissed his neck. He stepped out of his pants and carried me through the living room into the bedroom, the whole time sucking on my earlobe while I ground my cock against his rock-hard stomach. He gently set me down on the bed and took off my shoes, then pulled my pants and underwear off, dropping them to the floor. I sat up on my elbows, watching as he took off his shoes and socks, then his underwear. His cock was long, thick, and hard, and bent a little to the left. He had trimmed his pubic hair and his balls were shaved. He smiled then climbed onto the bed next to me. I turned and we kissed again, his tongue coming into my mouth while I reached down and put my hand on his cock. He pulled me on top of him, our cocks grinding together as we kissed. His body felt amazing against mine, his skin soft yet hard at the same time, the power of his muscles radiating through his skin.

"I want you to fuck me," he breathed into my ear.

Oh God.

I reached into my bedside table and pulled out a condom, opening the package with my teeth. I sat back on my knees while I slipped the condom on, then squirted some lube onto it. I put some lube on my fingers, sliding them into the crack of his ass until I found what I was looking for, and started spreading it around. His eyes closed. "Just do it, man," he breathed, spreading his legs farther and tilting his pelvis up.

I started slowly, placing the tip of my cock against his hole, gently applying a little pressure until the head went in. He tensed for a second, then relaxed. I went in a bit more, slowly, working my way in as he relaxed and got used to me being inside him. When I finally pushed all the way in, he gasped, tensed, and relaxed; his eyes opened wide, he grinned at me. "Wow, that feels amazing."

I started moving, slowly, sliding in and back out, then back in. With each deep thrust his beautiful body shivered and quivered, moans escaping his lips as I worked his ass, reaching up every once in a while to tweak his nipples, which obviously drove him insane. As I felt my orgasm rising within me I pounded faster and deeper and harder, and finally as my come started to build, he shouted out "Fuck! FUCK! FUCK!" and his entire body shook as he started shooting his own load. The sight of him drenching his chest with his come got me pushing harder and I screamed out as my entire body convulsed, my own load shooting into the condom.

I collapsed on top of him, my cock still inside him.

He kissed the top of my head. "That was amazing."

"Uh huh."

We lay like that for a few minutes, my ear pressed against his rib cage, listening to his racing heartbeat and his breathing.

Finally I sat up and pulled off the condom, dropping it into the trash. "Let me get you a towel. Or do you want to shower?"

"Can I shower in the morning?"

I smiled. "Oh, that can be arranged." I tossed him a towel and he wiped his chest. He tossed it back to me and I wiped my crotch down before getting back into the bed. He put his arms around me.

"Thank you," he said, kissing me on the neck again and nuzzling against my throat. "That was amazing."

"Yes, you were," I replied.

He smiled and yawned. "Do you mind if we sleep a little? I'm kind of worn out—the game and all." He winked at me. "And all."

"Sure."

He turned onto his side and I curled into him, kissing him good night on the mouth. He placed his head on the pillow as I turned off the lights. Within a few seconds he was breathing regularly.

I snuggled up against him and put my head on top of his arm. We fit together perfectly. I could lie like this forever. My friends weren't going to believe this—but then, I wasn't sure I did either.

It might just be a one-nighter; that was fine with me. I wasn't going to get ahead of myself and make plans for our future together or anything. But he wasn't leaving my place in the morning until I'd seen that big dick shoot another load all over him.

And on that note, I finally fell asleep.

Team Player

Brian Centrone

——

"It's the top of the ninth. Troy Rodriguez has just come up to bat. This is the Houston Ballers' last chance to turn this game around. Will he be able to do it, Chuck?"

"I don't know, Barry. Troy's had a tough season this year. He hasn't been living up to the manager's expectations. A strikeout from him could mean a trade."

"What a change in Rodriguez's playing since he was first signed to the Ballers. He was this team's golden boy."

"That was before he became the playboy he is today. I think all his—how should we say it, the kids at home might be listening—extracurricular activities have really affected his game. I mean, here we had a top player who's arguably in baseball's worst slump?"

"I couldn't agree with you more, Chuck. Maybe if Troy spent more time playing on the field than playing the field, he might have led his team to the championship this year instead of the doghouse."

"That's a harsh statement, Barry."

"Well, it has to be said."

"There he goes, he's at the plate. Look at that stance; he seems nervous."

"I'd be nervous, too, if this was my last chance."

"Here comes the ball . . . and . . . ohhh . . . strike one."

"Things are not looking good for our boy Troy out there. Two more misses and it's *hasta la vista* for Rodriguez."

"He's shuffling about. Seems like he can't find a good stance."

"I bet he's just buying time. He knows if he messes this up, that's it for him. He's outta here for good."

"Well, here's his chance for redemption. It's the second pitch . . . and . . . strike two! He's behind in the count—exactly where he doesn't want to be right now!"

"One more and he's gone . . ."

"But you know, Barry, the Ballers aren't totally at loss with Troy. Their new hitter, Joey Dumbfell, is really proving himself."

"I'm sure Troy must be feeling the choke with that one. His replacement's already starting to sweep him up and out."

"Here's the last pitch, we'll find out soon enough . . . and he's caught looking—that's it! It's over, Rodriguez lost the game and, most likely, his position with the Houston Ballers."

"The devastation that must be going on right now, not only from our boy Troy, but the whole team, not to mention the coach and manager."

"I'd hate to be in that locker room tonight."

"You said it, Chuck."

Troy Rodriguez entered the Houston Ballers' locker room with his head down and his guard up. He knew this day was coming, and now that it had finally arrived, he braced himself for the out lash about to come his way.

"Fucking twat, you lost us the chance at the goddamn championship, Rodriguez!" Samson Mills, the third baseman, slammed the locker door shut so hard it bounced back open.

"If you stopped sticking your dick in every cunt that walked by you and put more time into your game, we wouldn't be the laughingstock of the fucking league."

A towel flew across the room, landing at Troy's feet. He looked up to see who had thrown it. Michael Longbow, the team's starting pitcher, stood at the far end of the room, wearing just his jockstrap. "Use it to wipe up the blood when they're fucking done with you, Rodriguez. You know how I hate a messy locker room."

Troy gazed around to see what the other guys were up to, and more precisely, to see where his next attack would come from. Most of the lads were sulking instead of fuming, choosing to strip from their blue and gray uniforms and shower and change rather than take their wrath out on Troy.

As he stood back from the crowd, Troy noticed one player who seemed totally unfazed by the group's mood. Joey Dumbfell was going about his business of peeling off his snug new uniform with the merriest of attitudes.

Troy could only imagine the bliss that was going through the newbie's mind. Why the fuck wouldn't he be happy? He had come to replace the failing star hitter and tonight, he finally succeeded. Troy would be out by morning and Dumbfell would be the Ballers' next big thing.

"All right boys, listen up," Coach McNara whizzed by. "I know this is a major letdown both personally and professionally, but you can't let this get to you." Coach placed his foot on one of the benches in the middle of the room and leaned on his propped-up knee as he continued his sermon. "There'll be some big changes being made to the team over the next few days"—his eyes that had been roaming the crowd now rested on Troy—"and I want you all to be assured that change brings a better season for the Ballers! Now finish getting ready, have a good rest, and I'll see you all tomorrow for practice."

Coach headed out, stopping by Troy. "In my office when you're dressed."

Troy nodded his head, and when Coach had left, descended farther into the locker room.

He sighed deeply as he straddled the bench outside his locker, inhaling the musty, damp, and sweaty scents that clung for dear life to the air in the locker room. It was a familiar smell, one that Troy found both repulsive and comforting, and now he would most likely never get to smell it again.

It was his fault and he knew it. There was no one else to blame but himself. Troy had let his concentration slip. He wasn't training as hard anymore. Maybe he had gotten caught up in all the glory of being the team's golden bat. He had ignored the comments about him becoming cocky, flippant, arrogant. And when the press first started in about the various girls he was bedding, he found it humorous. What could he do? He was young and horny. He needed a lot of release from the pressures of playing professional baseball and there never seemed a shortage of chicks who were willing to help him out. Only now, it became part of the problem and was half the reason he was getting traded or sacked or whatever the higher ups had in store for him.

Rubbing his face with both hands, Troy sighed deeply before taking a look around the locker room. He was alone. Standing up, he began to strip out of his uniform, kicking off his cleats first, then yanking off his top, followed by sliding down his snug pants, his socks and stirrups coming off with them. Troy kicked at the pile of clothes before plopping back down on the hard wooden bench in only his jockstrap.

"Fuck," he shouted, banging his fist against the bench. Every muscle in his built body twitched. He was so angry with himself, with the whole situation. He banged the bench again before leaning back on it for a rest.

Troy studied the drop ceiling as he thought more about what had led him to this day. He focused on some dark brown stains that spread across a few of the tiles. They were the same color as his nipples, now grown hard from the chill in the room. Remembering the first time he ever lay down on this bench, Troy ran a hand up his naturally bronzed body, feeling every cut of his abs before reaching his nipple. He tweaked it a few times, the feeling arousing him.

When Troy first joined the Ballers, he found the atmosphere in the locker room electrified with sexual tension. Though he had been playing sports since he was a little boy, and every locker room he'd ever been in from adolescence to college had the same bustling tension, the Ballers' felt even more heightened. At first Troy couldn't figure out why and then one day it came to him. It was the grown men, fully aware and fully capable sexually.

He was so eager in those days to be liked, considered part of the team, that he'd do just about anything to fit in. Being so young and willing to please . . . Oh, God, did he remember. He remembered all of it, no matter how hard he tried to forget and put it past him. Every attempt to push it away brought him closer to it and instead of facing it, he pushed harder to get away from it. But he couldn't. He knew that now. He knew a lot of things now. Worse was that the memories still got to him, still turned him on, just as they were now while he lay on the bench, his free hand inching its way to his excited cock without him even realizing it.

Troy shut his eyes as his strong grip took hold of his own bat. It throbbed in his hand and he applied more pressure to satisfy it. He wanted to free it from the trap of his jockstrap and jerk his dark meat furiously.

He should do it; he needed the release.

Pinching his nipple harder, Troy let a soft moan escape his pouty lips. In one swift move, he freed his cock and pumped fast and hard. His breathing was heavy and his chest rose and fell with each intake and exhalation of breath.

He knew he wouldn't last long. His balls were already starting to pull up. He needed this. He needed it so much.

"Well, well, well, what do we have here?"

Troy shot up like a pole vault, his hands ripped from his body and any semblance of orgasm lost.

"Pulling your pud in the locker room again, Troy?" Mills laughed. "I didn't know you still did that."

"I don't," Troy spit out, trying to adjust his position on the bench while stuffing his now soft cock back into his jock-strap.

"That's not what it looks like to us," Longbow chimed in, coming around the corner in just a towel. He was still wet from the showers.

Mills, who was totally in the buff, walked in front of Troy.

"I thought you guys had gone." Troy averted his eyes from Mills's dangling package.

"We were just in the shower getting all nice and clean while you were getting down and dirty." Mills clutched his cock and pulled on it for emphasis.

"I don't think he was getting as dirty as he could, or used to," Longbow winked.

"I don't know what you're talking about." Troy was antsy to get out of the room and more so to get on some clothes. He wasn't sure if he should attempt to make a move or not. He desperately wanted to bolt, but did everything he could to play it cool until he saw an opportunity to escape.

"I think you do," Longbow egged on.

"Come on, Troy, for old times' sake," Mills cooed. "Just like when we were starting out."

"I said I don't know what you're talking about." Troy continued to look away, focusing his gaze on nothing in the distance.

"Don't tell us you don't remember?" Longbow chipped in, coming around the other side of Troy and placing his knee on the bench, his towel spreading open over this muscular thigh.

"How could you forget?" Mills traded grins with his pal. "You loved it when we spit-roasted you."

"Fuck off, Mills!" Troy snapped, jumping up to take on his teammate. He'd had enough. If he didn't act now, he knew he'd find himself in a situation he no longer wanted any part of.

"Now, now, Troy, let's not get testy," Longbow soothed. "We all know you're about to get the sack for sucking on the field. So before you do, why not have a suck in the locker room?"

The players chuckled.

"Yeah, Troy boy. Why not go out with a bang?!"

"A gang bang," Longbow threw in.

"Ooooohhh." Mills and Longbow high-fived each other like a couple of middle schoolers.

"I told you to fuck off." Troy positioned himself, ready for a fight. He stared Mills dead in the eyes, fist raring to go.

"Whoa, whoa. Hold up here, Troy boy," Mills stopped laughing. "We're just being friendly, that's all. We miss playing with you. Isn't that right, Michael?"

"That's right," Longbow agreed, shaking his head. "There was no better piece of ass on this team." He came up behind Troy and grabbed hold of him, pulling the hitter back.

Troy swung out, trying to free himself, but Longbow tightened his hold.

"Sit him down," Mills ordered.

Longbow did as instructed, forcing Troy down on the bench. Mills came up close, his stiffening cock in front of Troy's face. "Suck it!"

"You suck it," Troy spat out, and with a quick move, pushed back against Longbow enough to raise his leg and kick Mills with his foot. The force sent both players rattling against the lockers.

"Big mistake," Mills forced out, attempting to gain control of his breath.

"For you two, that is." Troy retrieved a bat from the corner of the room. "Now if you don't get the fuck out of here, I'll show you just how well I can still hit balls."

The players traded looks. Stumbling with their balance, the two grabbed at some clothes in their open lockers and staggered out without another peep.

When they were gone, Troy dropped the bat and fell onto the bench in tears. He was in total fear of what had just happened. Not so much of being hurt by Mills and Longbow, but of the emotions and desires that were aroused in him. Troy's cock was rigid and no matter how he tried to pass it off as the adrenaline pumping through from the attack, he really knew it was from Mills's pole poking in his face.

"Are you okay?" A voice asked.

Troy turned around to find Joey Dumbfell approaching him carefully.

"What do you want?" Troy bellowed at Joey.

Joey was standing right in front of him in only a towel. He had just come out of the showers and, despite the towel's efforts, was still wet. Droplets of water streaked down his baby face. The boy was only nineteen and had been picked up off his high school team. The other men used to joke that Joey was still a virgin, something the kid never confirmed nor denied, just laughed it off in the good nature the jab was presented.

"I just wanted to say I'm sorry."

"For what?" Troy stiffened up. Had Joey been witness to what had just happened between him and the guys?

"I didn't sign on to take your place. That wasn't part of the deal. I had tons of teams clamoring for me to sign with them."

He exhaled in relief. "So why'd you pick this one?" Troy watched the floor in fear that his eyes might give something away.

"Because of you."

"Me?!" Troy looked up at Joey and noticed how brilliant his blue eyes were. They beamed with excitement.

"You were like my idol. I wanted to be you. That's how I got to be so good at playing ball." He smiled.

"How do you feel now that you've out-mastered me?" His fear of being found out was replaced by bitterness. Joey's soppy confession was churning his stomach. He put aside the thought of the guys. The fact that he was about to be let go from the team because of this kid came rushing back to the surface with a force surely capable of knocking Mills and Longbow out.

"I've not out-mastered you, and I'm sure Coach doesn't think so, either."

"Since he's about to fire me, I highly doubt that."

"He's not going to fire you. I wouldn't."

"Oh? And why not?" Troy wondered if the kid was trying to annoy him on purpose.

"'Cause you're hot."

Troy stared at Joey in disbelief, and for the first time during their talk, realized that his face was level with Joey's towel-clad crotch, which was now tenting the thick, white, soft fabric.

"Ah, look, kid, I don't know what you're thinking, but you better stop."

"I'm not thinking, I'm acting. Don't you ever want to act on your feelings, Troy? Aren't you tired of fucking around with girls because you won't allow yourself another guy?"

"Now that's going too far."

"Just give in to it. You know you want to." Joey dropped his towel, freeing his rigid cock. It pointed right at Troy as if accusing him of a crime he hadn't yet committed.

"I may swing bats, kid, but I don't clean 'em." Troy tried to stay calm. Had Joey actually been witness to what happened after all? Were all three teammates in some sort of game together?

"Then by all means, grab hold . . ." Joey moved in closer, his fat, young, veiny cock inching toward Troy's full lips.

Troy swung his hand to slap Joey's meat away, but before he could even get a hit in, the newbie grabbed hold of Troy's arm.

The two players locked eyes, Joey's full of lust, Troy's full of fear, and as they continued to stare, Joey gently guided Troy's hand to his bat and balls, which Troy took hold of freely.

Joey moaned, relaxing his body.

Troy looked from Joey's eyes to his cock: the young flesh stretched over the engorged muscle: the low-hanging, full, hairless sac. Troy was enticed. It had been so long since he let a cock slip through his lips. As soon as he had made it big, he forbid himself his little indiscretion, but he never stopped craving it. If Mills and Longbow hadn't come on so aggressively, Troy might have actually bent his will to them, just as he had when he first started out on the Ballers. He looked back up into Joey's eyes. The boy was right in some way. He did keep hitting pussy as a way to quench his thirst for man meat, but it never satisfied him. Now that he was on edge already, and this kid was presenting him with a non-intimidating chance, Troy knew he needed to take it.

Jerking the long log loosely so that the skin gave with it, Troy opened his mouth. He wet his lips slightly before pursing them to kiss the bulbous head. The instant flesh met flesh, Troy was lost in desire. All his feelings from the past came rushing back just as quickly as the blood rushed through his cock, making it even harder. He grabbed on to his own wood while carefully sliding Joey's cock into his warm wet mouth.

The newbie pumped gently. Troy was in heaven. He missed sucking cock so much.

Clamping Joey's ass, Troy pushed the kid farther toward his face, allowing him to take all of Joey's fresh meat. He savored every inch of the hairless beauty. He ran the tip of his tongue around the head's rim, causing Joey to throw his head back and moan louder.

"Oh fuck, Troy."

Troy couldn't help but smile. The boy was going to be putty in his hands.

"My balls. Do my balls," Joey begged.

Licking the right nut, then gliding his tongue over to the left, Troy bathed Joey's sac with his spit. The boy was panting heavily, but Joey had seen and felt nothing yet. Mouthing Joey's balls with his full lips, Troy scooped both nuts up into his mouth, sucking on them until Joey had to pull away.

"God, you almost made me blow my load."

"We wouldn't want that yet, now would we?" Troy grinned.

Joey just nodded and looked at Troy in lust and awe. "I've been waiting for this day since I first realized the sight of you turned my dick hard," he gushed.

"I'll try and make it worth the wait," Troy chuckled. "Now turn around and let me show you what else my tongue can do."

Grinning from ear to ear, Joey obliged.

With the boy's round, firm ass in his face, Troy had no choice but to pry those smooth cheeks apart, exposing the prize he was after. Joey's pink puckered hole was so tight and sweet that Troy dove right in, licking, sucking, and fingering. He bent Joey over so he could have better access to the kid's home base. He shoved his face in, going mad on the boy's hole.

Joey was crazy with desire, groaning and moaning and supporting his trembling body against the lockers. He kept pushing back into Troy to get the hitter's powerful tongue deeper inside him, but Troy had something more powerful to stuff deep into Joey's dugout.

"You better brace yourself, kid," Joey instructed, pulling his face out of Joey's ass and standing up. "I'm gonna show you just how good I am with a bat."

Walking over to his locker, Troy pulled out his duffel bag and rifled through it until he found what he was looking for. Trotting back over to Joey with a condom and a bottle of Sex Grease in his hand, he resumed his position behind the newbie.

Spreading on a generous layer of the grease, Troy worked it into Joey's clenched hole, his fingers slipping in and out easily. Rolling on the glove and giving himself a generous amount of the grease, Troy stroked his bat before pressing it against Joey's base.

"You want this, kid?" Troy sneered.

"Please . . ." Joey turned his head so he could see Troy behind him.

It took a few years, but Troy was finally on the giving end of ass pounding. Mills and Longbow had never let him fuck them. They just used his hole over and over again. But now it was his turn to give what he had once loved taking.

In one swift motion, Troy had sunk balls deep into Joey. The kid let out a small gasp. Troy eased up. He pulled his thick dark meat out and slowly slid it back in. He was going to fuck Joey nice and slow so he could savor every moment.

"I love the way your ass grips my cock, kid. You done this before?"

"No," Joey said softly. "You're my first. I told you how I felt. I've been saving myself for you."

"Oh fuck, kid, that's hot." Troy picked up some speed, led on by the excitement of this discovery. "No wonder you're so tight. Urgh," he grunted, pounding into Joey, his balls slapping against the boy.

"Feels good, don't it?"

"Fuck, yeah, Troy. Pound me harder."

"If you're sure you can take it?" Troy asked, then slapped Joey's ass.

"I want to take it."

Troy smiled and went at Joey with full force. He gripped the kid's hips while Joey gripped the metal grating of the lockers. They shook with each thrust Troy gave Joey, which was followed by a grunt from Troy and a deep, lustful moan from Joey. The harder Troy pitched his cock into Joey, the louder the lockers rattled, and the louder their sounds got.

Joey was beginning to scream. He clutched his cock and started jerking it.

Troy knew he would erupt soon, but he wanted to make Joey come while he was still inside of him. He slowed down and started long-dicking the kid and slapping his ass.

"Oh, God, I'm gonna come!" Joey shouted, decorating the locker room floor with his heavy load.

The tightening of Joey's hole on Troy's cock when he came was enough to set Troy off. He pulled out of Joey, spun him around, yanked off the condom, and shot a hot load all over the newbie's baby face.

"What the fuck is going on here!" Coach McNara bounded in the locker room.

The players jumped at his roar.

Coach moved in close to the guys. "So this is what was taking you so long, Rodriguez."

Troy stuttered, but couldn't find a response.

"On the bench, both of you."

Joey picked himself up from the floor and took a seat next to Troy, who was looking particularly ill.

Coach paced in front of them. "You think this is acceptable behavior, do you?"

They remained speechless and motionless.

"Have nothing to say?" He stopped pacing and stood, looking down at them. "Well, I have something that will get your mouths open." Coach dropped his pants and pulled his cock out of his shorts.

Troy and Joey stared at Coach's soft cock, not knowing what to do.

"Come on, boys. Don't go all shy on me now. Why don't you show me what good team players both of you are?" Coach grinned and took hold of his dick, offering it to his players.

With a quick glance at each other, Troy and Joey both headed in for Coach's member.

"Oh yeah, now that's it," he moaned, as Troy lapped at his balls and Joey slurped on his knob. With the two guys going at it, it didn't take long before Coach was ready to explode.

"Take it!" he cried out as he blew his wad over their faces. When he was done, he took a deep breath and pulled up his pants.

The guys sat where they were, come dripping from them.

"Go get yourselves washed up," Coach ordered. He started to walk out of the locker room, but right before he left, he shouted, "I'll see you both at practice in the morning."

Troy looked at Joey with a smile on his face.

"What did I tell ya?" Joey gloated. He found a towel on the floor and wiped his face, then handed it to Troy to do the same.

"Come on," Troy got up from the bench, pulling Joey with him. "Let's hit the showers." He slapped Joey on the ass as the two made their way to get cleaned up.

"Hey, what are you doing tonight?" Joey asked as they left the locker room.

"You." Troy beamed and pulled Joey in for a deep, hard kiss.

Switching Positions

Brad Nichols

███████

I always get strange looks from people—family, friends, lovers—when I admit to being a huge baseball fan. Really, what self-respecting gay man likes sports? Um, have you seen some of those players? Hot, hot, and hotter—and that's just the top of batting order. Whether I'm watching from home on my giant flat-screen high-def television, or gazing from the luxury box seats at the stadium, I'm sometimes more interested in how a certain guy's uniform fits him than what he does at the plate. Jerk-off sessions have been plenty, though I've limited those to the stay-at-home variety. Nothing so blatant while at the game.

Until one day.

You knew that was coming, didn't you? What would be the point of all that exposition if I wasn't leading up to some fantastic sexual moment between me and my favorite baseball player?

I'm a wealthy man, and an indulgent one. After years of successful commercial real estate deals, I retired at the age of forty, content now to do whatever pleased me most. From April to September, and God willing October, baseball was my life. I had season tickets for every home game, and sometimes I would travel to another city to watch my team play, depending upon which city and who might be pitching. Or catching . . . I would bring dates, or just casual friends; no one steady and no one specific.

It was a day in August that brought me to the ballpark by myself.

The evening game was set to begin at 7:10, but I was getting an extra special treat, as I was tossing out the ceremonial first pitch. I had won a blind lottery for one of the team's charities and as my bid was the top one I got to toss out said pitch. I had dressed casually, in blue jeans and a rather preppy, white button-down shirt. This despite the fact that it was in the nineties at game time and I was sweating. But it's not everyday you're standing in front of forty thousand screaming fans (okay, granted, most of the fans weren't there yet and not many of them were screaming), but still, you gotta look your best. Especially with my name and face up there on the Diamond Vision.

So, there I was, standing just off the pitcher's mound, since I wasn't expected to actually throw the ball all fifty-five feet from mound to plate. The team's starting catcher was waiting for my pitch, so with a wind-up stolen from a Hollywood movie, I made my pitch. I guess my adrenaline was coursing through my veins, because I ended up throwing a hard strike, right across the plate. I heard a smattering of applause from the crowd, and then, as I went to shake hands with the catcher, I saw the surprised grin on his unshaven face.

"Nice pitch. Maybe you should be warming up in the bullpen, we may need you around the seventh inning. Or to close."

"Guess I was excited," I said.

We shook hands again, this time for the photographer. The moment was immortalized, suitable for framing. I would put it up on the walls of my country home. Truth be told, the catcher was my favorite player, and the chance to meet him, shake his hand, pitch to him, was well worth any investment, good cause or not. And of course in my mind, I had envisioned a different kind of pitching.

"Enjoy the game," the catcher said to me. He smiled again. "And thanks again for your generous donation."

"Hit a game-winning home run and I'll double the donation," I said, laughing.

"Don't tempt me."

Why not, he'd already been tempting me.

Anyway, I did enjoy the game because the good guys won, though not by much. It was a tight game until the eighth, and then it was broken open by a three-run homer by none other than my hero, my fantasy man himself. The catcher. Guess I had to get out the checkbook.

At the end of the game, I made my way toward the dugout, where the players were gathering up their favorite bats and slapping one another's butts and other slightly randy things that to me added to the homoerotic nature of the game. Just then the catcher saw me and he offered up the seventy-million-dollar smile all over again.

"So, I gotta pay up," I said.

"Guess so. Can I offer you a reward, perhaps the bat I used?"

"Wow, that'd be great."

"Come on with me, I already had the trainer take it to my locker. Not his job, but he looks out for me. Gets me stuff I might need."

"Are you serious . . ." I said, my mouth wide open.

He was, and so I hoisted myself over the dugout roof, onto the field, and then into the dugout itself. The catcher had removed his equipment, and so I got an up-close, unrestricted view of him. His thick wavy hair was slicked back, probably from sweating all night long. His face was covered with what looked like a few days growth of beard, and was highlighted even more when he bared his yummy white smile. I could just sink into him.

As we made our way down toward the locker room, I could hear the whoops and hollering of the full team of players, happy because they had not only won the game, but with the win they had first place all to themselves. Everyone seemed to be in a celebratory mood.

"You know, maybe I shouldn't take you into the locker room right after the game. The guys are probably changing and showering and stuff, you know—closed door antics not for public eyes."

"Oh, yeah, sure."

So he led me to a trainer's room, dominated by a massage table.

"Have a seat, I'll be right back with my bat," he said, guiding me to the table, this time actually touching me as he did so.

I guess he saw the expression on my face. He didn't say a word, and me, I couldn't have found one if I'd swallowed a dictionary.

"Maybe my bat is already here," he said.

Having a certain wealth brings with it a certain amount of self-esteem and confidence, and so with that and his very suggestive comment, I wasted little more time. I pressed my hand to his groin, felt how hard he was down there. From the cup, of course. Really, the hottest catcher in the league surely wasn't . . . turned on by me, was he? Yeah, he was.

He leaned in and placed a moist kiss on my lips, the scruff of his face brushing my chin. I opened my mouth to allow his tongue to explore, and I have to say, he mined gold the way he went at me. I kissed him back with as much energy and passion as I could muster, considering my heart was beating so fast I might have thought I was having a heart attack. That was okay, I'd already gone to heaven.

Our lips parted and the catcher backed away from me, and for a moment I thought our little sexual sojourn had come to an end. Instead, it was just beginning. He turned the lock on the trainer's room door and started to remove his uniform. I watched in awe, knowing that baseball players were usually in fantastic shape, especially catchers, who had to be known for their quick moves from home plate to second to throw out base stealers.

My catcher didn't disappoint. As he removed his jersey, I was exposed to a thick, muscular chest that was pleasingly covered with a thick pelt of black hair; his belly was equally fur-covered, with a trail that disappeared teasingly beneath his pants. I had seen him interviewed many times on television just after a game, but he never had his shirt off, just a T-shirt, and I could always see a teasing sprig jutting out from the collar. Now, my image of him was complete, and it was perfect.

I ran my hands over his chest, luxuriating in the downy softness. I had expected it to feel rougher, like his face.

"You like that, huh?"

"Great chest," I said, moving in for a lick of his nipples.

He finished undressing, with his spikes and pants joining his jersey in a sweaty, tangled mess on the floor. I gazed longingly at his thick, hairy legs, which as you might imagine befit the grueling position he played. I might have dropped down and licked his feet had he not been busy suddenly with his jockstrap. He tossed it away and a magnificent cock sprung to action, as though someone had announced that it was his turn at the plate. Get ready to swing.

It was then that I realized I was still fully dressed. Was I supposed to just undress as he had, or was this merely an exhibition game? He gave no indication that he wanted my clothes off; he just took hold of his cock in his own hands and with his eyes first locking on mine, finally looked back at his thick meat. Say no more.

Down on my knees I went, taking the bulbous, purple head into my mouth with an eagerness that reminded me of my youth, when anything was possible and dreams drove me to achieve my ambitions. Here I was now, living a dream, realizing an ambition, and I embraced it—no, I sucked it, and with all my might. With my tongue I caressed the long shaft, tickled at his thick bush of pubes, suckled at his low-hanging baseballs.

"Yeah, suck that bat," he said.

These baseball metaphors, I love them.

I did what I was told. For the next several minutes my mouth bobbed up and down on his thickness, taking the whole thing to the back of my throat, then to the tips of my lips, and back again. Fast, furious, I could hear him breathing harder and harder, like he'd just hit one into the gap and could smell a triple. Me, I was hoping for a home run, perhaps an inside the parker. Finally, I could tell he was getting ready to come. His hands gripped at my hair, and he let out a tremendous sound, a volcano getting ready to erupt.

Thick spurts of come shot out of the eyelet of his cock, drenching my face and dripping down onto my preppy white shirt. As the catcher milked the last of him, he smiled down at me.

"Looks like that shirt is all soiled. Guess it's gonna have to come off."

I needed no more incentive. I unbuttoned my shirt and tossed it on his uniform, then followed it with my pants. Finally, I stood naked alongside my own naked fantasy, my brilliant, sexy, furry-chested catcher, and I had to wonder, what the hell could possibly happen next.

As the catcher, he makes the calls, he directs the pitch. And so I let him. And it turned out that the old adage in baseball is true, when someone says, "What I really want to do is pitch."

"I'm gonna fuck you, man," my catcher told me.

"Yeah, a fastball, right down the middle," I said.

He laughed at that one, and then he bent me over on the massage table until my bare ass was primed and ready. From a cabinet inside the trainer's room, my catcher withdrew a bottle of lube and a condom; guess that trainer did look after his, uh, needs. Thoughts swirled in my mind of the things this room had seen, if that's the kind of stuff they keep here. Here I was, about to be added to the stories these walls would hold.

I watched as he rolled the condom all the way down his long, beautiful cock, and then as he rubbed some lube on it. Next I felt the cool sensation of lube hitting my ass cheeks, followed by the touch of his cock head at my hole. He was going to take me from behind. My sphincter puckered at the very thought, and then that thought was lost by a concentration on my part to allow his thick cock to penetrate me, and, to switch sports a moment, to go deep. Pain gave way to an intense pleasure, and I waited for him to truly engage my ass by fucking it hard.

He leaned down, burying his cock until it could go no further. His chest pressed against my back, and I could feel the thick hair brushing against me. It felt so good, so soft and fuzzy, my cock nearly shot a load right then and there. I told him how good that felt and he nuzzled in more and told me to wait, that I'd end up with a fucking rug burn before he was done pounding me.

He wasn't kidding, because just then he began to slide in, slide out, slide in, slide out, each new thrust exponentially intensifying, until he was grunting and I was screaming and he was pounding and I was receiving. A frenetic rhythm attached itself to us, and for I don't even know how long, the fucking continued, lasting seemingly longer than the game itself. I held back as long as I could, wanting him to go into extra innings before the game was decided on a big, powerful blast.

I couldn't hold on any longer. I felt my cock welling, expanding. I felt the pressure mounting. My catcher was close too; his strokes were shorter, tighter, his breathing pent up like a geyser getting ready to blow. With his cock still pumping my sore ass, with his hairy chest scraping against my raw back, his breath hot on my neck, I gave in to this glorious moment and announced I was coming. I did, seconds later, an explosion ripping through my body and shooting cannon after cannon of white, sticking come all over the table, the floor, the foil wrapper of the condom that lay neglected on the floor.

Barely able to catch my breath, my catcher decided to shoot his load again, and this time I felt it deep within me, the huge head of his cock expanding the walls of my ass further as each spurt shot and shot some more. He kept fucking until every drop seeped out of him. At last his fucking ceased, and he sweetly pulled out of me.

"Man, that was hot," he said. "I love pitching."

"Being a catcher ain't so bad, either," I said.

It had only taken nine innings from that ceremonial first pitch to the final out of the game, but I realized in that time my beautiful catcher and I had ended up switching positions.

Nothing ever happened again between my catcher and me. I still go to all the home games, but when the season is over and winter sets in, I retreat to my country home, and there on the wall, I stare at the photograph of me shaking hands with the catcher. His smile is ever-present, but in my mind I'm able to see the rest of him, his fabulously furry chest, his rock-hard cock. My dick twitches every time.

And sometimes I go for the bat. Not mine, his. Because I did get that game-winning bat of his.

"Something to remember me by," he'd said at the time.

As if I could forget him—or his bat.

ABOUT THE CONTRIBUTORS

SHANE ALLISON has had stories published in *Ultimate Gay Erotica, Hustlers, Best Gay Love Stories* and many other anthologies.

ARMAND works full-time and spends much of his free time writing erotic stories, poetry, and fiction. He is currently working hard to publish his first novel and lives by himself in Ohio.

A native Californian, **BEARMUFFIN** lives in San Diego with two leatherbears in a stimulating ménage à trois. He writes erotica for *Honcho* and *Torso*. His work is featured in *Alyson's Friction* and *Ultimate Gay Erotica* anthologies.

LEW BULL is a South African writer who enjoys the experiences of traveling; has been published in *Secret Slaves, Ultimate Undies,* and *Tales of Travelrotica for Gay Men;* and has had writing accepted for the following anthologies: *Dorm Porn 2, Treasure Trail, Ultimate Gay Erotica 2007, Tales of Travelrotica for Gay Men 2* (Alyson Books) and *Superheroes* (Starbooks), to name a few.

BRIAN CENTRONE has an M.A. in novel writing from the University of Manchester. Before moving to the U.K., he attended SUNY/Westchester Community College, and Fordham University in New York City, where he started a gay sex column for the campus newspaper, upsetting many people. Brian is currently hard at work completing his novel.

CURTIS C. COMER lives in St. Louis with his partner, Tim, their cat, Magda, and lovebird, Raoul Gomez. His stories have appeared in the Alyson anthologies *Starf*cker, Best Gay Love Stories 2005* and *2006, Ultimate Gay Erotica 2005, 2006* and *2007, Dorm Porn 1* and *2,* and *Treasure Trail.*

ERASTES lives in Norfolk, U.K. He writes homoerotic historical romance because someone needs to. He likes classical music, noisy clubs, walks by the Norfolk Broads, and cheese. He likes cats too, but cheese is better on toast. His first novel, *Standish,* was published in November 2006. For details see www.erastes.com.

RYAN FIELD is a thirty-five-year-old freelance writer who lives and works in both Bucks County, Pennsylvania, and Los Angeles. His work has appeared in anthologies and collections for the past ten years, and he's a regular contributing writer and editor for www.bestgayblogs.com. He's currently working on a nonfiction book about gay bloggers and exhibitionism.

TODD GREGORY is a New Orleans-based writer who has been published in numerous anthologies and Web sites. He has also edited several anthologies, including *Blood Lust* (with M. Christian), *His Underwear,* and *Rough Trade* (both forthcoming in 2007). He is currently writing an erotic thriller titled *Sunburn,* which he describes as a "cross between James M. Cain and John D. MacDonald, with gay characters."

T. HITMAN is the nom de porn of a full-time professional writer who knows a thing or two about the sport of baseball. Since 1996, he has published over a hundred fifty erotic short stories for gay readers, in such places as *Men, Freshmen, Dude, Torso, Mandate,* and in enough anthologies to fill an entire bookshelf, and baseball is the favorite theme for many of those sweat-drenched crotch grabbers. A diehard Red Sox fan whose dream of a World Series title was realized in 2004, he is also the author of the baseball-centric, bestselling Alyson novel, *Hardball* (1999). He has also visited the hometown dugout at Fenway Park more than once, and just like every great player past and present, has walked the long, dank tunnel to reach it.

MORRIS MICHAELS, JR. is a lover of all things "apple pie, men, and baseball!" Not always in that order, however! Ivy educated, he has published several tales detailing erotic adventures—his own as well as those of his friends—as he is not above wallowing in the gutter on occasion and enjoys both cerebral and more physical pursuits.

BRAD NICHOLS is the editor of *Tales of Travelrotica for Gay Men* and *Best Gay Love Stories: New York City.* He loves eating hot dogs while at the game and is not related to . . .

JOEL A. NICHOLS was born and raised in Vermont. In 2007, stories of his will appear in *Dorm Porn 2* (Alyson), *Tales of Travelrotica for Gay Men 2* (Alyson), *Second Skin* (Alyson), *C Is for Co-ed* (Cleis), *Got a Minute* (Cleis), *Distant Horizons: Queer Science Fiction* (Haworth), and *Sex by the Book: Gay Men's Tales of Lit and Lust* (Green Candy Press), and have appeared in *Full Body Contact, Just the Sex, Ultimate Undies,* and *Sexiest Soles.* He won second place in the Brown Foundation Short Fiction Prize 2005. In 2002, he was a Fulbright Fellow in Berlin. Joel studied German at Wesleyan University and has a creative writing M.A. from

Temple University. He lives in Philadelphia with his boy-friend, works for a porn Web site, and teaches college English. http://www.joelanichols.com.

NEIL PLAKCY is the author of *Mahu* and *Mahu Surfer,* mystery novels set in Honolulu, and co-editor of *Paws and Reflect: Exploring the Bond Between Gay Men and Their Dogs.* His fiction has appeared in many publications, including *Blithe House Quarterly, Verbsap,* and *In the Family,* and the anthologies *My First Time 2; Men Seeking Men; Cowboys: Gay Erotic Stories; Tales of Travelrotica for Gay Men; Best Gay Love Stories: New York City; Ultimate Undies;* and *By the Chimney with Care.*

SIMON SHEPPARD is the editor of *Homosex: Sixty Years of Gay Erotica,* and the author of *In Deep: Erotic Stories, Kinkorama, Sex Parties 101,* and the award-winning *Hotter Than Hell.* His work also appears in well over two hundred anthologies, including many editions of *The Best American Erotica, Best Gay Erotica,* and *Ultimate Gay Erotica.* He writes the syndicated column "Sex Talk," hangs out at www.simonsheppard.com, and never watches baseball games.

JOHN SIMPSON is the author of *Murder Most Gay,* a full length e-book carried by Renaissance E Books. Simpson has also written "The Virgin Marine," "The Acropolis of Love," "The Tower," "The Serpent," and "Locker Room Heat," all short stories, for Alyson Books. In addition, he has written numerous articles for various gay and straight magazines, and two full-length nonfiction novels.

A writer and personal trainer living in Vancouver, Canada, **JAY STARRE** uses his fitness and sports experiences to inspire erotic fiction for gay men's magazines including *Men* and *Torso*. Jay has also written steamy stories for over thirty-five gay anthologies including the *Friction* series for Alyson, *Full Body Contact, Ultimate Gay Erotic 2005* and *2006*, and *Tales of Travelrotica for Gay Men*.

CHARLIE VAZQUEZ was born and raised in New York City, and self-published his first queer erotic novel, *Buzz and Israel* (2004, Fireking Press). His shorter erotic and comical fiction works have been published in Alyson Books' *Straight? 2* (2003), *Best Gay Love Stories: New York City* (2006), and *Tanglefoot* magazine's issue number one (2004). His second full-length novel is just a baby, but he likes it a lot. He loves e-mail, especially from other writers and clowns. Contact him via www.firekingpress.com.

SHANNON L. YARBROUGH is the author of the book, *The Other Side of What*, and has had several other stories featured in Alyson anthologies recently. In school, he threw like a girl and took up clarinet instead. The closest he gets to playing sports these days is tossing a tennis ball to his dogs in the backyard. He lives in St. Louis, Missouri, and does enjoy a Cardinals game from time to time on the television during baseball season.